A SICKNESS IN THE SOUL

An Ashmole Foxe Georgian Mystery

WILLIAM SAVAGE

Ridge & Bourne

"A SICKNESS IN THE SOUL"

BY

William Savage

This is a work of fiction. All characters and events, other than those clearly in the public domain, are products of the author's imagination. Any resemblance to actual persons, living or dead, is unintended and entirely co-incidental.

PROLOGUE

"Many people wear masks. Some to hide their feelings, some to conceal their identity, and some to hide that most hideous curse of mankind: a sickness in the soul."

I t is often said that, in the last few moments of your existence on this earth, the whole of your past life passes before your eyes. All Jonathon Danson saw and felt was a heavy blow to his face, which sent him sprawling backwards in his chair. It was closely followed by a crushing pain in his chest. After that, he felt nothing ever again.

The Reverend Jonathon Danson D.D. left the Dissenting Academy to become a minister. Unfortunately, he proved to be one of profound mediocrity. His manner was dull and pedantic. The fires of his enthusiasm burned but fitfully. As a result, the once flourishing congregation in his chapel was soon reduced by two-thirds, then by nine-tenths. The few left — mostly elderly widows and portly retired merchants — snoozed in contentment through his rambling sermons. None could understand more than one word in three. Danson never used one short word when three long ones would do; never a plain phrase when an obscure one could be found. He filled his sermons with Greek and Hebrew quotations. He made excursions into the most obscure corners of the Scriptures. He even added lengthy expositions from the works of theologians long dead and justly forgotten.

Danson's only true interest lay in what he termed 'the elucidation of hidden knowledge'. Had he been able to remain in academia, he would have seemed no more than one eccentric among many. However, he had few financial resources. At the age of twenty-six, poverty forced him to find employment as a chapel minister — a role for which he was neither suited nor capable.

To supplement his meagre stipend, Danson took in pupils. He taught them just enough literacy and mathematics to follow their fathers into the world of commerce. His other legacy to these pupils was even more lasting: a conviction that all learning was torture. Being in his school was like becoming trapped in the catacombs while still alive.

Through all this, Dr Danson pursued 'hidden knowledge' with the fervour of a hunting dog scenting a whole warren of rabbits.

Finally, at the age of forty, fortune smiled upon him. A distant cousin died. The Danson family was noted for failing to produce heirs. The cousin's considerable wealth thus descended upon Dr Danson as the nearest, indeed the only, relative available.

At once, Danson resigned his ministry, to widespread relief, and bought himself a substantial house in Norwich. There, he determined to devote the rest of his life to his passion for obscure byways of research.

He paid a carpenter to turn one room in his new house into a substantial library, and then called him back to block one of the windows for yet more bookcases. He hired a butler to answer the door and tell people the doctor was not at home. Then came a cook to prepare regular meals — he believed his brain functioned best on a full stomach — and a kitchen maid to help her. From the Overseers of the Poor, he hired two young women to serve as housemaids. Last of all, he married.

This first Mrs Danson died, possibly from boredom, after four years of marriage. A few months later, Danson married again, mostly to avoid having to deal with domestic affairs. He had little faith in his ability to direct or keep his servants, a fact amply proved several times since his first wife had passed away. Thereafter, he devoted himself completely to his researches. He also began spending still more money on books.

These were not, of course, ordinary books. 'Hidden knowledge' was not to be found in the volumes any gentleman of learning might own. Danson bought books that dealt with alchemy. Thick volumes on astrology, numerology, and anything else he could find to do with the occult. Many were in Latin, some in Ancient Greek and a few in Hebrew. They held strange diagrams and symbols. They spoke of the mysteries of the Kabbalah and introduced him to the writings of Hermes Trismegistus. He began to wonder if he dared conjure up spirits. Could not they impart yet greater understanding and open up still more deeply hidden pathways to spiritual knowledge?

Once married for the second time, Dr Danson paid little attention to his wife. He wanted a housekeeper, not a friend or a lover. Most would have expected her to turn elsewhere for affection. If she did, her husband never noticed. It's unlikely he would have cared enough to pay attention if he had. All that concerned him was that the house should run like clockwork and his meals should appear on time. He paid what seemed necessary to run his house and gave his wife whatever she wanted for herself. Since she wasn't vain, greedy or demanding — what she spent on herself was tiny compared to the amount he was spending on books — he was well content. He supposed she was too, if he ever thought about her happiness at all. The couple thus lived free from obvious discord and any social obligations.

All might have continued on its stable course had not a day arrived when a stranger came to the house. Earlier that morning, Dr Danson informed Archibald Gunton, the butler, to his considerable surprise, that he was expecting a visitor. When he arrived, the butler was told, he must be admitted immediately and without question. He would await the man in his library.

The man came and spent barely twenty minutes with Dr Danson. No one saw or heard him leave. It was not until the butler entered the library about an hour later that he found the reason. His master lay slumped back in his chair, his mouth and eyes wide open. On his face, there was an expression that the butler later described to his mistress as being 'as if he had looked into hell itself'. At his feet were his wig and a small dagger; the one which he usually kept on his desk. There was blood on the left side of his chest. It was obvious at once that the Reverend Dr Jonathon Danson, scholar of the occult and seeker after hidden knowledge, was dead.

As the news spread in the neighbourhood, two schools of opinion formed. The majority, considering Dr Danson's circumstances, announced that it was plainly a domestic crime. An elderly rich husband takes a pretty, young wife, who was penniless before he married her. 'Murder!' they whispered amongst themselves. 'Stands to reason, don't it?' A sizeable number reached a different conclusion; one based on rumours of the man's strange interests. 'Witchcraft!' they muttered, or 'devilry!' Either way, that group were certain the powers of evil had come to claim one of their own.

❄❆❄

TWO NIGHTS LATER, AND IN A PLACE IN THE CITY FAR REMOVED from Dr Danson's elegant dwelling, another man stood and looked down at the body of his latest victim, wrinkling his nose in disgust at the stench and filth all around him. Parts of Norwich might rival London for beauty and architectural splendour, but this was not one of them. The great church of St Peter Mancroft might stand scarcely fifty yards off, but this noisome alleyway belonged to the other part of what was still England's second city; the part where the poor lived in hopelessness and squalor. This was the other England. A place where people struggled for survival, where crime was everywhere and murder almost an everyday occurrence.

Not murder done with such style though. Not a man killed while he slept by a single thrust from a dagger deep into his heart. Not a proper assassination.

If the killer wondered why he was being paid to deal with a homeless wretch like this, he kept such thoughts to himself. He prided himself on being a professional. It mattered nothing to him whether his selected victim came from the highest ranks of society or the lowest. Both would receive the same treatment.

He pulled the rags aside, which the man had used to try to cover himself, and looked at the body. Quite a young man, he guessed, though the life he was living had aged him a good deal. Thin too. No sign of drink, which was strange. Usually vagrants like this always had some flask or bottle of filthy, low-grade liquor to keep out the cold.

A noise startled him, and he crouched, ready to fight or run.

There it was again. This time he could identify it as the wooden clapper the night-watchmen carried. Coming closer too. This was no time to linger, if he wanted to avoid detection.

The assassin stooped once more and pulled the rags back over the dead man. Then he took his knife and carefully wiped the blade clean of blood, before slipping it back into the sheath at his waist. Time to disappear as stealthily as he had come.

A rat, on the hunt for food, stopped and sniffed the air, catching the warm smell of fresh blood as it did so. It looked around carefully, always on the alert for danger. Nothing. It was alone in this alleyway, which formed part of its regular hunting territory. Its whiskers twitching, the rat slipped through the shadows until it found the source of the smell. Then, crouching in the dark, alert as ever, it started to lap.

I

Jack Beeston had been Norwich's long-term principal gang leader for many years, until Ashmole Foxe finally secured his conviction on a long list of capital offences. In the first few months after his execution, the number of crimes committed in the city fell to levels that were unimaginable before. The remnants of his criminal grouping split into factions, each one headed by a lower-ranking subordinate, each determined to take over Beeston's role. They were so busy beating and killing their rivals they had little or no interest in regular criminal activities. The citizens of Norwich thought it was heaven.

Samson "Sammy" Ross's men killed two of David "Smiler" Hayes's principal supporters, then narrowly missed killing Hayes himself. Hayes plotted revenge. Matthew "Growler" Spetchley's bully boys raided the house where Ross lived. They left his body hanging in the outhouse, hoping to fake his suicide. That left Hayes and Spetchley. It wasn't long before attacks by each group left a good number of both gang's members dead, crippled or severely wounded.

Meanwhile, the people of the city observed events with rising satisfaction. "Let them kill one another" was the general attitude. "It reduces their numbers and stops them causing trouble for the rest of us."

The only exception to the belief in the virtues of this ongoing process of dog-eat-dog was Mr Ashmole Foxe, the aforementioned amateur catcher of criminals. His objection was not on moral grounds, nor was it based on a belief that no one should take justice into their own hands. It was simply practical. It was clear to him that neither Hayes nor Spetchley would be able to defeat the other. Both would realise this, and a truce would be arranged. When that event took place, as surely it must, the city would have two criminal gangs where there had once been only one. Since each would harbour a deep sense of ill-will against the other, what had begun as direct confrontation would change into an ongoing attempt to out-do their rival in committing ever more daring and profitable crimes against the rest of the population.

During one of their periodic meetings to discuss potential additions to the alderman's library, Foxe mentioned his concerns to his long-time friend and customer, Alderman Halloran. Halloran also served as Foxe's link between himself and the mayor of the city and the wealthy merchants who made up the Mercantile Society. They had taken of late to referring to Mr Foxe anything of a potentially criminal nature likely to upset the welfare of Norwich and its businesses. So far, he had not let them down. Facts were unearthed, culprits tracked down and the wheels of justice set in motion. Why Mr Foxe? Simply because, in the absence of either the police force or other investigators, someone was needed to do the job. Who better than a young man of ample wealth who possessed an enquiring mind and the time to indulge it? A young man who had offered a means of livelihood to the widow of a notably unsuccessful bookseller, a Mrs Susannah Crombie, and found someone with all the energy, knowledge and judgement needed to run his bookselling business almost without his involvement. Only the aspect of the business relating to rare and antiquarian books remained firmly in Foxe's own hands. That was what had brought him to Alderman Halloran's house in Colegate that day. Halloran was an ardent book collector and relied on Foxe to keep him supplied.

They had spent more than an hour discussing various volumes

which might be of interest to the alderman. Now it was time to move on to other matters.

The alderman was not impressed with Foxe's gloomy view of the consequences of Jack Beeston's demise.

'Are you not being unnecessarily pessimistic?' he said. 'So far, the results of this rivalry have been positive for our city as a whole. Why should there be a truce between Hayes and Spetchley? As we all know, they hate each other. That won't change. Even if one manages to emerge triumphant, this long drawn out struggle will leave them both seriously weakened.'

'We can only hope so,' Foxe replied. 'On the other hand, ...'

'I hope you are not suffering from melancholia,' the alderman interrupted. 'You haven't been to the theatre of late, according to the manager, nor did you attend either of the last two balls at the Assembly House. It's not like you to miss opportunities like those. What's more, Mrs Crombie mentioned to me that your servants have begun to worry about you. No new "pets" they tell her, since that girl went to work for Lady Cockerham. Even your style of dress is less fashionable of late. Look at you now. Where is the heavily embroidered waistcoat and all the gold and silver piping on your jacket? Where is the rich lace at your cuffs and at your throat?'

It was true, of course. Without noticing it, Foxe had been sinking into something like respectability.

The answer to Foxe's state of mind would have been obvious, had the alderman been privy to Foxe's recent movements. For weeks he had been spending more and more time with Lady Arabella Cockerham. At first, this surprised him. He put it down to a need for relaxation and intelligent conversation. He usually felt some lassitude at the conclusion of a demanding case. Lady Arabella was kind, sharp-witted and managed to comfort him without appearing to do so. Being with her cheered him up. After a while, going to her house in Pottergate became a habit. Then, to his surprise, he found himself growing fond of her. He began to wonder whether he should not marry and settle down, as his friend Captain Brock had done.

Anyone who knew him would have deemed this a preposterous idea. Foxe had spent all his life, from the onset of puberty until the present day, engaged in a single-minded pursuit of sex without commitment. Why change all of a sudden? He was just thirty years of age and had no difficulty finding fresh bed-mates whenever he wished. He had an excellent housekeeper and the thought of children under his feet appalled him. Even so, the notion stuck in his mind. One evening, almost on a whim, he had assumed a serious expression, interrupted their conversation and proposed marriage to Lady Arabella. He assumed she would accept on the spot.

Instead, she laughed in his face. She had, she told him, married once before and had no intention of repeating such a disagreeable experience.

Foxe, stung by her cheerful rejection of what he should have realised was a foolish approach, chose instead to stand on his dignity. He nodded and left in a state of high dudgeon.

It wasn't long before he regretted his stupidity. He was now shut off from Lady Arabella's company. He would also be unable to find occasions to enjoy the energetic charms of her maid, Maria. Feeling too embarrassed, and too proud, to make any apology or try to re-establish himself in Lady Cockerham's good books, he sulked. He moped about his house, feeling sorry for himself and annoying everyone from Mrs Crombie to his apprentice, Charlie Dillon. That lad, eager to copy his master in every way he could, had started to cast his eye over all the girls of his acquaintance — much to the dismay of Florence, the kitchen maid.

It was in this unhappy state of mind that, one evening, shortly after his talk with Alderman Halloran, Foxe sat at his desk and wrote to his former lover, Miss Gracie Catt.

My dear Gracie,

It seems so long since we have been in touch. Indeed, I fear this letter may never reach you. Since Kitty has become the talk of the theatrical world, I imagine her services are in demand throughout the realm. Indeed, you may already have left the address to which I am directing this missive. Do you ever think of returning to Norwich? I am sure your many friends here would rejoice at such news. I am sure I would.

My own life continues much as before, somewhat dull and undemanding. Sometimes I fear I am sinking into a morass of normality. I can only hope and pray that a new mystery comes along which will demand an unusual effort on my part. That seems most unlikely. Norwich has become far more law-abiding than it was, thanks to the demise of Jack Beeston. There hasn't been a killing or any other serious offence in weeks, if you omit the various gang members attacking one another. With nothing to excite me, I must soldier on as best I can.

Please let me have news of you and your sister when you have a moment. I miss you both and you may be assured of my continuing regard.

I am, as ever, your devoted friend,

Ashmole Foxe

ON AT LEAST TWO COUNTS, POOR FOXE WAS SOON TO REGRET EVER sending this letter.

THE FIRST REASON FOR REGRET OVER THIS MISSIVE BECAME APPARENT almost at once. On the day before, the one on which Dr Jonathon Danson, D.D. was sent to meet his maker, Mr Ashmole Foxe also had an unanticipated visitor. Alfred, Foxe's manservant, brought in the man's card. It was not informative. All that was printed on it was his name, "Mr Anthony Smith", and his address, "Cambridge".

'Show him into my library, Alfred,' Foxe said. 'It's possible he wants to buy or sell some books, which makes it a suitable place to receive him. You'd better ask Molly to bring some refreshments too.'

The man who came in seemed to be trying to make himself as forgettable as possible. He was of average stature with the kind of face you might see on the street a hundred times a day. His dress was sober, though Foxe noted that it was made of fine cloth. He wore an unremarkable wig, plain blue stockings and good shoes, though not of the very best quality. Even his voice was without any noticeable accent.

After the usual preliminaries, accompanied by accepting a dish of coffee, Mr Smith proved to be in no hurry to state his business.

Instead, he looked around at Foxe's modest library with the eye of an expert surveying colts at a Newmarket horse sale.

'Before knocking at your door, I took the time to enter your bookshop and peruse some of the stock there. Well-chosen, I must say, and most carefully presented. Your library, sir, is not so extensive, yet it contains some fine bindings. From what I can see, without moving from my seat, it also holds more than a few rare and desirable books. To be expected in a bookseller, perhaps. Yet I have known several who, like certain wine merchants, have little taste for what they sell. Your reputation as a bookseller of taste and discernment is assuredly justified.'

'I thank you, sir,' Foxe replied, wishing Mr Smith would come to the point. 'I can take little credit for what you saw in the shop. My partner, Mrs Crombie, deals with that side of the business. I am pleased to say she rarely requires my help in choosing suitable volumes.'

'So I understand. You are most fortunate in that respect. It must allow you to concentrate on dealing in rare volumes. Even so, I gather that too takes up little of your time. For the rest, you take an interest in looking into unexplained deaths. An unusual hobby even for a wealthy man, if I may make such an observation without offending you.'

'You have done a good deal of research into myself and my business,' Foxe said. He was beginning to feel annoyed by this display of prior investigation. 'You have the advantage of me in that respect. You knew you were coming. I was not informed of your visit in advance, thus denying me any opportunity of anticipating your areas of interest.

'I perceive you are annoyed with me, Mr Foxe. It is perhaps deserved. Let me explain myself without further preliminaries. As you will have seen from my card, I have come from Cambridge. There I have the honour to be a member of a group of scholars and bibliophiles linked to the colleges of the university. My colleagues and I heard of you through our contacts amongst serious book collectors. I have therefore come here today to see if you would be able to help us. We have a need for a particular volume for our little group's somewhat specialist collection.'

'If it is erotic or pornographic literature you are seeking, sir,' Foxe said stiffly, 'I must inform you that I do not deal in such matters.'

Mr Smith smiled. 'We never thought you did, Mr Foxe. Our interest lies elsewhere, I assure you. We seek out works published by the earliest pioneers in the study of chemistry and other aspects of natural philosophy. Unfortunately, many of these writers also dabbled in less respectable subjects. They wrote on matters such as magic, alchemy and astrology, as did Sir Isaac Newton himself, as I'm sure you will know. As a result, their writings are often viewed with suspicion and they have garnered more than their fair share of detractors. It is true that much of what they wrote is tainted with notions of the occult. That is unfortunate, but it does not lessen their usefulness in understanding how we have come to our present state of knowledge.'

Foxe, always prey to unbounded curiosity, could not leave this statement unexplored.

'You and your colleagues are serious about such research, Mr Smith? Surely matters such as alchemy have long been discredited. As for magic and mystical ideas from the Jewish Kabbalah and the like, are they not now seen as little more than gibberish? On a level with witchcraft and the conjuring up of spirits?'

'What you say is correct, sir. Yet there was a time when such topics were the subject of serious and conscientious study by men of proven ability. If these scholars — we are not afraid to call them what they were, Mr Foxe — kept their activities secret, it was mostly for fear of ignorant persecution. The established Christian churches have for centuries treated all seeking such knowledge in the harshest manner. Many were tortured and burned at the stake for suggesting the church was not the sole source of truth about this world and the heavens above it. Were these poor wretches more deluded than the pious hypocrites who prided themselves on the atrocities they committed in the name of their god?'

Foxe certainly agreed but felt such a question was best left unanswered in dealing with a stranger. It was time to turn the conversation towards less dangerous waters.

'Can you at least tell me the nature of the particular books in which you are interested?' he asked. 'To be frank with you, sir, I encounter few such titles. I know of no one who holds many such titles on their shelves, let alone seeks them out. The collecting of pornographic books may be reprehensible, but the reason for their popularity — even amongst those who might be expected to avoid them — is plain enough. Are not the kind of books you mention mere relics of a less enlightened age?'

'I admit it is easy to think of them as such, and to dismiss my friends and I as cranks.' Smith had lost nothing of his ease and good temper. 'Let me explain. Our interest is three parts historical and one part scientific. What you are pleased to call this more enlightened age has come about through the determination the writers of alchemical and similar books possessed. They wished to understand the wonders of the universe. They wished to discover its laws and patterns. Of course, much of the knowledge they pursued so eagerly turned out to be hopelessly in error or of no practical use. They did not know that at the time. How could they, until they had tried it for themselves and found it wanting? Even today, we are able to uncover fresh ideas amongst their findings. New paths for exploration using better-grounded approaches to scientific endeavour.'

By now, Foxe had decided that Mr Smith and his friends should be taken seriously, both as scholars and as potential customers. It was time to get down to business.

'Let us return to the purpose of your visit,' he said. 'Can I take it that there are certain titles in which you and your group have a special interest?'

'Certainly,' Smith replied. 'Indeed, there is one book we are most eager to find and purchase for our library, if we can.'

'What can you tell me of this book?'

'The book we are looking for is called "*A Treatise on the Nature of Matter and its Transformation by Various Means*". It was written by a certain Ebenezer Tyrwhit and published via a select group of subscribers in the year 1697. It sounds innocuous enough, but its author was condemned for heresy by the Bishop of London and forced to flee this land. Have you ever seen or heard of a copy, Mr Foxe?'

'No. Should I have?' That sounded ungracious, but Foxe was temperamentally wary of anything which smacked of the supernatural.

'We dared to hope so. We have heard a whisper that there may be a copy somewhere in Norwich, probably in the private library of some scholar of the occult. We are not rich men, but we would be willing to pay a most generous price, if a copy should be for sale.'

'May I ask the source of your information?'

Once again, Mr Smith smiled. Foxe decided he must be well used to receiving rebuffs. Despite his prejudice against all those who took an interest in 'hidden knowledge' and similar superstitions, Foxe could not help respecting — even liking — the man.

'You may ask,' Smith said, 'but I regret that I am unable to answer in any detail. I do not doubt your integrity, Mr Foxe. Nor your own good sense. Nevertheless, we have learned to be wary on behalf of our friends and contacts. There are still some in this world who seek to bolster their beliefs and sense of self-righteousness by persecuting any with whom they disagree. Many of those who supply us with information have been subject to public ridicule — and worse — in the past. It is our practice to keep their names and locations entirely secret. All I can say is that we received this information from one or more sources whom we have every reason to trust.'

Like all men of that time, Foxe was well aware of the ease with which ranters and bigots could whip up a tempest of ill-informed and malicious prejudice. Nearly all of it was directed against innocent people and cloaked with a veneer of religious or patriotic fervour. He had several good customers amongst the small Jewish and Catholic communities. Several had suffered in this way, as had various other groups who had fled to Norwich to escape violent persecution overseas. They went in constant fear of rioters stirred up by religious and political fanatics. If you were of their number, you took care to live as inconspicuously as possible.

'I will not press you, Mr Smith,' Foxe said. 'Your pardon if I appeared to do so. I will accept your assurance that your information is as reliable as any such information can be. Unfortunately, I have never heard of the book you seek. Nor do I know of anyone who might meet your description of the person who is said to own a copy. I deal with many book collectors in this city, but no one matching this description. I imagine such a person would have his own sources through which to get the volumes he required. There is no reason why he should come to me, especially if the subject matter of his research was something he might wish to prevent becoming general knowledge.'

'But you will contact me at once, should you hear of it?'

'I can give you my word on that, Mr Smith,' Foxe said.

'Thank you, sir,' Smith said. 'Our information on the possible location of a copy of this volume may prove to be in error. All the same, we are convinced the forgotten corners of private libraries are the only places where books of this kind may now be found. At one time, it wasn't unusual for members of the gentry and aristocracy to dabble in esoteric knowledge. Most did it for the thrill of engaging in what was forbidden. Few were genuine scholars. The interest soon ebbed and what books they possessed now lie disregarded in their libraries. Certain antiquaries as well were drawn to the notion of uncovering hidden knowledge in ancient mysteries. Since theologians and other churchmen condemned such activity as consorting with the forces of evil, they too kept their interest hidden. Do you not think it sad that most people fear what they do not understand? That was why innocent old women were called witches and attacked. It was from the belief that the secrets they possessed — folk secrets handed down from past generations — were used to hurt and destroy, not to heal. You will look, won't you? We know you have privileged access to the libraries of several members of the nobility.'

'I have already given you my word,' Foxe said. 'I will do my best, though I can promise nothing.'

'That is enough, Mr Foxe,' Smith replied. 'I am glad to have made your acquaintance, sir. My visiting card I know is not very informative, but any communication addressed to me via the Porter's Lodge at St George's College will always reach me.'

Needless to say, Foxe's curiosity was stimulated to white heat by this visit. He would certainly search for the book, though he had no notion of where to start. In the meantime, he was determined to discover all he could about his visitor and the strangely-titled volume he sought.

Other demands intervened and he was forced to set his search aside until it slipped from his mind entirely.

'The fact is, something has come to my notice which I think might interest you,' Alderman Halloran said.

Two days had passed since the visit from Mr Smith. Firstly, Foxe had been compelled to spend a whole day attending to important correspondence. Most were items which he had contrived to ignore because he knew how tedious it would be to deal with them. Now Alderman Halloran had sent a message asking Foxe to call on him at his earliest convenience.

Foxe, leaning on the word "convenience", interpreted this to mean, "when you can manage to get around to it without disrupting your day". It was therefore late in the afternoon when he presented himself at the door of the alderman's fine house in Colegate. Now, they were seated, as usual, in the alderman's library. Each time he visited, Foxe admired the fine oak bookshelves, broad desk for study and comfortable chairs either side of the fireplace. It was a room he loved to spend time in.

'You said when we spoke last that you were bored. You'd like a good mystery to get your teeth into,' Halloran said. 'Very well. The mayor was contacted at about eleven this morning by a Mrs Katherine Danson. Her husband is — or rather, was — a reclusive writer of philosophical words. The man was found dead in his study shortly before ten. His Worship has passed the matter to me and I thought you might be interested in helping me catch the murderer.'

'I suppose I might,' Foxe said, displaying no enthusiasm whatsoever for the task. He didn't want to get involved in some cock-eyed mystery that would turn out to be a boring domestic crime. What he wanted was something difficult to get his teeth into.

'I wouldn't normally bother you with this sort of thing,' Halloran went on, 'if you hadn't been at something of a loose end. It's not something that would have interested me much as a magistrate either. Probably a domestic crime. But you did say ...'

Would he never get to the point? Foxe remained silent and waited.

'It's like this,' Halloran said. 'The man who's been murdered is — was — a bit of an eccentric. He called himself a scholar, but no one I've spoken to has ever heard of him. He didn't give lectures or publish books or pamphlets either, to the best of my knowledge. All I know is that he's something of a recluse, who's recently married a young wife.'

Fox groaned inwardly. Old husband, new young wife. It was a terrible cliché. There was bound to be some lover in the background. The wife and the lover had conspired to get rid of her husband. How boring!

'That's not all,' Halloran went on. 'He had a distinct reputation for pursuing unusual topics. Seems he was interested in strange, philosophical things. Not a regular philosopher, and certainly not a typical retired churchman, for all that he was a Doctor of Divinity. To sum up, he is, or was, a retired dissenting minister with an interest in things strange and esoteric. Anyhow, I thought it would be right up your street. As I said, it's not something that particularly interests me. His wife sent a servant to report his death and the mayor asked me to look into it. Usually, that's the end of the matter. I put the required notices offering rewards for information into the paper, a few cranks reply and the business is filed away as unsolved. I have notified the coroner, of course. It's really up to him now. Unless the wife manages to bring a prosecution, we'll never know who killed him.'

'Why was it you thought I would be particularly interested?' Foxe asked.

'Mostly because of the man's strange interests, coupled with a complete lack of obvious clues as to who killed him and why. By all accounts, a man who was so dull that people fell asleep talking to him. Few did, of course, what with him being a recluse. He doesn't seem to have had an enemy in the world, at least not that anyone knows of. The servant who was sent to the mayor informed him there was no sign of someone entering from the outside. Nothing taken either. It's hard to imagine why anyone would want to kill such an eccentric old fool. Unless the wife did it, of course.'

'He was poisoned, I suppose,' Foxe said. 'That would be the typical way for a woman.'

'No,' Halloran replied. 'Not poisoned. Stabbed through the heart. There's also the matter of the mysterious visitor he had just before his body was found.'

It was at this point, Foxe started to pay attention. The visitor hadn't been mentioned before. Yet, if it was obvious that he had done the deed, why should Halloran still call him in?

'What can you tell me about this mysterious visitor you mention?' Foxe asked.

'Almost nothing. You'd better go and talk to the wife, although she apparently never saw the man. The butler let him in.'

Butler? How could a retired minister from some dissenting group afford to keep a butler?

'What does the butler say?'

'No idea. The wife sent one of the other male servants to tell the mayor about the killing and the mayor simply passed the message on to me.'

'How many servants did this man keep?'

'The usual number, I suppose.' Halloran had a wealthy man's disinclination to bother himself with domestic matters. It hadn't occurred to him that few retired ministers could afford the number of servants he had himself.

'Where did he live?'

'On Pottergate, I believe. I wrote down exactly where.' He got up and began to rummage in the mass of papers on his desk.

Pottergate? Maybe this retired minister came from a wealthy

family? Perhaps his new wife was an heiress? Pottergate was where Lady Arabella lived. It was not quite as good an address as Colegate, but both were lined with the dwellings of rich merchants, bankers and the like. Pottergate?

Halloran found what he was looking for and passed Foxe a scrap of paper. 'I've told you everything I know,' he said. 'All I can suggest is that you go and talk to the wife and find out as much as you can. That is if the case interests you. There's no pressure to take it on, if you don't want to.'

'Thanks. I might as well have a look at it,' Foxe said, hoping he sounded grudging. In truth, his curiosity had been well and truly sparked by the butler and the address. 'I've got nothing else particular to do at the present time. Won't the man's wife be very upset at this stage? She won't want to talk to me yet.'

'Again, I have no idea,' Halloran said. 'Go and find out. Sometimes these young wives can be extraordinarily callous towards an elderly husband. Most of them are expecting — probably hoping — they'll be wealthy widows as soon as possible. Then they're free to look for a younger and more interesting husband. As far as the mayor is concerned, this murder has taken place at a most inconvenient time. He and the rest of us in his inner circle are trying to discover how a substantial amount of money has been embezzled from the city treasury, and by whom. That's much more important than the death of some old fool who dabbled in matters best left well alone.'

After he left Halloran's house, Foxe found he was turning the matter over in his mind. There was something deuced peculiar about the whole business. A retired minister living on Pottergate and keeping a butler and other male servants? Male servants cost serious money. A recluse who went out and found and married a young woman, presumably as a second wife after the first had died? Damn it! He'd forgotten in his astonishment to ask whether the wife was pretty. A plain woman would only be likely to attract men hoping to benefit from her husband's death. Pretty ones found bedfellows with ease, rich or not. What about this 'mysterious' visitor? Reclusive scholars didn't admit casual visitors, did they? If he was expected, why did the minister's wife not know who the man was?

Foxe decided he wouldn't go and see the wife right away. Better to find out all that he could about her, her background and her behaviour since she married this odd husband. That way he could prepare his questions in advance. It would also give the lady time to compose herself — always assuming she was actually grieving.

As soon as he reached his house, he turned aside into his book-shop. Under Mrs Crombie's management, the shop had become a centre for social contacts and one of the main clearing houses for gossip in the city. If anyone could tell him what the world knew about this ill-matched couple, she could.

Foxe swiftly explained to Mrs Crombie the gist of what the alderman had told him and asked her to add what she knew. She didn't disappoint him. She admitted her knowledge was superficial in this instance, then proved to be a mine of information.

For a start, she explained that the retired minister — his full name was Dr Jonathan Danson — had lost his first wife some three or four years past. Around eighteen months ago he had married a new, very young wife. Her background? This had been the subject of gossip for a while, though it was hardly that unusual. The word was that she had worked in a fashionable bordello of the kind which catered exclusively for the well-heeled. After his wife's death, Danson had gone there several times, probably more for companionship than anything else.

'Dr Danson must be sixty or more, if he's a day,' she told Foxe. 'I've never met the man himself, but that's what people tell me. Not a very well-preserved sixty-something either. His new wife will be almost forty years younger than that. I suppose she married him for his money. Either that or to get away from having to go with any man who could pay.'

'He's wealthy then?' Foxe asked.

'Must be. The madam of that bordello wouldn't have let him enter otherwise. He also lives on Pottergate and keeps servants.'

'So I understand,' Foxe said. 'Family money, is it?'

'That's another odd thing,' Mrs Crombie said, warming to her subject-matter. 'Folks say he was as poor as the proverbial church mouse until a few years ago. Just another of the many ministers of some chapel or other. The sort who've infested this city in recent years.' Mrs Crombie was a staunch member of the established church. 'Don't ask me which dissenting group had hired him. All I know is people say he was a poor preacher — far too dry and scholastic. He also turned out to be somewhat prone to harbouring strange notions about religion, even for a dissenter. In the end, only a congregation who were desperate would consider him. He rarely stayed long with any of them.'

'An inheritance?'

'Who knows?'

'What about the wife? Is she pretty?' Foxe asked.

'It's typical of you to ask a question like that,' Mrs Crombie said, laughing. 'I've not set eyes on her either, but people say she's plenty comely enough, though not a beauty. Always cheerful and good-natured though. No one seems to know much more. As I told you, the husband is — was — a recluse. His wife is one of those women who rarely ventures far outside the household. She's not a reader either. I've never seen her in my shop.'

My shop, Foxe noted, with an inward smile. Well, he had made Mrs Crombie his partner in the bookselling business — or a good part of it — and she'd done him proud. He supposed it really was *her* shop nowa-days, even if he did still own it and everything in it and it was his father's name over the door.

Having obtained as much information as he could from Mrs Crombie, Foxe turned to his other main source of information on what went on in the city and amongst the people who lived there. The groups of children who lived on the streets knew much more than the other inhabitants guessed. He had long had an excellent relationship with them. In part that was due to his open-handed generosity. In part, it stemmed from the fact that he was prepared to take what they told him seriously. Most people simply snarled and kicked them out of the way. Foxe knew they lived rough and managed to get by through begging, stealing and, in the case of the girls, casual prostitution. Some of the prettier boys too. It didn't make them stupid or evil. They did it because there was nothing else they could do. His current apprentice, Charlie Dillon, had once been a street child himself and their unofficial leader. Even now, although he served Foxe and lived in part of the stables behind his house, he exercised considerable authority amongst them.

Foxe thanked Mrs Crombie for her help and walked through into the workroom, feeling sure he would find Charlie there. From the start, the boy had shown a particular interest in bookbinding and printing. Foxe had the old printing press which his father had used renovated. He also invested in organising for some of his skilled printer and bookbinder contacts to give Charlie lessons in both skills. Both had proved good investments. Charlie also served as Foxe's link to the various street children who lived and slept wherever they could in the city. Once he had been amongst their number himself, until Mr Foxe had rescued him and taken him into his own household. Despite his new-found respectability, the boy still had considerable standing amongst the street children, a status enhanced by his master's use of him to hand out pennies. This small investment had usually paid handsome dividends. The children could go anywhere either unobserved or disregarded by everyone. They also had sharp eyes and ears and quick wits, all three honed by the precarious lives they lived. They were better than any team of Bow Street Runners at discovering whatever Mr Foxe wished to know.

Foxe found Charlie exactly where he had expected him to be — sitting at the bench working on the repair of a badly-damaged book from the circulating library Mrs Crombie had established. It was the work of a few moments to explain what he wanted and ask Charlie to contact the street children. They would soon find out all he wished to know about Dr Danson and his household.

'I'm particularly interested in the relationship between the retired minister and his wife,' he told the boy, 'as well as any rumours there are concerning both their backgrounds. I also need to know whether he had contact with any of the wealthy men from groups like the Quakers, the Presbyterians or the Independents. It's possible he didn't. Danson had an interest in unusual — even blasphemous — areas of study.'

With that, Foxe returned to his home, satisfied he had done all he could for the present. It would soon be time for dinner.

❦

BY NEXT MORNING, FOXE HAD DECIDED THAT HE NEEDED TO involve himself in investigating the death of Dr Danson, if only to satisfy his own curiosity. It had bothered him on and off all evening and far into the night. If he tried to walk away now, his mind would give him no peace for days to come. He'd suspected this would be the outcome. That was why he'd already done what he could to prepare himself by talking to Mrs Crombie and setting the street children to work. Halloran knew his Foxe. If he'd seemed to give him a choice in the matter, it was little more than a courtesy.

It would be a little time before he could expect what he'd begun to bear much fruit. In the meantime, he could still go to see Danson's widow. It wasn't ideal, but it might help to talk to her and her servants, if possible, while events were fresh in everyone's minds.

He therefore set aside his morning ritual of visiting his favourite coffeehouse and turned in the opposite direction. He was heading for Pottergate.

Alderman Halloran had given him clear directions, so he should be able to find the correct house without asking further. However, once he arrived his confidence in Halloran's directions suffered a severe blow. He was where he had been told to be, but what now stood before him was a splendid, modern mansion of no less than seven bays fronting onto the street. Everything looked fresh and well cared for. The house was built of fine brickwork, with ashlar facing on the corners and window openings. The windows were large and all filled with glass. The imposing front door before which he stood boasted a gilded brass knocker in the shape of a lion's head. Was this really the home of Dr Danson, retired dissenting minister?

It was indeed, as the footman who responded to Foxe's knock at the house next door soon assured him.

Foxe retraced his steps and wielded the lion's head knocker with some care. Even so, his knock seemed to resound through the house like a cannon firing.

The door was opened by a stately butler wearing full livery. The man's appearance and demeanour were better fitted to the country mansion of a duke than the city home of a mere Doctor of Divinity. The fellow bowed, took Foxe's visiting card and asked him to wait in the hall while he went to ascertain whether Mrs Danson was receiving visitors.

Foxe stared around in awe. The hall was lofty and superbly proportioned. It was also decorated with fine plasterwork. The furnishings were of fine mahogany, made by a superb craftsman. There were mirrors and paintings of undoubted quality, though Foxe noticed in passing that none of them were portraits. Opposite the door, a broad staircase swept up to the first floor in a single elegantly proportioned curve. Even the bannisters were finely shaped, and wasn't that an Axminster carpet on the treads? Even since it had become known that the new monarch, His Majesty King George III, favoured Axminster carpets, they had become *de rigeur* amongst the fashion-conscious rich.

The final touch to all this costly grandeur came in the form of several large Chinese vases, interspersed with marble busts and classical bronzes. Everything had that carefully understated way of proclaiming the wealth of its owner that he would have expected in the house of an aristocrat of the most refined taste; one with forebears amongst the gentry stretching back hundreds of years, not a retired minister of humble origins.

The butler returned to inform Foxe — this butler surely never simply told anyone anything — Mrs Danson would see him in the withdrawing room. The two of them, with the butler in front and Foxe trailing numbly behind, turned to the left to pass through a richly appointed dining room. Its deep windows to the street stood opposite long mirrors with brass sconces between them, each holding no less than four long candles. The table, glittering with a display of silver, was of darkest mahogany. Foxe wished he could have afforded one like it.

The withdrawing room was no less imposing. Here, the walls were covered with rich crimson damask and the furnishings were once again of walnut and mahogany, obviously fashioned by a master cabinetmaker.

In stark contrast to the magnificence around her, the young woman who awaited Foxe was simply dressed. The dark dress she wore was made of fine material, sure enough, Foxe had an eye for such things.

Even so, it was simply cut and lacked any decoration beyond a narrow band of lace at the neck and on the cuffs. She might be newly widowed, but she had clearly decided not to assume full mourning clothes. He could not believe she had nothing more suitable, for her dress was of dark blue damask over an underskirt of cream silk, sprigged with tiny flowers. She wore no jewellery beyond a single pearl brooch. Her head was covered by a simple cap of cream linen. She was as elegant as her house.

Was she beautiful? By no means, though she could have been described as comely enough. Foxe's initial impression was almost wholly favourable. She displayed a simplicity which was most attractive. Her gaze was calm and direct. Best of all, she responded to his bow with an elegant curtsy, indicating with a graceful gesture that he should take a seat. In turn, she seated herself on the other side of a small table. Foxe was a connoisseur of women. Whatever Mrs Danson's background, she was a woman of quality. Something innate in her shone through to prove it. Foxe was more and more impressed.

He waited until his hostess had seated herself, then sat where she had indicated. After that, he opened by introducing himself and offering his condolences on her loss. He had come on behalf of the mayor, he told her, who had requested him to look into her husband's death. She nodded, her face grave, and they next indulged in the usual polite conversation on such occasions — the weather, the prospects for the harvest and suchlike. Thus, it proceeded until a maidservant brought in a tray set with cups, sugar and a pot of coffee and Foxe and his hostess took refreshment.

All this time, Foxe had been observing Mrs Danson discreetly. Her manners were excellent and her voice was carefully modulated, with no trace of either a city or a country accent. Her demeanour was suitably grave, given that she had recently been widowed, but, beyond that, she displayed no greater sign of emotion. When Foxe told her that the mayor had suggested he might be of assistance to her in discovering her husband's murderer, she displayed neither surprise nor pleasure. She merely nodded and told him that she would be grateful for any help he could offer.

Was she numbed by her loss? Bewildered by being thrust suddenly into the role of widow? Foxe did not think so. He felt sure what he was seeing was an act; a role deliberately assumed to divert unwanted sympathy or attention. He could not at that time have explained what it was, but something about her convinced him there was steel behind this gentle, unassuming facade.

'I am afraid I will need to ask you many questions, madam,' Foxe said, 'both of yourself and other members of your household. Some may seem intrusive or even impertinent, but I assure you all will be necessary if I am to help you.'

Mrs Danson nodded. 'I will answer if I can, sir, although I have little or no knowledge of my late husband's affairs. As for the servants, I will instruct them to give you every assistance and answer your questions truthfully.'

'Thank you,' Foxe said. 'May I start by asking whether your husband had any known enemies?'

'Let me be frank with you,' she replied. 'If I don't tell you, others soon will. My husband and I were married about a year-and-a-half ago. Before that, I was employed in a bordello. How I came to be there is of little relevance, though I will tell you if it becomes necessary. Dr Danson visited that establishment several times after his first wife died, generally choosing a different companion each time. One day, he chose me. He must have liked me for each time he came after that he asked for me in particular. So much so that the other girls took to calling me "The Minister's Wife". One day, he suggested we should marry.'

'You accepted.'

'Not at once. I did not enjoy my life in that place, but I had become used to it. Being no great beauty and unwilling to offer any of the "special services" some men demanded, I often went for hours without any callers displaying the slightest interest in me. Those who did were usually elderly and required little beyond a comforting feminine presence. Still, it was not a good life nor one with much to offer me after the beginning.'

'Why did you stay?' It was an impertinent question, but Foxe's curiosity would not allow him to stay silent on the topic.

'You could say I had little choice. That was, however, only part of the truth. At the start, I took whatever the house offered. I learned to speak well, I learned good manners and proper deportment. I learned how to pour tea elegantly and make polite conversation. I even learned how to dress like a lady, even if no real lady would have accepted me as other than I was.'

'Then Dr Danson asked you to marry him. Surely he was much older than you?'

'That didn't bother me. I spent much of my time with elderly men. In some ways, I preferred them. Young ones expect you to pretend to experience ecstasies from their clumsy fumblings. Old men know their limitations and are grateful for kind words, caresses and tolerance for their lack of vigour. They know you only sleep with them because they pay you. Young men like to assume you let them keep thrusting and gasping away because you enjoy it.'

Foxe had never thought of that.

'Dr Danson was known to be a recluse,' his widow continued, 'and he was also known to be wealthy. After some thought, I decided he would be able to look after me well. His wants would also be modest, and I would not be expected to appear in society to suffer nothing but snubs and sneers. I also believed I could make him a good wife. I asked for little and tried to look after him as well as I could. I found, to my surprise, that the management of servants was not as difficult as I had feared. To my even greater surprise, I discovered most of them enjoyed working in this house.'

'I am sorry to ask this, but can you tell me the source of your husband's wealth? I understand he was not always a rich man.'

'I have heard that as well. Unfortunately, he never discussed such matters with me. He gave me a regular allowance for housekeeping and paid the servants' wages. I accounted for all expenditure regularly and to his apparent satisfaction. He also gave me a set amount of pin money and an allowance for clothes. Everything else he dealt with himself. He was not extravagant in his expenditure, Mr Foxe, but not niggardly either. Only in one area did he seem to expend large sums without limit.'

'What area was that?'

'His library. That was where he spent nearly all his time and that was where he died. When you have finished questioning me, I will tell Gunton to take you there.'

'Gunton?'

'Archibald Gunton, the butler. He takes his duties very seriously, but he is not such a rigid creature as he appears. He scared me at first, but we have come to understand each other. If there is anything else you should know beyond what I can tell you, he is the person to ask.'

Foxe's head was buzzing with questions, but he needed time and space to digest what he had been told already, not yet more surprises. He therefore thanked Mrs Danson for her candour and said he had no more questions for the moment.

'Then I have some for you, Mr Foxe,' the lady said. 'Your visiting card describes you as a bookseller. What is a bookseller doing involving himself in the investigation of a crime involving people whom he has never met?'

'That is a long and involved story, madam,' Foxe replied. 'I am quite willing to answer your question fully. However, I must beg your indulgence to postpone my response to another time, when we both have greater leisure available.'

'I will hold you to that, sir. You are not the only one possessed of boundless curiosity. My second question is simpler. Who was it that suggested you come here?'

'His Worship the Mayor, as I told you, via an intermediary.'

'That is what surprised me. Gunton, who bore my message to His Worship yesterday, reported that the man seemed barely interested.'

That was typical of the present mayor. The man loved the status and trappings of the role but avoided any duties which might demand actual effort. Even so, Foxe thought it best to give a more diplomatic answer.

'It is the responsibility of the family of a murdered man to launch a prosecution, madam, not the magistrate. He did not wish to leave you unsupported, so he made sure I knew about it and could offer my help.'

Mrs Danson looked at Foxe for what felt like a long time, though it could have been no more than a few moments.

'A most careful answer,' she said at last. 'My husband has been dead barely a day and already I am learning many new things. Very well. With your help, Mr Foxe, I may yet surprise His Worship a good deal — as I suspect I have surprised you. Let us hope so. Poor Gunton was much discomfited by the mayor's response. I have no idea whether he liked his master, but he had a lively sense of what he felt was due to him as a gentleman and a scholar. The dead can receive no comfort from us, but I would be glad to feel that Gunton's outraged feelings could be pacified.'

Foxe said nothing. He was too astonished and confused. By this point, he wished only to escape and recover himself. However, it was not to be.

'One last point,' Mrs Danson said. 'Not a question this time but what may prove useful information. A stranger came to this house yesterday. I did not see him, since he asked for my husband. According to Gunton, the man was expected. My husband had given instructions he should be admitted without delay. Since, as usual, Dr Danson was in his library, that was where Gunton took the visitor. On his return downstairs, Gunton sent one of the maids up with a tray of refreshments. She told him later that she had found her master and his visitor already deep in conversation. "They was lookin' at some o' they old books together" were her exact words. Gunton tells me he did not see the man leave, but you can verify that with him.'

She stood up and pulled the bell-cord to summon a servant. After a short delay, Gunton came in person, obviously expecting to be instructed to show Foxe out. If he was surprised at being told to take Mr Foxe to the library, allow him to explore as he wished and answer all his questions fully, he didn't show it. He simply bowed an acceptance of his instructions and walked to the door, where he waited for Foxe to join him.

As he entered Danson's library behind the magisterial form of Archibald Gunton, Foxe couldn't suppress a gasp of awe and admiration. The room must have run across almost the full width of the house. There were six huge windows looking out onto the street, each equipped with a narrow seat where you might catch the full light on some poorly printed page or written manuscript. The ceiling was at least the height of the hall below and richly plastered. No wall coverings were necessary since every wall, including those between the windows, was covered by book-shelving from floor to ceiling. At the far end was a large desk, flanked by two globes on mahogany stands. Opposite the windows stood two upholstered chairs, either side of a fireplace decorated with a magnificent surround of carved marble. Inlaid below the mantle was a thick band of what looked like blue jasper. The only other furniture consisted of a round mahogany table, flanked by two splendid chairs, also in mahogany. It was a library fit for a duke — or the king himself. How the devil had Danson afforded it?

For a few minutes, Foxe simply wandered from one side of the library to the other. He looked at the shelves of books and read some of the titles. Sometimes he took one down, carefully and reverently, to look at the binding or the title page and frontispiece. He was familiar with almost none of the books he leafed through. What to make of, "*Declaratio academica de gaudiis alchemistarum*" by Abraham Kaau, an academic paper of 1738. "An Academic Declaration of the Joys of Alchemy", was that what the title was in English? Foxe's grasp of Latin was rudimentary. "*Sermo academicus de chemia suos errores expurgante*" by Herman Boerhaave, published in Leiden in 1718. "An Academic sermon about Purging Chemistry of Its Errors". Was that a correct translation? Then, at last, a book in plain English: "*The Sceptical Chymist*" of 1661 by the famous Robert Boyle. And so on, and so on. Books translated from Arabic, the works of Aristotle: ten volumes bound in white vellum. A cornucopia of rare and exotic items to delight the bibliophile.

If Foxe's mind had been in a tumult before, it was now a mass of confusion, spiced with rampant envy at all that lay around him. Finally, and with the greatest reluctance, he tore himself away from his inspection of this dazzling repository of volumes and turned to ask the butler a question.

'May I ask you where you found your late master, Mr Gunton?' Foxe's polite speech and use of the title 'mister' won the butler over in an instant. He did not unbend, but the look in his eye as he replied conveyed both surprise and respect.

'In this chair beside the library table, sir.'

'Was there anything on the table?'

'Just the tray with the coffee pot and cups. I ascertained that both cups had been used when I cleared them away later.'

'No books had been left there?'

'None.'

'Yet Mrs Danson said the maid had said that your master and his visitor were examining several books they had set out between them.'

'That is so, sir. I imagine the master had put them all away. The master was most particular about his books. He always returned them to their correct places on the shelves himself. He would never have allowed any of them to be placed on a table where there was coffee, or anything else which might stain them.'

'Thank you, Mr Gunton. It is clear that you are most observant.' This won Foxe a slight but perceptible relaxation in the butler's stance. 'What are you able to tell me about the visitor whom you brought into this room?'

'I formed the opinion that he was expected, sir. Dr Danson did not, save on rare occasions, receive any visitors and certainly not in his library. On this occasion, however, he informed me he was expecting someone that morning who should be shown into his library without delay.'

'When did your master tell you this?' Foxe asked.

'On the previous evening. I cannot be certain when or how his visitor had made the arrangement for that day, sir, but Dr Danson did receive a letter some days earlier. He opened it in my presence and I observed it produced unusual excitement when he read it.'

'Can you describe this visitor, Mr Gunton? What name was on his card? What impression did he make on you?'

'As I recall, his card gave his name as Mr Cornelius Wake of Golden Square, London. However, if I may be frank with you, I didn't like the look of the man. There was something false about him, as if he was acting a part in the theatre. I also became convinced that English was not his native tongue. He spoke it too precisely and sometimes used an odd way of pronouncing certain words. Whatever his origin, the gentleman, to my mind, was almost from foreign parts. The name on his card was not his real name either. In my experience in service, sir, which is extensive, I have developed an instinct in such matters.'

'I believe you, Mr Gunton. One last question. Is everything as it was on the day your master died?'

'It is. Nothing has been touched, save for the removal of the tray, as I mentioned. The master had some system of his own for arranging his books. The servants were forbidden to touch any of them, on pain of immediate dismissal. Apart from one thing, that is. The master kept a dagger on his desk, for slitting the pages of new books I believe. That was what was used to kill him, sir. It was taken away with his body.'

Foxe thanked the butler for his help and asked to be taken back to Mrs Danson, so that he might take his leave. His mind had been full before he came to the library. Now it could not accept any more information without bursting.

As he thanked the lady and prepared to leave, Foxe remarked that Dr Danson had possessed a remarkable library.

'It was my husband's pride and joy, Mr Foxe. He loved it with a passion he never displayed towards anything — or anyone — else. He spent nearly all his time in that room, and he was forever procuring fresh books to add to his collection. To be honest, aside from his obsession with them, I know next to nothing about those books. Nor would I have wished to. They were exactly like my husband, sir: dusty, dull and filled with incomprehensible nonsense.'

'You took no interest in his researches?' Foxe asked

'None. He would not have welcomed such interest even if I had. He was a secretive man by nature, Mr Foxe. Never more so than when it concerned his library or whatever so-called researches occupied his mind. Sharing was foreign to him. Most nights he stayed up late reading or writing notes by candlelight, while I went to bed. Most days he shut himself away and appeared only for meals — and not always then. As you must have guessed, Mr Foxe, I did not love my husband. I regret his death, as I would the death of any human being, but no more than that. If I urge you to find his killer, it is a combination of curiosity and a proper regard for justice that drives me. It is nothing else, I assure you.'

3

Despite his confusion and weariness of mind, Foxe was denied the chance to return home immediately. Halloran had told him the inquest on Dr Danson was to be held that afternoon at the Guildhall. Foxe decided he needed to attend, if only to discover what might have come to light during the necessary medical examination. At least he might be able to find time to order his thoughts during the routine parts.

Since Foxe arrived late, when the clerk to the court was about to open the proceedings, he had to sit on the front row of chairs. He would have preferred to be at the back, from where he could look around and note expressions and overhear whispers. It was not to be. The best he could do was snatch a brief look at the public benches as he entered. Why were so many people present? It must, he thought, be because the dead man had surrounded himself with an air of mystery. It was soon proved this was a false hope. The onlookers who expected to discover shocking and fascinating secrets were going to be disappointed.

The coroner opened the inquest with the usual matters: the formal identification of the deceased and the finding of the body. For this purpose, he called the butler, Mr Gunton. The man stood stiffly erect as he gave his evidence, all the while contriving to suggest outrage at being compelled to do so.

Next, Mrs Danson took the oath. She was asked to explain whether there had been anything unusual about her husband's state of mind, health or behaviour prior to his murder. Foxe noted that, in deference to public expectation, she was now dressed in black and heavily veiled. He would have accepted a large wager that many of those present had come to see her. Her previous life was well known in the city and the gossips had been busy elaborating upon it. They too were quickly disappointed.

She spoke firmly and precisely from behind her veil. Foxe had to admire her. She must have known that ugly rumours were already circulating, implying she had a hand in her husband's death. Yet here she was, standing erect and giving her evidence in a firm, calm voice. Many a wife of better breeding and impeccable virtue would have displayed far less courage and good sense. In successive answers to the coroner's questions, she denied noticing any change in her husband's manner, refuted the suggestion that he had shown either anxiety or fear in the days before his death and stated that she knew of no enemies who might have wished him harm. When it came to the matter of her husband's unusual visitor, the coroner jumped on her words. Could she give the court a description of the man? She could not, since she had not set eyes on him.

At that point, the coroner asked her to stand down and recalled Gunton.

'The gentleman gave his name as Mr Cornelius Wake,' the butler said. 'I understood he was expected. That is all I can tell the court. I had never seen him before and do not know the purpose of his visit.'

'What did he look like?' the coroner asked.

'As to his appearance, sir, it was largely unremarkable. However, I did reach the conclusion he came from foreign parts. Mostly, I should add, due to his tendency to speak in a stilted manner.'

This was much more to the audience's liking. An excited buzz arose. Several turned to their neighbours and stated, as a positive fact, that foreigners were well known to be behind most crimes in the city. Heads nodded all around.

The coroner banged his gavel several times and demanded silence on pain of having the public expelled from the rest of the proceedings. That reduced the crowd to angry mumbling and earned him a good many hostile looks. However, nothing more of note could be drawn from Mr Gunton. The coroner's further questions about Mr Wake met with monosyllabic answers and an air of barely-concealed scorn.

Next came the medical evidence. Foxe began to take greater notice. That the cause of death was stabbing, he knew already. The weapon was also evident, since it had remained in the wound. However, when asked if he could offer any further evidence, the surgeon who had carried out the autopsy sprang one surprise.

'I probed the wound with a thin rod,' he said. 'The blade had entered between the ribs on the left side of the deceased's chest, leaving a small tear in his waistcoat and shirt. It had been directed forwards and slightly downwards. Thus, it had passed through the muscles of the chest wall before piercing the left ventricle of the heart. Death would have been instantaneous — had not the victim already been dead.'

'Already dead! Are you sure? You'll need to explain that remark more fully,' the coroner asked.

'Simple,' the surgeon said. 'A dead body does not bleed. A moderate amount of blood had leaked from the site of the wound, sir, but no more than that. Had the blow with the dagger been the cause of death, the whole of the area around and below the wound would have been soaked.'

'Can you estimate how long Dr Danson had been dead when he was stabbed?'

'Not long, in my opinion. Had there been an appreciable period between death and the blow being struck, there would have been no blood at all. The amount of liquid blood found indicates it would have been no more than a few minutes.'

The coroner shook his head in bafflement. 'Are you saying the assailant killed the man by some other means, waited several minutes, then stabbed him to make sure?'

'Only the murderer could answer such a question, sir. What I can say is that the man died from a heart attack and then, a little later, was attacked violently. Considerable force was used to drive the blade home. From the angle at which it penetrated, I would imagine the assailant was standing, while the deceased was seated where he was found.'

'Please explain why you believe great force was used?'

'We know the weapon used had a sharp, thin blade, but one which was rather short. To be honest, I am amazed it managed to penetrate as deeply as it did. I therefore attribute that fact to the violence with which it had been forced home.'

'Can you provide any evidence about what caused Dr Danson's heart to fail at precisely that time?' the coroner asked.

'My guess would be the blow the man had received to the face, perhaps accompanied by a severe shock. Heart attacks may arise at any time, especially in the elderly. Of course, a severe shock puts additional strain on the heart and may precipitate such an event. There was definite pre-mortem bruising about the lower part of the face. That must have been from a heavy blow, in my opinion.'

'By a fist?'

'That is the most likely answer.'

'Would it have been enough to render the man unconscious?'

'That is harder to say,' the surgeon replied. 'In combination with shock and excitement, the normal beating of the heart might have been interrupted. That alone would be enough to cause the man to faint. I cannot say for certain whether the blow alone would have knocked him unconscious. Given that a heart attack followed soon afterwards, it might very well have done so.'

The coroner was forced to be content with that. He therefore wound matters up swiftly. The jury were asked to return a verdict and he reminded them that they could only name the murderer if they had clear evidence to support their assertion. In his opinion, they did not. It might have been the mysterious Mr Wake, but there was nothing to prove it.

Foxe admired the coroner for his judicious words. The jury were probably longing to blame the killing on the mysterious foreigner. Hopefully, this stern injunction would dissuade them from doing so.

He was proved correct. After the briefest of retirements, the jury dutifully recorded a verdict of "murder by person or persons unknown". They were then dismissed, and everyone dispersed. As they filed out, many people of the audience directed angry glances towards the chair where the coroner had been seated. Whatever the law, they were quite sure they knew who the murderer was. After all, Foxe heard several tell their neighbours, foreigners were always killing one another on the slightest excuse, weren't they? It stood to reason one of them would do it again, even in England.

FOXE HAD MUCH TO THINK ABOUT. WHY SHOULD SOMEONE ATTACK Danson, render him unconscious and return several minutes later to kill him with the dagger? Of course, if his victim had been unconscious from the blow, the murderer might well not have been aware he had already died. The obvious answer was that the killer had spent that time looking for something to steal. Then, to make sure he would not be identified, he decided to finish the old man off. The problem with that explanation, of course, was the fact nothing had been taken or even disarranged. According to Gunton that is. Could he be lying? Could he be protecting someone? The affair had now become hopelessly confusing!

Foxe was denied more time to puzzle over what he had heard by a chance meeting. As he was walking away from the Guildhall, deep in thought, he encountered one of his better, if rather occasional, customers. William Buxton, a prosperous corn merchant, was a man with many contacts in the city, as Foxe knew. He was also well connected with the Presbyterians who used the new Octagon Chapel. If anyone would know about the Reverend Jonathan Danson, D.D, in his days as a minister, it would be Mr Buxton. Fortunately, he had no especially pressing business. He readily accepted Foxe's invitation to partake in a pot of coffee in a nearby coffeehouse.

Once they were seated and supplied with drinks, Foxe broached the subject uppermost in his mind.

'Danson?' Mr Buxton said. 'What can I say? I know you shouldn't speak ill of the dead, but the plain truth is that the fellow was an old fool. He'd tried being a proper Christian minister and serving a congregation. No good at either, if you ask me. For a start, he was one of the most boring speakers anyone had ever encountered. He was passed from congregation to congregation, eventually ending with one so small they could barely pay him enough to live on. Back then, he was too poor to afford better than an old coat spotted green with mildew and shoes with holes. His poor first wife relied mostly on handouts of old clothes from kind members of their congregation.'

'When did things change for him?' Foxe asked.

'About the time his first wife died — around four years ago that was — Danson received a small legacy. Not much, as we all thought at the time, but enough to let him resign from his last congregation and bury himself in a rundown house somewhere near the castle. As I heard it, he then lost his faith and his wits and started to dabble in alchemy and various sorts of magic; thought he was going to discover the hidden secrets of the universe in a pile of mildewed books written by long-discredited authors. Damned dangerous, I call it. Start tinkering with the spirits and demons and you don't know where you'll end up.'

'Did he continue preaching at all?' Foxe asked. 'I know there are some former ministers who either preach on occasion or give lectures on their areas of study.'

'Who would have had him? No respectable chapel would let him in through its doors. As for public lectures, anyone foolish enough to attend would die of boredom. No, he became a kind of recluse. Lived with his old books and a half-crazy woman to act as his cook and housekeeper. Each was as mad as the other.'

'Do you know where his wealth came from?'

'No idea. People were amazed. One minute he's living in poverty, the next he's leased a fancy house and hired a small army of servants.'

'Perhaps his legacy was larger than you all thought?' Foxe said.

'Must have been, I suppose. If so, why did he wait so long to start throwing his money around? There were dark rumours about him before. His startling rise in the world produced a further mass of speculation. The commonest rumour was that he'd finally found the Philosopher's Stone and begun changing lead into gold. Stuff and nonsense, obviously.'

'Can you recall exactly when the man began to act as if he were rich?'

'About eighteen months or so ago,' Buxton replied. 'Not long before he married again.'

'I know you don't approve of the subject of his so-called researches,' Foxe said, 'but do you know if he was genuine in his scholarship? For example, where did he obtain his degree of Doctor of Divinity? Neither the universities of Oxford nor Cambridge would have accepted him. They require all those studying or teaching there to be practising members of the Church of England.'

'One of the Dissenting Academies I would imagine,' Buxton replied. 'Maybe the one in Daventry. Either that or he invented it himself to try to make his ideas seem more impressive. So far as I know, he was never a member of the established church, let alone an ordained one. I think his father was a petty tradesman. I don't even know where he had later obtained the money needed to undertake a lengthy period of study. A wealthy patron or relative, perhaps?'

'His congregation, when he had one, must have believed in his learning, surely.'

'He certainly acted like a scholar. That's true enough. Still, you could check up on his degree status easily enough. The extent and quality of his scholarship would be much more difficult to estimate. His study lay in such odd areas. I can't imagine many people could begin to assess how sound it was. All I can tell you is that none of the leading men of learning in this city — men like our own minister or Dr Priestley, for example — were willing to give him the time of day. What's your interest in the man, Foxe? He's dead, so you can't sell him any of your over-priced books.'

'I didn't even know he collected books until I went to his house yesterday,' Foxe said. 'His library is quite magnificent, you know. If he collected it all recently, it must have cost him a fortune.'

'You've been to his house, have you? Did you meet the pretty Katherine?'

'His wife — or rather his widow now? Yes, I did. To be honest, she surprised me.'

'You know she used to work in a bordello?'

'She told me so herself,' Foxe said. 'Quite open about it too.'

'It sounds as if she impressed you,' Buxton replied, smiling. 'Not easy to do in your case, I imagine.'

'She did,' Foxe said. 'I found her sensible, frank and a good deal quicker in her mind than you might imagine.'

'Could be a business opportunity for you there, Foxe. The new widow will hardly want to keep all those weird books. She might well be willing to let you find buyers for them, if you play your cards right. Don't tell me you hadn't thought of that!'

'Of course, I had, Buxton, but the day after her husband was found murdered was hardly the time to discuss it. And don't be so cynical about the kind of books Danson collected. More people are interested in books on such subjects than you might think. I had a visit from one such person only a day or so ago.'

'Well, you should know, if anyone does. Did Danson buy books from you or was that beyond even his purse?' The price Foxe asked for the books he sold was a perennial subject of banter between them.

'Never. Wherever he found his books, it wasn't from me or anyone else I know in the trade.'

'Got anything new I might be interested in?' Buxton asked. 'I might just have a small amount of money to spend on the right volumes.'

After that, the talk was all of books and bindings, until the two parted around half an hour later.

❧ 4 ❧

The matter of Dr Danson's death was beginning to interest Foxe a great deal. Unfortunately, before he could get any further, news reached him there had been another murder. this one had taken place at the end of a masquerade ball at the Assembly House. Even worse, the murdered man was a member of the aristocracy. Halloran and the mayor were bound to want him to get involved. Dammit! Just when he felt sure he was on the way towards making a breakthrough in the murder of Danson. Why, oh why, did he ever complain life was dull or wish for a new mystery to liven things up?

Like many of the wealthier citizens of Norwich, Foxe had been delighted with the new Assembly House. Thomas Ivory, the city's leading architect and builder, had designed and opened it in 1754. Since then, he had attended many assemblies, balls and routs in the building. It had proved a great success and Foxe had enjoyed himself immensely most times he had been there. The building itself was elegant and finely proportioned. Inside, the decoration was of equal quality, for Ivory had not stinted at any point. Events there also offered Foxe two things he dearly loved: one was dancing, at which he fancied himself a master, and the other was the chance to show off — an activity in which few in the city could even hope to surpass him. There was, of course, the added bonus of the presence of a large number of pretty women. Going to a fashionable ball at the Assembly House was guaranteed to raise Foxe's spirits to peak levels.

There was, however, one type of ball that Foxe disliked — the masquerade. He was proud of his good looks and something of a dandy in his dress. To spend the evening wearing a mask and a costume of some kind did not appeal to him in the slightest. That, and his temporary lack of a suitable partner, had accounted for his absence from the masquerade that Saturday evening. He had therefore not been present when Lord Frederick Aylestone, the youngest son of Viscount Penngrove, was found murdered in a room away from the main hall itself.

Poor Foxe had not yet completed his breakfast when a messenger arrived from Alderman Halloran. His master, he told Alfred, was requesting Mr Foxe's attendance on him. He should come with all possible speed.

When he arrived, Foxe tried to divert the alderman's attention by telling him that he felt sure he was on the track of Danson's murderer. That produced scarcely a flicker of interest, so he added an idea which had only occurred to him that very morning. He suggested the murder of the reclusive scholar might be connected to the embezzlement from the city treasury which Halloran had told him about.

Halloran dismissed even that with a wave of his hand.

'I have far more important matters on my mind, Foxe,' he said. 'Viscount Penngrove has already been in touch with the mayor and frightened the fellow half to death. He seems to feel the city and its government are somehow to blame for what took place.'

'What nonsense!' Foxe said. 'It was a private event, surely. Besides, Lord Aylestone must have been more than twenty-one years old and quite capable of deciding for himself where to go and what to do.'

'Don't be naive, Foxe. Viscount Penngrove is rich, extremely influential where it matters most and looks down on the leaders of this city as mere tradesmen. He's angrier than a nest of wasps that have been poked with a stick and he's looking for someone to take the blame for his son's death. The mayor's desperate for you to do your magic and come up with the culprit, before the viscount has him drummed out of office.'

'What can I do?' Foxe asked. 'I wasn't even there.'

'It's a great shame you weren't,' Halloran said, 'but your absence is hardly relevant. You don't need to have watched a murder take place to work out who did it.'

'Even if I had been present, I don't see how that would have saved young Aylestone,' Foxe said. 'I loathe masquerade balls anyway.' He knew he sounded petty. Halloran simply ignored him.

'His Worship has asked me to urge you to take a special and urgent interest in this matter,' he said. 'Viscount Penngrove, as I just said, is a man of considerable influence at court. The mayor feels his poor opinion of our city could best be raised by presenting him with the means to bring a successful prosecution against whoever killed his son. As quickly as possible too.'

Foxe protested that he already had an investigation underway; one which promised to be more than usually complex to unravel. Once again, Halloran was unimpressed.

'Please do as the mayor asks, Foxe,' he said, 'if only for my sake. If I have to tell him you've refused to get involved, my life will be a misery.'

'I'm surprised Aylestone was at the ball at all,' Foxe said. He knew he would have to get involved, but he wasn't going to give in easily. 'He has a reputation for being far too serious for such entertainments. Hasn't he got himself involved with some puritanical minister who thinks godliness and misery are one and the same thing? You do know Aylestone was the author of that pamphlet? The one denouncing the theatre as the principal source and support for all lechery, vice and godlessness in the city, don't you? The boy was a fool, as well as a killjoy of monumental proportions.'

'Penngrove told the mayor he'd commanded the young man to be there, in the hope he might find a potential wife amongst those present. When his son protested that to attend such a vulgar entertain-ment would be inappropriate for someone known to be serious about his religion, his father was ready with an answer. Lord Aylestone was to wear a mask covering a good part of his face. He was also to be dressed, quite inappropriately, as a Harlequin. His son had thus been led to believe his true identity would remain concealed. He just had to remember to leave before the point at the end of the evening when everyone always displayed their true identities.'

'All the aristocracy are interested in is getting heirs to ensure the family holds onto their estates,' Foxe grumbled. 'They sell their children like cattle at an auction. Balls like that are part entertainment, part marriage market. Eligible daughters are paraded around like prize heifers, while their mothers seek out suitable husbands for them.'

'Now you sound like one of those seditious radicals,' Halloran said. 'We all know how it's done. Stop being silly, please. Do as you're asked and find out who killed this fellow. Then you can go back to whatever you're involved in at present, the mayor will be happy, and I'll have time to enjoy my books again.'

How could Foxe do anything else but agree?

❧

HALLORAN'S DEMAND TO FOCUS ALL HIS EFFORTS ON THE MURDER OF Lord Aylestone only increased Foxe's bout of bad temper. He had now gone for more than ten days without any female company in his bed, though he could have found some anytime he wished. The trouble was, he discovered, he didn't have the heart for it. As a result, his servants had begun to question Molly, the housemaid, after she had been to fold back the shutters in her master's bedroom. Two heads on the pillow meant a cheerful and relaxed atmosphere in the house. One head signalled another day of sour looks and outbursts of irritation.

Foxe could not have explained the reason for this unaccustomed continence. He'd thought many times of spending time in a suitable bordello. He could also follow his past practice and go to the theatre. There he could usually charm one of the younger actresses into coming back to his house after the performance. The real reason why he did neither was simple. What he needed was comfort and loving attention, not a night of sexual athletics. Whatever the source of a temporary bed-partner, Foxe knew in his heart what they all wanted: as good a time as he could give them, followed by a suitable reward — money or an expensive present — at the end. He'd gone down that path many times in the past and knew how the business went. Of course, in the days when Kitty and Gracie Catt were his constant sources of female company things had been different. The sisters had provided an ideal balance. Kitty was excitable and sexually voracious; Gracie, the elder, was calm, attentive and warmly appreciative of his presence. Sadly, the two of them had left Norwich for good, and that was that.

By the time Foxe dined that evening with his oldest friend, Captain Brock, his mood had descended from simple misery into the deepest self-pity. Brock's wife, Lady Henfield, was away visiting the home of her former brother-in law, the Earl of Pentelow, so Brock had come on his own. The two had met less frequently since Brock's marriage, which was a matter of regret for them both. Since retiring from a glittering naval career, Brock had tried to settle down but the draw of the sea and ships proved too much for him. With Foxe as a sleeping partner to provide the initial capital, he had built up a thriving business in a fleet of wherries running between Norwich, Great Yarmouth and Lowestoft. These small, flat-bottomed and sail-driven boats served to transport goods to and from the deep-water harbours on the coast, using rivers like the Wensum and the Yare. They were the lifeline of Norwich's overseas trade and Brock's fleet were accounted as the best and most reliable of the wherries.

Hardly had they exchanged greetings that day when Foxe started complaining about the mayor's demands.

'Halloran expects I'll rearrange my activities to keep the mayor from pestering him,' he complained. 'He never considers the amount of time I'm forced to devote to his investigations; nor the stupidity of young men in getting themselves murdered. Viscount Penngrove is a pompous, arrogant bully and his son was a useless fool. Lord Aylestone, curse him, was too idle to devote himself to anything worthwhile and too dim-witted to do anything else. If I'm to be honest, I'd have to say that whoever killed the fellow did the world a favour.'

'You only dislike him because he tried to get the theatre closed down,' Brock said mildly. 'He's typical of the youngest sons of the aristocracy. They know they'll have to support themselves eventually, given that the eldest always inherits the title, the estates and almost everything else. Yet their families never think to equip them with any skills beyond dancing, drinking, horse riding and gambling. Unless they manage to marry an heiress, most of them spend their lives in well-deserved obscurity. Few actually prosper.'

Foxe ignored him. 'It's my own fault,' he said. 'I shouldn't have tempted fate by saying I wanted a good case to occupy my mind. As soon as I had one — the death of Dr Danson — along comes Halloran. The fellow tells me — almost orders me — to leave that alone. Instead, I'm to rush off and investigate the death of this blue-blooded nitwit. A man who was worth little to himself or anyone else. I should have refused, of course, but I'm too easy-going.'

Brock had by now had more than enough of listening to Foxe whine.

'Pull yourself together and stop behaving like a spoiled child!' he snapped. 'Whoever the victim was, he didn't deserve to be murdered, did he? Besides, everyone knows you can't resist poking your nose into any unexplained killing. You'd have been furious if Halloran and the mayor hadn't called you in or had gone to someone else. Now, behave yourself or I'm going to go home right now. All this self-pity is enough to curdle any sensible person's stomach. My dear wife and I attended that masquerade ball, even if you didn't. If you'll stop ranting, I'll tell you exactly what I saw.'

Foxe could be a self-regarding misery at times, but he was never a fool. He closed his mouth and waited to hear what his friend had to say.

'For a start, everyone knew Viscount Penngrove had forced his son to attend in the hope some suitable young woman would take his fancy. Aylestone was still single and his father was well aware of his short-comings. His son's best hope of making anything of himself was to marry a woman with brains, backbone and money as well. Someone who would take her husband in hand and stop him wasting his life on religious bigotry.

'Naturally, it proved to be an abject failure, as you would expect. Aylestone was morose and uncommunicative from the start of the evening. Far from meeting any potential brides, he lurked on his own at the edge of the dance area. He refused to join in the dancing or go to the card-room and socialise. One or two hopeful mothers attempted to introduce their daughters to him. All were snubbed, often rudely. The only time he became animated was when he saw a couple dressed as a shepherd and shepherdess and learned they were an actor and actress from the Norwich Company of Comedians. Adam Bewell, I think it was, and a Miss Catherine Marsh. The sight of them made Aylestone furious. He demanded that they should be ejected, saying they polluted the occasion and disgraced the others present by their attendance.'

'How did the Master of Ceremonies deal with that?' Foxe asked, becoming intrigued despite himself.

'Despite the efforts of those around him,' Brock replied, 'Lord Aylestone could not be quieted. Anyone else making such a commotion would have been turned out into the street. The Master of Ceremonies didn't dare do that to Viscount Penngrove's son. Instead, he quietly asked the other two to leave of their own accord for the sake of peace and good order. I understand he promised to refund what they had paid for their tickets and give them more tickets, gratis, for the next assembly ball. He was almost certain Aylestone wouldn't be present again. His father would be too embarrassed by what was happening and would make sure he stayed away. Since, by this time, Miss Marsh was in tears, the two agreed and left. I imagine Bewell escorted the lady home.'

'What about Lord Aylestone?'

'His father was furious and bundled his son out of the main room and into a small annex as quickly as he could. Aylestone's outburst had caused a kind of stunned silence. Even the musicians had stopped playing. We could therefore hear a good deal of the tremendous rebuke the young man was getting for his behaviour. In the end, Viscount Penngrove ordered Lord Aylestone to return to the event and behave in a more seemly manner.'

'Did he?' Foxe asked.

'If he did, he stayed well out of sight,' Brock told him. 'Even he must have realised that he'd made himself a public spectacle. Whatever he did, I didn't notice him for most of the rest of the evening. Nor, I imagine, did anyone else.'

'You didn't see him again at all?'

'Almost at the end of the evening, most of us caught a quick glimpse of the fellow. He was standing at the edge of the stage where the musicians were playing, staring glumly into the main hall. At that point, he was still wearing his mask.'

'How did you know it was him then?'

'His Harlequin costume was quite distinctive. None of the other people dressed as a Harlequin looked anything like he did.'

Foxe considered this for a moment, then posed a final question. 'Do you know how and when his body was found?'

'It must have been about the time the final dances of the evening started,' Brock said. 'Two people went into the room where Viscount Penngrove had taken his son earlier. Probably to indulge in some amorous activities behind a curtain which hangs there. You'll recall it. It covers a space where chairs and tables are usually stored.' Foxe nodded in agreement. 'That's where they found Lord Aylestone. He had been stabbed in the chest and was quite dead.'

'How long was this after you'd all seen him at the side of the stage by the musicians?'

'I'd estimate about fifteen or twenty minutes. Certainly no more.'

'Pah!' Foxe said. 'To think Halloran dragged me away from a sensible mystery just for this!'

'Are you telling me you've solved it purely on what I've told you tonight?' Brock's voice was heavily tinged with scepticism.

'Not everything, but the main part. It's blindingly obvious.'

'Not to me it isn't.'

'Look, it's perfectly plain who killed Aylestone and why it was done. I don't yet have enough to convince miserable sceptics like you and Halloran, but that's just a matter of digging a bit deeper in the right places.'

'Who did it then? If you're so clever, explain who it was and how you know.'

'How I know is because I listened carefully and used my brain. Reasoning, Brock. Simple reasoning from cause to effect. You could do the same if you tried. In fact, I'll leave you to do just that while I work out the rest.'

'Which is?'

'Exactly how the killer went about producing what he hoped would convince everyone it had nothing to do with him. Once I have that, I'll have enough to take to Halloran and give Viscount Penngrove the explanation and the evidence he needs to ensure a conviction. You're right. No one deserves to be murdered, however much better off the world will be without him. If I didn't believe that, I'd keep my ideas to myself and avoid sending another poor fellow to the gallows.'

AFTER ALBERT, HIS VALET, HAD COLLECTED FOXE'S CLOTHING AND left him alone to settle down for the night, Foxe found himself too anxious in his mind to find sleep right away. He wasn't thinking about Lord Aylestone's murder. What he'd said to Brock contained a good deal of bravado, but he was still convinced he knew what had happened. All that was left was to be able to prove it to a jury. What was worrying him was he couldn't delay the boring business of collecting that evidence. He'd get no peace from Halloran and the mayor until he could present them with the complete answer.

In the meantime, poor Mrs Danson would think he had lost interest in investigating her husband's death. It was a measure of the esteem in which he held her that he determined the very least he could do was to visit the lady himself and explain the circumstances. At the same time, there were at least three important questions he'd failed to ask on his earlier visit. What could she tell him about the letter the butler had mentioned? Did her husband have any regular visitors and, if so, who they were? Oh yes. Did she know he had a weak heart?

As soon as it was late enough in the morning to make his visit with proper politeness, Foxe went back to the house in Pottergate. He needn't have worried. The moment he began to explain to Mrs Danson what must draw him away temporarily from his search for her husband's killer, she interrupted him.

'Mr Foxe. I'd guessed before you came that you'd have to look into the death of Lord Aylestone. The needs of the aristocracy and upper gentry always take precedence over everything else, don't they? That's the way of the world. You needn't apologise.'

Such clear-headed logic left Foxe somewhat in awe, and he hurried on to cover his confusion. What could she tell him about the mysterious letter her husband had received? Was he correct in assuming it had told him his visitor would come on that particular day?

'I know nothing about any such letter, Mr Foxe,' she said. 'I would not have seen it when it arrived, and my husband never discussed any of his correspondence with me. If he kept anything of that nature, it would be in the desk in the library. I'll ask Gunton to bring you the keys, so you can look for yourself.'

'Thank you, madam,' Foxe said. 'I cannot stay long enough to do that this morning, but I will take you up on your kind offer as soon as I am free to do so. My second question is quite simple. I believe your husband was stabbed with a dagger he owned. Do you know where it was kept?'

'He was killed with such a weapon, Mr Foxe. A small dagger of foreign make he'd been given at some point in the past. You'll need to ask Gunton where it was kept. I'm afraid I have no idea. I'll call him.'

The butler was called, confirmed what his mistress had said and explained the implement in question was usually kept on the master's desk.

Mrs Danson dismissed Gunton with a nod and turned to Foxe. 'Do you have any further questions?' she asked him.

'Just two more, madam. Did your husband have any regular visitors?'

'I believe I said before that my late husband was a reclusive man. Generally speaking, visitors of any kind were not welcome. Gunton was instructed to inform any who did come that his master was too engaged in his studies to receive anyone. The only regular visitor was Mr Craswall, the apothecary. He came perhaps once each month and sometimes spent an hour or more with my husband.'

'So, you knew about his heart? You were aware your husband was in poor health?'

Mrs Danson smiled. 'He imagined he was. He was always complaining about one ailment or another. I doubt there was much wrong with him. There's a saying that a creaking door lasts longest, Mr Foxe. In my late husband's case, he creaked and groaned sufficiently to make himself immortal. He never mentioned heart problems though.'

'May I ask if the apothecary was treating him?' Foxe said. 'Some people who think themselves ill consume various medicines in large amounts.'

'I can be quite certain in saying he was not being treated by Mr Craswall,' Mrs Danson replied. 'My husband had strange ideas about medicine, as about so much else. He would never have paid for the services of a physician or purchased any medicines from the apothecary; neither for himself nor for me. He preferred to rely on various strange concoctions based on recipes taken from the old books he read. Sometimes he mixed them himself in the kitchen, much to the cook's annoyance. Most smelled dreadful!'

'He gave them to you?' Foxe was appalled by the thought.

'I can assure you I would have nothing to do with such nonsense. I either managed to collect enough from my pin-money to pay for my own treatment or consulted Mistress Tabby, the Wise Woman. I understand that you know her, Mr Foxe?'

'Indeed, madam, I do, and hold her in high esteem.'

'The feeling is mutual. After your previous visit, I sent my maid to ask her what she could tell me about you.'

Seeing the surprise on Foxe's face, she wagged a finger at him, like a schoolmistress giving a slow pupil a playful rebuke as encouragement.

'You aren't the only one who can enquire into people's backgrounds, as I'm sure you have been doing in my case. Happily, for you, the reply I received from the Wise Woman was quite positive. Had it been the other way, you would have found the door to this house closed firmly against any further entry on your part.'

5

Later the same day, Foxe returned with the greatest reluctance to the matter of the murder at the masquerade ball. He decided to pay a visit to the nearby Theatre Royal — now re-christened "The Grand Music Hall" to avoid sanctions from the authorities. That was thanks to Lord Aylestone's strident reminders that the venue had neither received an official licence to charge entry to the public to see the plays presented there, nor sought approval from the monarch before styling itself "Royal". The name change dealt with the latter point. The former was handled by claiming the public were paying only to watch various musical interludes — now grandly entitled "concerts". The plays were given gratis between the music.

Foxe was an important patron of the theatre, so the manager was delighted to receive him. He remarked that they had not seen enough of him in recent weeks, adding that several of the young, female members of the company were more than eager to make Foxe's acquaintance.

In the past, Foxe would have been pleased by such a comment. That day, however, it was not to his liking. He replied somewhat stuffily that his time had been much occupied with other matters. He also felt sure the actresses concerned had better things to do than think about him.

The manager, bewildered but swiftly aware that he had made a serious gaffe of some kind, bowed and merely enquired how he could be of assistance.

'Tell me what you know of Lord Aylestone,' Foxe demanded gruffly.

'The poor fellow murdered at the masquerade?' the manager said. 'All too much, I'm afraid. Lord Aylestone used to be something of a devotee of the theatre, until he had his heart broken by an actress. She accepted his gifts and led him to believe she doted upon him, then eloped with a sergeant in the militia. Instead of reflecting upon the fickle affections of young ladies, his lordship blamed the theatre, for some incomprehensible reason. He convinced himself her mind had been warped by the need to play heartless jades in certain plays. That and the continual changes of character demanded by taking a variety of roles as the programme demanded.'

'An odd explanation,' Foxe observed. 'Does that particular actress still perform here?'

'She does not. As I told you, she eloped, and we have not seen her since. I imagine she must have left the stage entirely. It all happened perhaps five or six years ago. Lord Aylestone was maybe fifteen at the time. Sixteen perhaps. The loves and hates of youth tend to be violent, do they not?'

'And the man she ran away with?'

'A Welshman, from Pembrokeshire, I believe. Not an actor at all, as I mentioned. Men of that type seduce silly girls wherever they go and leave them behind just as readily.'

Foxe scowled. 'From what you tell me, the noble lord was becoming eccentric even in his youth,' he said. 'Not that he didn't have legitimate cause for complaint.'

'Had he stopped at holding such obviously silly beliefs — aimed, I'm sure, at avoiding the need to accept he had never actually engaged her affection — the matter might have been shrugged off. He was hardly the first to suffer such a fate, nor will he be the last. Sadly, he next fell under the influence of a dissenting preacher with strong puritanical ideas. Members of that particular preacher's congregation had already become a decided nuisance. They were always trying to accost people coming to the theatre and handing out pamphlets denouncing plays as works of the devil. With Lord Aylestone now amongst their number, they grew ever bolder. They persuaded him to write to the Lord Chancellor, claiming the theatre was putting on plays in defiance of the law ...'

'Which you were,' Foxe said drily.

'Of course, Mr Foxe. As you well know, nearly all the theatres in the land do the same. They get around the law, as we do, by claiming to promote and charge for musical concerts. They just happen to have "dramatic entertainments" provided, entirely gratis, in the course of the evening's programme. What Lord Aylestone was doing was trying to make the authorities enforce the law in literal terms. If he could do that, the theatre would be closed down and the shareholders fined. All the actors and actresses would also be put out of work. It's unthinkable!'

'Did you fight back?'

'What could we have done? In legal terms, he was correct. We kept our counsel and hoped the authorities would see sense. Fortunately, that proved to be the case.'

'Did that make Lord Aylestone and the others give up?' Foxe asked.

'Far from it. They had scurrilous pamphlets printed, denouncing the theatre as "the source of all evils and abominations" and "the devil's recruiting ground". These they tried to hand out to our patrons as they arrived. Our players have been insulted in the street and called harlots and molly-boys. We thought it would finally die down and the bigots find other targets for their bile. Now, I expect, they will be back in double measure.'

'What did the players themselves think of Lord Aylestone?'

'Exactly what you might imagine. They invented scabrous names for him and rained down ever more imaginative curses on his head. But actors are usually cheerful and resilient folk, Mr Foxe, as you know. They have to be able to cope with the constant ups and downs of their profession. Of late, they had turned the noble lord into a figure of fun; a bogeyman to be mimicked, not a serious threat to anyone.'

'Would anyone amongst them have wanted him dead?' Foxe said.

'All of them, I think, but only in a jocular way. You know, sir. People would say things like, "I wish someone would drop a brick on the fellow's head from a tall building and put an end to him for good." It wasn't serious. No one would have attacked him or anything like that, let alone stoop to murder. It was play, nothing more. Like the person playing the villain in some drama who kills one of the characters. Make-believe only. I'm afraid you must look elsewhere for your murderer, Mr Foxe.'

'Was Adam Bewell in the theatre at any time on that evening, do you know?'

'He was not. I can be sure of that, since the theatre was closed and secured against unauthorised entry. Several times in the past, thieves have broken in and stolen valuable items of property. We now make it extremely difficult to break in. During periods when there are performances, we also employ a night watchman.'

'Are there performances going on at present?'

'Certainly, sir. I still hope to see you in the audience one evening soon.'

⁂

FOXE COULD DO NO MORE THAT DAY. HOWEVER, HE HAD BEEN TOLD that the inquest on Lord Aylestone was to be held the next morning. The coroner had wanted to hold it earlier but that had failed as so many people had tried to cram into the hall to listen to the pandemonium that ensued. He had to postpone the hearing until he could find a venue capable to taking such large numbers.

Foxe therefore determined to attend his second inquest in as many days. He joined the crowds who flocked to the Assembly House itself the next morning. Few went to listen to proceedings. What attracted the majority was the chance to gawp at the building where the crime had taken place. As a general rule, ordinary folk were never admitted.

When he got there, Foxe found entry was being controlled. Most idlers and anyone deemed to be a vagrant were turned away. Even so, there must have been at least two hundred members of the public present to hear the coroner bang his gavel and open the proceedings.

The first item was to confirm the jury had observed the body, as the law demanded. Next, Viscount Penngrove's butler gave the necessary evidence of identification. It was clearly unthinkable to ask the man himself to perform such a menial task. After that, a well-known local physician, a man of some eminence, gave evidence concerning the cause of death.

Had the audience been less set on drama and more attuned to understanding medical evidence, they would have realised — as Foxe did — that the physician's dry and scholarly account of his findings, heavily larded with Latin, provided enough to allow an accurate reconstruction of the events surrounding Lord Aylestone's death.

He began by stating the cause of death. Stripped of the confusing medical terminology it amounted to a stabbing in the chest. He then added that he had been somewhat surprised by the earlier state of the body. What he was referring to was how it had been at the time it was found, or shortly afterwards.

'Please explain why you have made that remark, Doctor,' the coroner said at once.

The physician seemed taken aback at this demand. He was not used to having what he had said questioned, nor of needing to explain his meaning to anyone. Still, after a lengthy pause to re-order his thoughts, he explained. When the corpse was found, he had been summoned from a friend's house, where he had been engaged in playing whist. It was some little distance from the Assembly House and he estimated he had not arrived until almost two hours after the alarm had been raised. By then, the corpse was cold to the touch and rigor mortis was almost established, as he would have expected. However, the corpse had already been quite cool when found and the limbs showing signs of stiffening.

'What do you make of that, sir?' the coroner said. Foxe wondered why he didn't ask the physician how he knew the state of the body so long before he had actually arrived.

The physician blinked in surprise. 'Isn't it clear enough?' he said. 'A dead body cools gradually. On death, a corpse is at first limp and flaccid. Rigor mortis, the stiffening of joints and muscles, usually sets in between two and six hours after the point of actual death. Its onset too is gradual, until the corpse becomes almost totally stiff. Then it wanes again. I would not have expected the dead man to stiffen at all in the short period between the last time he was seen alive and the time he was found. However, the onset of rigor can be affected by the temperature round about. The place in which the body lay was quite warm, and the body itself was further concealed behind a curtain. It is possible, I suppose, that rigor had come on more quickly than usual.'

'Is there anyone present who can give the court clear evidence of the time when the victim was last seen alive?' the coroner called out. On being assured that the Master of Ceremonies and several members of the audience were present and could do so, he signalled to the medical examiner to continue.

'I should remind the court, sir,' the physician said, 'that I was not present on that evening. My comments as to the state of the body when it was found were made based on the findings of a medical man who was present. He spoke to Viscount Penngrove and the noble lord passed what he had said on to me. I made only a cursory examination when I first arrived. I did not examine the body fully until the next day.'

'Most irregular!' the coroner spluttered. 'This is mere hearsay, doctor. I cannot admit it into evidence unless it is vouched for by the physician who you say was there at the time. Is that gentleman in the court?'

Silence.

'Does anyone know where he may be found?'

The clerk to the court stepped forward — most reluctantly, Foxe thought. With much hesitation, he explained that, unfortunately, the man was not present at the inquest. Nor could his evidence be sought.

'From what I have been told by those who encountered him that evening, sir, he was visiting from London. He said he intended to depart to return home on the first mail coach the following morning.'

'God's teeth!' the coroner exploded. 'Did anyone think to make a note of this man's name or ask where he lived?'

Another silence.

'Is Viscount Penngrove present?'

A tall man with a long, bony face stood up slowly. 'I am here,' he said. 'I wish to God I were not.'

Whether this was an understandable comment about needing to attend an inquest on one of his sons, or an expression of disgust at being forced to sit, hugger-mugger, with tradesmen and other common people, was not entirely clear.

'Is it true, your lordship,' the coroner said, 'as the medical examiner here has said, that this physician no one can name made a remark about the temperature of your son's ... body ... and the extent of ... um ... stiffening?'

'Something like that,' Viscount Penngrove drawled.

'Exactly as reported, my lord? Nothing else added and nothing omitted?'

'Can't recall. Rather upset by it all, as you might imagine.'

The coroner struggled bravely forward. 'You did not ask for this physician's name or his address?'

'I am not in the habit of bothering myself with the personal details of tradespeople,' came the viscount's cold reply. 'I passed what I could remember on to the fellow now on the stand. Up to him after that.' He then sat down, making it clear he would entertain no further questioning.

The coroner's face had now assumed something of the colour of a ripe plum and he was breathing heavily. He would have very much liked to point out to this haughty aristocrat that the law required him to answer whatever questions were put to him. Fortunately for his future career as coroner, he remembered who he was talking to and kept his mouth tightly shut. It was the medical examiner who now bore the impact of his frustration.

'Doctor,' the coroner snapped. 'Let me make it perfectly clear that you are here to give evidence in your professional capacity. That means confining yourself to matters you actually saw for yourself. It does not mean confusing your own evidence with items picked up second or third hand. Is that clear!'

The physician bowed his head. 'I am sorry, sir,' he said. 'I thought to explain an anomaly of which I believed the court should be aware.'

'A supposed anomaly!' the coroner snapped. 'Nothing more.' He turned to the jury members and fixed them with a malevolent glare.

'Members of the jury,' he said loudly. 'The comments made by the medical examiner about the temperature and stiffening of the corpse *before he had examined it...*' A pause to recover his failing dignity. '... are to be disregarded as mere hearsay, incapable of verification. The clerk will strike them from the record, and you will ignore them.'

'Moving on, Doctor — if you can stick to facts known to yourself this time — what can you tell the court about the nature of the weapon used?'

'When I first examined the corpse, sir, I was shown a weapon which had been found beneath it. It was a short-bladed dagger with an unusually large hilt. Nine times out of ten a man would have survived a wound inflicted by a blade of that type. Since the blade was short, it would have been difficult to drive it in deeply enough to reach a vital organ. This time the victim was unlucky, and the attacker had used exceptional force. I found the blade had been driven into the chest between the ribs and penetrated deeply enough to reach the heart, thus causing immediate death.'

'Have you ever seen a similar dagger before?'

'No, sir. It was altogether strange. It was as if the hilt and guard were of full size and the blade something more like that of a large penknife. I believe the clerk has brought it for the jury to see for themselves.'

'At last, actual evidence,' the coroner muttered. At a sign from him, the clerk passed the oddly-shaped dagger to the foreman of the jury, who passed it around between the others. After that, the physician was dismissed — though without the usual thanks for his services.

The next person called to give evidence was a stout wine-merchant. He explained that he had spent most of the evening seated in a place from where he was able to observe the door into the room where the deceased had been found. After the somewhat animated conversation between the noble viscount and his son, he had seen the father return to the main hall. He had not seen Lord Aylestone do the same. The court needed to understand that he had not watched the door continuously. People kept coming up and talking to him. Twice he got up to fetch food and drink. Several times his wife returned from where she had been in conversation with a group of her friends to enquire whether he was bored, just sitting there. Each time, his attention had been distracted for several minutes or more. Lord Aylestone could have left the room where he had been with his father during any of those periods.

'Why were you sitting there for such a long period?' the coroner asked him.

'Thanks to my gout, sir,' the wine-merchant responded, 'even walking or standing is painful. Dancing would be quite beyond me.'

Asked whether he had seen anyone else enter or leave the room during that time, the merchant explained he had seen several people do so during the course of the evening. Some were obviously servants. He was not sure about the others.

Finding the man could be no more specific, the coroner called the Master of Ceremonies for that evening.

'Can you throw any light on the previous witness's evidence that he saw various people enter and leave the room where the corpse was found?' he asked.

'Indeed, sir. On that occasion, the room was being been used to store visitors' outer clothing until they might need it again. So many had attended, and the wind was so keen that evening, that our usual facilities for storing coats and cloaks were filled early on. Most patrons were content to allow our servants to take charge of their outer garments. In exchange, they received a ticket by which the correct ones might be claimed later. However — perhaps because they antici-pated a crush as all started to leave — some asked if they might deposit their garments themselves. They, or their servants, were then directed to the room in question. Between the servants of the Assembly House, the patrons' servants and even some patrons them-selves, there would have been constant movement in and out through that door. Exactly who went there and when is impossible to answer.'

'Exactly when was the noble lord last seen alive?' the coroner asked. "How long was it before his body was discovered?'

'Lord Aylestone was last seen alive at about ten minutes before midnight, sir. Many of those present, including myself, observed him standing at the side of the stage and peering into the room. Although he was still masked, the costume he had been wearing was quite distinctive. He had been wearing it when he first arrived, and he was still clothed in it when his body was found. No one else on that evening had worn a remotely similar costume. The body was discovered just after twelve-thirty in the morning.'

The Master of Ceremonies was the final witness. When he had left the witness's chair, the coroner quickly summed up. He ran through the likely timings once again. Assuming the murder had taken place soon after he had last been seen, that left a gap of barely half-an-hour before the discovery of Lord Aylestone's body. He had been killed by a single thrust from a dagger. They had all been able to see that weapon for themselves. The exact state of the body when it was found could not be fully established, due to the inability of the court to hear evidence from the one person who might have been able to provide unambiguous testimony.

All most unsatisfactory, the coroner grumbled, but there was nothing he could do. However, it could make no difference to the verdict. The man had either killed himself or been murdered. Since no evidence had been brought forward to suggest the former, he urged the jury to deliver a verdict of murder by person or persons unknown.

They swiftly complied.

❧ 6 ❧

Foxe returned home after the inquest in a thoughtful state. Nothing he had heard had changed his initial opinion about this murder. He was confident he knew more or less how it had happened. Yet certain points had somewhat shaken his confidence in the details of the hypothesis he had formed. If they were correct, the identity of the killer was again in doubt. Too many people had gone in and out of the room where the body had been found to fix suspicion on any of them. The reappearance of Lord Aylestone towards the end of the evening also troubled him. The facts could not be easily challenged. Too many witnesses had seen him. There was also the matter of his distinctive costume, the fact he arrived wearing it and that it was still on his body when he had been found.

Everything pointed to the murder taking place in that short period between his reappearance in the hall and the discovery of his corpse. A period of less than an hour. More than enough time for him to have met his death, followed by the killer hiding his body where it might well have remained safe for many hours. Only the amorous intentions of two of the guests had resulted in its discovery.

The difficulty lay in the medical evidence. Unless the observations of the unknown doctor from London were discounted, this version of events could not be reconciled with the state of the corpse when it was found.

Foxe swore under his breath. Now this business too was turning into a complex mystery. He had been certain he had deduced all the answers more or less exactly. Now he was not so sure. He'd told Brock the death of Lord Aylestone would be easy to unravel, given a little more time. It looked as if he might have to eat his words.

What to do next? He could try to get further evidence from others who had been present at the masquerade ball. He could question those who ran the stagecoaches to try to find the name of the London doctor. Both sensible next steps. The trouble was, neither appealed to him in the least. Despite Halloran and the mayor, Foxe was determined not to set aside his investigation of Dr Danson's death. He would continue with it secretly, if he must. Surely he could devote one evening to satisfying his curiosity about Danson and his new wife? No one would ever know.

Having made up his mind and thrust all scruples aside, he ate a hasty dinner, then sought out the bordello where Mrs Danson said she had worked. In the days when Gracie Catt was madam of the most exclusive bagnio in Norwich, he'd gone nowhere else. Not that he'd ever made much use of the girls she employed. She and her sister were more than enough for him to cope with. Generally, he'd visited in the guise of a dancing master, giving the girls lessons in deportment. The bordello he was visiting now had not been amongst the most elite establishments at the time. Since Gracie had left the city, however, it had risen in status and now stood near the pinnacle of fashionable houses. Foxe owned the building in which it was situated, as the madam knew. She would be sure to answer his questions openly.

The place he sought was not far from his own house, but Foxe still hired a torch-bearer to go ahead with a flaming torch to light his way. The streets of Norwich could be dangerous for anyone on their own, though Foxe had no need on this occasion to venture into the most perilous areas. After less than five minutes, they stopped outside a handsome brick building. It might have been the residence of a wealthy merchant. Foxe knew it had been built scarcely twenty years before for precisely that purpose. However, the merchant in question had suffered heavy losses as a result of a shipwreck and been forced to leave for a more modest dwelling. At around the same time, the fashion had shifted. Rich merchants, like Alderman Halloran, now lived to the north of the city. The house where Foxe stood had now mostly passed into the hands of professional men. Others, like this one, had come to serve for other purposes where a discreet façade and a respectable address were an advantage.

'I don't believe you've ever visited us before, Mr Foxe,' the madam said, ushering him into her inner sanctum and offering him a glass of what proved to be excellent brandy. 'We usually deal only with your attorney. I know we are not behind with the rent, so your visit this evening intrigues me. I hope you do not bring us bad news.'

'Not at all, madam,' Foxe said. 'I come in search of information, not to bring any.'

'Do you not have time for a little relaxation first? All our girls are beautiful, naturally, and all highly accomplished in the arts of love. I am sure they would be eager to show you what they can do to give you pleasure.'

'I don't doubt it, Mrs Ross,' Foxe replied. 'Your establishment has the reputation of being the finest in this city. However, as I said, it is information I am seeking this evening, not female companionship.'

'Very well, if you insist. Perhaps later ...?'

Foxe left the invitation unanswered.

'I need to ask you about a particular lady,' he began. 'One who I have been told once worked here. Her present name is Mrs Katherine Danson. I'm afraid I don't know her maiden name, or the name under which she worked.'

Mrs Ross giggled. 'Maiden name! Not the most appropriate term for any of my ladies! Even though some have remained maidens for an amazing period of time and in defiance of the number of times they have been deflowered. A few may arrive as maidens, but none remain so above a day or two.'

'Mrs Katherine Danson?' Foxe reminded her.

'Yes, I well remember Katy. Katy Stubbings she was when she came to us. Pretty girl. Pretty ways too. We presented her as Martha and dressed her as a servant girl. You'd be surprised how many of our more respectable gentlemen secretly lust after their female servants. Maybe you wouldn't though.'

'I make it my fixed resolve never to act in a way that would cause problems in my household, Mrs Ross. Any master who rogers his maids — even with their agreement — loses all respect. Marry, if you want a regular bed-mate at home. Otherwise, seek your pleasures elsewhere.'

'Very wise, Mr Foxe. Alas, the men I speak of simply fear to indulge their adulterous urges in their own households,' Mrs Ross said. 'They're afraid they would lose their reputations as churchwardens, chapel elders, parsons, or even bishops! Here we assist them to act out their fantasies in safety. Katy had been a servant, I believe, before she ran away to avoid being raped yet again. She told me she liked men and enjoyed being properly pleasured but wasn't going to stay with such a brute. I assured her that any man who was unduly rough or used force here, save only for those who pay heavily for the privilege with certain of our ladies only, would be ejected at once and banned from returning. I have female servants, Mr Foxe who have the strength of any man. They also have my full permission to treat such animals as roughly as they wish, short of murder. I doubt anyone would want to experience their anger a second time.'

'I don't doubt it,' Foxe replied, his imagination running riot over the damage several furious Amazons might inflict on their victim. 'But to return to Mrs Danson ...'

'Katy was sweet-natured and quiet, which made her a favourite amongst our older customers. She was happy to fuss over them all evening. Some wanted to enjoy her as a man does with a woman. Some expected her to undress in order to admire her figure. A few never tried to go further than kissing and cuddling. To be truthful, she was more a provider of comfort and flirtation than anything else. They liked her. The other girls liked her. I liked her.'

'So, Dr Danson simply came along, took a liking to her as well, and asked her to marry him?'

'More or less. He was one of those whose demands were very simply met. He missed his wife. Not in a carnal sense, I understand. More as a warm, consoling presence. Katy told me he liked most to

fondle her breasts and kiss her nipples, rarely venturing below her
waist for any purpose. She liked him well enough to marry him for the
security he offered. I was sorry to see her go, but I understood. This is
not business for the long term. Once you are past your bloom, few men
desire you. The few who will accept you want things most women are
loathed to provide. You either manage to marry, become a madam like
me, or end your days on the streets.'

'She was eager to end her time here?'

'Not eager, I would say, but realistic. She might have continued for
several years more. She had definitely kept her looks and her figure. Dr
Danson simply gave her an opportunity she was loathed to miss. I
assumed she would marry him, then seek out younger lovers to provide
what he was unable to give her. However, there was another reason for
her departure.'

'What was that, Mrs Ross.'

'Her last few months at the bordello were spoiled by the antics of
her younger brother. He turned out to be not only an unpleasant rogue
but a criminal. She told me she thought she'd escaped him for good,
then he turned up out of the blue. At once, he started to threaten her
and tried to sponge off her earnings. She wouldn't provide him with
the money he wanted, so he attacked her, right in this house. Fortunately, my servants heard her screaming. I had him ejected on the
instant in the manner I explained before. Since Katy was popular with
everyone here, I expect they did not hold themselves back. I did not
enquire, but he never returned. Instead, as I understand it, he returned
to a life of petty crime. Then he was caught stealing silver and
sentenced to death. In view of his age — around seventeen, I believe
— his sentence was commuted to transportation to our American
colonies.

'That's all I know,' she concluded. 'I believe Mrs Danson has never
sought to conceal her time with us, which is most unusual. Most of
those who marry invent their earlier lives when asked. As I said, she
was a lovely girl and I liked her a good deal. Now, if you're sure I can't
call one or two ladies who are still not engaged this evening ...'

Foxe wouldn't have been Foxe if he hadn't wavered, then given in.

Sally she said her name was; a raven-haired beauty whose manner of speech Foxe found difficult to understand. Some kind of foreigner, he decided, though she spoke English well enough. There was also the fact that, in moments of high passion — and there were several of those — she kept calling him "cariad", or something like that. Otherwise, she was lissom, enthusiastic and athletic in her love-making, though a little too noisy at times.

As he was leaving some two hours later, Foxe asked Mrs Ross about the young woman's origins. She said that Sally and her family had travelled from somewhere in Wales seeking work. Her surname was simple enough — Jones — but they'd called her Sally because her Christian name was so odd. She couldn't even recall it exactly. When she'd told them, they'd all been too busy laughing to remember.

As he lay in bed that night — quite alone this time, and deliciously exhausted — Foxe decided he couldn't afford to take another whole day away from the matter of Lord Aylestone without risking the good relationship he had with Halloran and, through him, with the mayor. Besides, Mrs Ross's words had satisfied his immediate concerns about Mrs Danson. His liking for the young widow had increased and he saw no reason to assume she was anything but genuine in what she told him. On the other hand, the revelations about her brother intrigued him greatly. It was time to enlist the help of the street children in finding out more.

7

Sally's charms had swiftly restored Foxe to his normal self and must also have given his brain a boost, for he awoke next morning with an important idea fully formed in his mind. What if the unknown physician who first attended Aylestone's body was right and the man had been killed much earlier in the evening than everyone supposed?

It was high time to pay a visit to the Assembly House and talk with Mr Hinton, the man who had been Master of Ceremonies that evening.

Mr Hinton recalled the events of that evening all too clearly. He began by telling Foxe that Viscount Penngrove had been unpleasant from the moment he arrived. His son had been worse, if that were possible. His Lordship was merely cold, haughty and demanding. Plenty of aristocrats behaved as he did, and you became used to it. His son, Lord Frederick Aylestone as he kept reminding everyone, was not only pompous and morose, but full of complaints. He disliked the music, calling the players "rustic amateurs". He refused to take any part in the dancing, which he insisted was "the pointless capering of those destined for hell's flames". He especially loathed his brightly-coloured costume, although it seemed his father had had it made for him. According to the man's valet — who was forced to sit all evening in the draughtiest area near the outside door, just in case his master might discover a sudden need for him — his master had tried in every way possible to avoid attending. When asked to select a costume, he had chosen the most unsuitable ones he could think of. Oliver Cromwell was probably the most outlandish, followed by John the Baptist. In the end, his father had recalled an elaborate Harlequin costume he'd seen not too long ago and had an exact copy made for his son to wear. Where had he seen it? Probably at some theatre in London.

Then, to crown it all, the wretched fool had caused a scene. It had forced him to ask a perfectly innocent patron, a Mr Bewell, to leave to avoid more unpleasantness. He knew one should not speak ill of the dead. Still, he found it very difficult to feel anything other than relief that he would never have to encounter the man again.

'When you asked this Mr Bewell to go, did he do so right away?' Foxe asked.

'As far as I know, he did,' was the reply. 'I asked if I should call a servant to get Mr Bewell's outdoor clothes, and those of the young lady who was with him, since she was extremely upset by what had happened, but Mr Bewell told me it would be quicker if he fetched them himself. It seemed he'd left them in the room vacated by Viscount Penngrove and his son. Many of those who had arrived later than the rest had found our normal storage for their clothes already full. I'd therefore instructed our people to tell their servants to use that other room instead. I doubt if Mr Bewell had a servant — he is, I believe, an actor, though an up-and-coming one — and he probably took their outdoor clothes there himself, rather than wait for one of our servants. They were harassed and overworked by this time. The evening was colder than we all expected and so many people will insist on making their appearance on such evenings at the last moment.'

'You said Viscount Penngrove and his son had already left that room by this time.'

'Indeed, the noble lord had taken his son there to remonstrate with him in the strongest terms. We could all hear it.'

'Did they come out together?'

The Master of Ceremonies took his time to think that over. 'I believe not,' he told Foxe at last. 'I definitely saw Viscount Penngrove come out, but he was on his own at that stage, as I recall it.'

'Did you see Lord Aylestone come out of the room after him?'

Another pause for memory. 'No, not exactly, but his father had ordered him to return to the main hall in a most peremptory way. I assumed the fellow had taken a moment to compose himself. When Mr Bewell returned with his clothes and those of the lady, he made no mention of seeing anyone in there. I'm sure of that. He was wearing his own cloak and had the lady's over his arm. All he said was that so many sets of clothing had been piled up, it had taken him a good time to find Miss Marsh's and his own.'

'And at the end of the evening?'

'I was far too busy helping the most important guests summon their servants and reassume outdoor dress to take any notice.'

'Was this Mr Bewell the only person Lord Aylestone quarrelled with in the course of the evening?'

'By no means! The fellow had been causing upset from the moment he arrived. Instead of taking part in the dancing or talking with the ladies, he sat on his own, passing loud remarks about anyone whose attire or behaviour displeased him. Loud enough to be heard clearly by his victims, I mean. A number of ladies were picked out for their "immodest" dresses. They were treated to biblical quotations containing the words "whore" or "harlot". This was interspersed with imprecations against "ungodly behaviour" and mentions of hell fire. Then there was that earlier incident.'

'What incident was that?' Foxe asked.

'I did not see it myself. However, several people told me they had seen Lord Aylestone jump up and heard him say he had just seen the very man who had stolen his ladylove from him years before. The one who was the actress. He was heard to declare it was high time the worthless knave got the hiding he deserved.'

'Did anyone see who he was referring to?'

'Not to my knowledge, Mr Foxe. Besides, I'm sure he must have been mistaken. As I heard the tale, the man in question had been serving in the militia. He would hardly have returned to Norwich wealthy enough to purchase a ticket for our masquerade. On the other hand, I suppose he might have been an officer, not a mere soldier. Many a young lady has had her head turned by the sight of a young officer in a fine, red coat.'

Since Mr Hinton could add no more, Foxe took his leave and went next door to the theatre. He was lucky enough to find both Bewell and Miss Marsh there. A final rehearsal for the next evening's production was about to take place.

Mr Adam Bewell proved to be a man of somewhat unremarkable appearance without his costume and make-up. Foxe judged him to be around thirty or thirty-five years of age, still youthful in his face, but beginning to gain a little weight. Miss Marsh was younger, perhaps no more than twenty-five. Comely enough, though her hair was somewhat lank and her complexion sallow. As soon as Foxe introduced himself and explained the purpose for seeking them out, she excused herself, saying the experience was still too painful for her to talk about it. Mr Bewell could speak for her, since she had seen little after that beast, Lord whatever-his-name was, had so grossly insulted her. They had left and Mr Bewell had escorted her home, where she had disrobed and cried herself to sleep.

Mr Bewell agreed that he had done as the lady said, then gone to his own lodging and retired for the night.

'I'm interested in what happened immediately after Lord Aylestone and his father had their argument,' Foxe said. 'I believe the Master of Ceremonies asked you and Miss Marsh to leave.'

'He did,' Bewell replied, 'but in a most gracious and apologetic way. I felt for the poor fellow. He could hardly eject the viscount's son, though I imagine that was exactly what he longed to do. It was also quite likely Lord Aylestone would be unable to restrain himself if he encountered us again. I don't know what the stupid man has against theatrical performances, other than simple religious bigotry. A few ministers of religion share the ridiculous idea that the theatre fosters immorality and vice. Most who do confine themselves to boring their congregations with sermons on the matter or writing silly pamphlets.'

'What did you do on agreeing to leave?' Foxe said. 'Did you go straight away?'

'We both needed our cloaks. The servant who took them when we arrived had put them in that kind of annex room, since the main repository for clothing was full. Mr Hinton — he was serving as Master of Ceremonies — offered to summon a servant. However, Miss Marsh was extremely unsettled by Lord Aylestone's crass behaviour and wished us to leave as swiftly and quietly as possible. Rather than wait, I went to retrieve our cloaks myself. That's all there was to it.'

'Did you leave as soon as you returned with your outdoor clothing?'

'Certainly,' Bewell said. 'There was nothing to detain us.'

'Was Lord Aylestone still in the room when you got there?' Foxe asked.

'There was no one there,' the actor said. 'It did take me some time to find our cloaks though.'

'Did you look behind the curtain into the recess which is there?'

'What curtain?'

'And did you return to the Assembly House after that?'

'What for? The response of Lord Aylestone to our presence had sickened me. I had lost any appetite for dancing and no longer had a partner. I've already told you Miss Marsh was desperate to go home, so we left as quickly as we could. She's already confirmed I saw her home, after which I went to my own lodgings.'

'Can anyone vouch for seeing you there?'

'I imagine the landlady must have heard me come back. Ask her.'

By the time Foxe was able to tell Mrs Crombie all he had learned that day, the good temper of the morning had deserted him.

'I thought this business of Lord Aylestone was going to be simple,' he said to her. 'Now I'm faced with suspects I hadn't expected. That's to say nothing of the gentlemen whose ladies had been insulted by the young fool. Any of them might have decided to take their revenge and gone too far. Then there's the matter of Lord Aylestone saying he'd seen the man who had stolen his girl.'

'He might well have sought the fellow out, taken him somewhere private and tried to take his revenge,' Mrs Crombie said. 'Especially after he knew he'd been publicly humiliated by his father. Maybe he hoped to repair his loss of face, or something equally silly. If the man

had been a soldier, he would know how to defend himself. Lord Aylestone probably tried to start a fight and came off worst.'

'Do you know anything of the incident with the actress, Mrs
Crombie? Was the man she ran off with an officer?'

'I've heard him described as a sergeant, a lieutenant and even a
captain. You know how it is with these tales. People love to elaborate.
What they don't know, they make it up.'

'Indeed, they do,' Foxe said. 'It's quite common for the younger
sons of wealthy gentry families to purchase commissions in the militia
or the yeomanry. Less expensive than regular army commissions, with
the added advantage of being restricted to serving in Britain itself. The
uniform is just as handsome too.'

Mrs Crombie smiled. 'It's the uniform that draws the eyes of
impressionable young women. Fellows like that strut about as if they
had been fighting the French single-handed. Many a foolish young
woman has lost her heart — and other things — to an officer in the
militia. It's said sailors have a girl in every port. I think militia offi-
cers probably have several in every town where they have been
stationed.'

'Do you speak from experience?' Foxe asked her, grinning despite
his attempt to keep a straight face.

'I was young once, Mr Foxe. When the militia paraded in the city,
my friends and I were usually amongst the crowds admiring the
display.' She paused. 'I'll not satisfy your curiosity by saying any more.
I'm surprised you weren't tempted to get yourself a uniform.'

'I didn't need artificial aids to attract young ladies,' Foxe said. 'As
you know very well...'

'Enough!' Mrs Crombie said, turning her back on him. 'If you've
only come in here to boast, I suggest you leave now and find someone
else to listen to your nonsense. I have work to do.'

'Have pity on me,' Foxe said, laughing. 'I need to find something to
boast about. I may have to go to Alderman Halloran and tell him Lord
Aylestone was killed by an unknown man, who may or may not have
been an officer or a sergeant in the militia at one time; a man who now
cannot be traced because the trail has gone cold. Imagine him
suggesting the mayor gives Viscount Penngrove the same answer. The

only way His Worship could avoid a roasting would be to say it was all that fool Foxe's fault.'

⊗⊗

DESPITE ALL HE HAD SAID TO MRS CROMBIE, FOXE DIDN'T FEEL quite satisfied with Adam Bewell's answers. It wasn't just that they clashed with his earlier thoughts about what had taken place, it was more of an intuition. There was something too glib about the man's speech. Maybe he had done exactly as he said, but Foxe couldn't fit it together to his satisfaction, bearing in mind what else he had discovered. Everyone he'd spoken with so far was certain Lord Aylestone must have returned to the main room after being so loudly rebuked by his father. Yet no one reported seeing him until much later in the evening. The obvious conclusion was that he had either stayed in the side room for some time, composing himself, or he had gone elsewhere in the interim. Was it so?

Bewell had been the one whom Lord Aylestone had insulted so openly. He was also the only person who could be proved to have entered the room shortly after Viscount Penngrove had been seen to leave it. Yet, he had told Foxe he had seen no one when he entered. He had even denied knowing about the curtained recess. Could he be believed? The man was an accomplished actor after all. The term "playing the innocent" might be literally true in his case.

Foxe tossed ideas back and forth in his head all evening, until he felt the problem must drive him mad. Where had Lord Aylestone been between the time his father left him in the side room and the point when he had been seen looking back into the main hall? Where could he have been? The Assembly House had no upper floors. Beside the entrance, the principal hall and the cloakroom, there were few places to go. The privy? He could hardly have spent the best part of two hours there. Besides, he would have been seen, surely. The kitchens? They would have been busy with servants going to and fro.

Perhaps he had left the Assembly House altogether. Gone for a walk to clear his head. Possible, Foxe supposed, but not likely. None of the servants had mentioned him asking for his outdoor clothing part way through the evening. It had been a chilly night. He could hardly have wandered about Norwich, dressed as a Harlequin, without attracting a good deal of attention, even if he had ignored the cold. In the end, Foxe gave up and went to bed with a bad headache and a stiff brandy to help him sleep. He needed more evidence from someone.

Next morning, Foxe returned to the Assembly House and sought out some of the servants. He especially needed to find those who had been dealing with arrivals and departures on the evening of the masquerade ball.

He was able to find most of them in time. Unfortunately, none were able to tell him anything new. All confirmed that the actor, Adam Bewell, had left with Miss Marsh exactly as he'd told Foxe. They were also positive he had not returned later. The doors were always manned and none of them had seen him enter again. Whatever Foxe's uneasiness, Bewell's alibi was solid. He left when he said he did and was not there again that evening.

One or two of the servants told Foxe they had been in the main hall itself at various times during the evening. None had seen Lord Aylestone between the time his father had taken him into the side room and his appearance by the musicians' stage. Nothing Foxe said could alter their certainty of this. They might not have seen him before that night, but all swore they would have recognised his distinctive Harlequin costume. Their unanimity, therefore, ruled out any earlier time of death.

When Foxe asked about the supposed confrontation with a former member of the militia, most either shook their heads or repeated the same tale as he had heard from Mr Hinton. No one had seen such a confrontation; nor had any of them heard anything of that nature.

Despite spending almost two hours questioning everyone who might possibly had seen or heard anything relevant, Foxe had to come away virtually empty handed. He was able to glean only one extra fact. It too served only to confirm that Lord Aylestone was alive just before midnight. A servant who had been assisting departing guests with their coats and cloaks said Lord Aylestone had come to ask for his cloak. When was that? About fifteen minutes before the Master of Ceremonies announced the formal end of the evening. Was he sure it was

Lord Aylestone? Quite certain. He'd known it was Aylestone by his affected speech and because he was dressed as a Harlequin. That particular version of a Harlequin, Foxe asked? Definitely. He'd seen the costume Aylestone had been wearing when he arrived and this one was identical.

'Can you tell me exactly what Lord Aylestone said to you?' Foxe asked. There was a slim chance something in his words might have indicated what he had been doing earlier.

'He said he was leaving early, sir, and was in a hurry. His father was still in the main hall and not yet ready to depart. They had planned to leave together, so he'd had to send his servant to find another suitable coach to take him home by himself. I was to bring him his hat and cloak and do it "on the instant". Those were his exact words.'

'What did you do next?'

'I hurried off as fast as I could to collect his lordship's things and bring them back. Oh yes, there was one other thing he said. He told me a friend was leaving with him and I must collect that man's cloak and hat as well.'

'How would you recognise it?'

'His lordship described both, right down to the place where they would most likely be.'

'Was that in the side annex room?' Foxe asked him.

'No, sir, in the main cloakroom. Well, not the noble lord's attire. We didn't start using the other room until well after the viscount's servant had brought us their cloaks and hats. I believe the other man's was in that side room, just inside the door.'

'What did Lord Aylestone do after you brought him the cloaks he wanted?'

'He put draped both cloaks over his arm and held the hats in his hand. Then he went back into the main ballroom. I supposed he had gone to find his friend.'

'Did you see him again?'

'No, sir. I assumed he must have left as he said he would do.'

'One last question. Did he mention the name of the friend who was to leave with him?'

'No, sir, he did not.'

Another dead end. As Foxe walked the short distance back to his house, he was forced to conclude that he could proceed no further. Unless he could find new evidence, he would have to tell Halloran he'd done his best but found nothing useful. He hated being beaten, but there it was.

Unless ...

It was an extremely long shot, but there remained one source of evidence he hadn't explored. Many of the street children would have been hanging around outside the Assembly House. Some would have been begging. Others would have lurked in the shadows in the hope of picking the pockets of the more drunken guests when they departed. Charlie could put out the word. Tell them his master wanted to know if any had noticed someone coming back to the Assembly House late that evening.

It wasn't much, but it was worth a chance. With any luck, the children might soon report something in response to his earlier questions about Mrs Danson's brother. When they did, Charlie would ask them about the night of the masquerade ball.

8

As it turned out, Foxe got more fresh evidence than he had bargained for. Unfortunately, none of it concerned the whereabouts of Lord Aylestone.

When he went into his shop that afternoon to look for his apprentice, Charlie rushed up to tell him some of the street children had already been to the back gate of the house.

'There's been another murder, Master,' the boy burst out in high excitement. 'Another man dead! The children want you to look into it.'

Foxe stifled a groan, turning it into a loud sigh.

'I need no more murders to look into, Charlie. I have sufficient problems already. Tell them I will do what I can, but it will have to wait a while.'

'But, Master!' Charlie protested. 'You have to talk to them now. This one's important...'

'All murders are important to someone,' Foxe replied testily, 'if only the victim. Now, please stick to telling me what you have learned about the matters I sent you to ask the children to find out. No! Not another word, and stop bouncing up and down like that. You're making me feel nauseous.'

If Charlie was crushed by Foxe's words, he didn't show it. He did mutter something under his breath — probably something mutinous — but then did as he was asked. The street children, he told his master, had been extremely busy on the tasks set them. Some had travelled the city spreading the word and questioning other vagrants. Others quizzed those in the dark alleys and back streets who knew most about Norwich's busy criminal underworld. The girls had even talked with all the tarts they knew, always a potential source of gossip.

As a result, Charlie could now give a full report on George Stubbings, Mrs Danson's younger brother. Almost from the time he could walk, the fellow had been a reckless wastrel. A man willing to turn his hand to almost anything which did not involve actual work. At first, he had sponged off his sister. When she refused to give him more money from the little she earned as a servant, he'd turned to other women. Soon, they began to avoid him. He was known to be violent when he couldn't get what he wanted any other way. After his sister had run away from a brutal, lascivious master, he'd spent a good time trying to find her. The general view was that he'd hoped to put the poor girl on the streets and act as her pimp. However, she'd eluded him by going to a bordello instead.

Like all of his type, Stubbings also dabbled in petty crime. However, his speciality was always the use of violence, not guile. He tried demanding payment from some of the market traders in return for not burning down their booths. They banded together and gave him a severe beating. Then those who regularly collected payments on the same basis did the same. Finally, he took up with Jack Beeston, becoming one of his all-purpose thugs. By the time Beeston was arrested, young Stubbings had developed a well-deserved reputation for acts of cruel and mindless violence.

Happily for the inhabitants of Norwich, Stubbings next made an incompetent attempt to free his master from the castle gaol. He used the simple expedient of banging on the outer door and viciously assaulting the warder who came to see what all the noise was about. Not only was the warder tougher than he seemed, there were other warders within earshot. After a ferocious fight, in the course of which two other warders were injured and one killed outright, Stubbings was overpowered. He was thrown into a cell and charged with assault and murder. At the next assize, he was duly convicted and sentenced to death. Since he was then still barely seventeen years of age, an indulgent judge wrote to the king, recommending mercy. Stubbings' sentence was commuted to fourteen years' transportation.

The most recent gossip was that Stubbings had managed to escape from custody while being transferred to the prison hulks at Portsmouth. Once again, he'd killed a prison guard, so a price had been set on his head. Where he had gone was uncertain. Some claimed he'd been seen back in Norwich. If that was so, he'd need to keep as hidden as he could. There were plenty of people amongst the city's underworld who would recognise him and turn him in to get the reward.

Foxe took a small handful of pennies from his purse and told Charlie to distribute them amongst the children as a reward.

'Tell them there's more to come,' he said, 'if they can find anyone who saw a man going back into the Assembly House very late on the evening Lord Aylestone was killed. Quick as they can, please.'

'I will, Master,' the lad said. 'Now can I tell you about the other mystery they want you to solve for them. The other killing. Please! I promised them I would.'

Foxe dithered, then gave in. It would never do to make the boy break his word. Nor was it in his interests to upset the children themselves. He sighed and nodded his head in assent

'One of their number, I suppose' he said. It was always a possibility. Living as they did, they were vulnerable to all kinds of violence.

'No, Master. It's a man they called "Uncle". Someone they said was kind to them, even though he was poor and lived on the streets, just as they do.'

Foxe groaned inwardly. The very last thing he needed was a murder involving some vagrant. Still, he knew his conscience wouldn't let him walk away from considering any unexplained death — especially if it was truly a murder.

'Where did they find him?' he asked. 'What makes them sure he was killed and didn't die from some sickness, or simply from cold and starvation?

'They told me they'd tried to wake him, but their hands had come away covered in blood. They think he was stabbed.'

'Stabbed! Who'd kill a vagrant living rough on the streets?'

'That's what they want you to find out. Mistress Tabby wants you to find out too. When I went to deliver a parcel of books, I met two of the children on their way here to ask for your help, Master. They told me they'd first called Mistress Tabby, hoping she could give the man some medicine to stop his bleeding. She went with Bart to the place where they'd found him. When she got there, she said it was too late and to send for you at once.'

Foxe had been going to do what he could for the children anyway. With Mistress Tabby involved he had no choice. She would have known at once if the man had died naturally. If the children said he had been stabbed and Tabby hadn't contradicted them, it was certainly true. By sending for Foxe at once, she'd made that message clear. This was no ordinary killing, no fight amongst vagrants or self-inflicted wound. If the Cunning Woman said he should get involved, that was more than enough for Foxe.

❦

Miss Tabitha Studwell, Cunning Woman and herbalist, Foxe's first lover and now his staunch friend and counsellor, was waiting for him when he reached the place where the body lay. She had her servant, Bart, with her; a huge fellow, simple of mind but possessing the strength of three other men. With him to protect her, Mistress Tabby could venture into the worst, roughest parts of the city. Lay a finger on his beloved mistress and Bart would break both your arms.

'I want you to find out who killed "Uncle", as the children named him, Ash. From all I have heard, he was a good man; one who didn't deserve to die in this way. There's something badly amiss in this affair. I can feel it. Something more than the fact of a brutal death. Something or someone . . . truly wicked.'

'But I'm already investigating two other murders, Tabby,' Foxe protested. 'You know that. I really don't have the time to take on a third. I agree it sounds odd ...'

'Wicked, I said. Not odd. Wicked. Now stop whining and pay attention. This is important.'

The man, Tabby told Foxe, had been found lying in a gap between two ramshackle buildings in a foul alleyway, just off the marketplace. He must have been sleeping there. He had tried to cover himself with a few rags and there was a folded coat under his head.

'I told Bart to bring him where the light was better,' she continued. 'It's no use. I've already done what I can to examine him,' Mistress Tabby said, 'but it's too dark and I am not going to kneel in the filth on the ground. He's dead, but I can't tell you much more, save that when I felt the left side of his chest my hand came away smeared with blood. I need Bart to take him somewhere where I can make a proper examination.'

'Tell him to bring the body to my house,' Foxe told her. 'That's the closest point. I've an outhouse in the garden which might be a suitable place.'

Bart picked up the dead man as if he weighed no more than a child and they walked in a kind of procession. Bart led the way with his burden, Foxe and Mistress Tabby immediately behind him. Next came Charlie Dillon and a gaggle of street children. It wasn't the cortège a man might have wished for, but everyone who followed him was at least genuine in their sorrow.

When they reached the outhouse, Foxe told the street children to wait outside while the Cunning Woman did her work. Charlie and Henry, Foxe's groom, found two trestles and some planks to construct a makeshift table. That done, Bart, with the gentleness which surprised those who didn't know him, stretched the dead man out on its surface.

Mistress Tabby opened the dead man's shirt and peered closely at his chest. Looking where she pointed, Foxe could see a small wound on the left-hand side where the blade of a knife or dagger had entered. Even when they'd stripped and cleaned the body completely, the Cunning Woman could find no other wounds. What she did find, however, underneath a filthy rag that the man had been wearing around his throat, was a fine chain around his neck, from which hung a pendant. She handed them to Foxe. As he took it from her, he gave a gasp, then bent his head and looked at them closely.

'Gold,' he said, 'both chain and pendant. Worth a good deal, I'd say too. Look, there's a coat of arms engraved on the pendant.'

He held it up to catch what light there was, turning it from side to side and muttering under his breath.

'Family coat of arms for certain. Not one I recognise though. I'll take it with me. I know someone who can help me identify it. Now why would a homeless vagrant be wearing such a thing?'

While Foxe had been examining the pendant, Mistress Tabby had continued to examine the dead man, gently parting the front of his shirt to get at the place where she thought the fatal wound must be. When she had found the spot, she probed the wound itself, using a thin piece of stick she'd found in a corner.

'From the angle and depth of the wound, Ashmole,' she said, 'I think it was made by a thin, narrow blade. Perhaps something like an Italian stiletto. Whatever was used, it was done expertly. The killer inserted the blade between the ribs on the left-hand side of the body and drove it straight into the man's heart. Death would have been instantaneous. This poor fellow, thin as he is, didn't die from disease or the cold. He was stabbed through the heart with a single strike.'

Her immediate findings were confirmed later, almost word for word, by the local surgeon who gave the medical evidence at the inquest.

'A single strike, straight to the heart, using a thin blade like a stiletto,' Foxe said. 'This isn't some commonplace killing. This man was killed by a professional. Who would make such a neat job of it? Yes!'

Mistress Tabby waited.

'Brunetti,' Foxe said after a moment. 'It's got to be his work. He uses some kind of Italian stiletto. Luigi Brunetti, Italian. Makes his living as a hired assassin. You've surely heard of him.'

Tabby shook her head.

'Brunetti came to Norwich with his family many years ago. They were honest folk, my father told me, but their son ran wild. He still lives in the city, more's the pity, living by his wits. He's an expert card sharper. He also dresses up and pedals fake medicines. In fact, he'll do just about anything for money. However, his main trade is committing murders for money. He'll do it for anyone who pays him enough. A stiletto has always been his weapon. If this was Brunetti's work, we'll never prove it. The man is much too cunning for that. He probably crept up on the dead man while he was asleep.'

'Why should anyone pay an assassin to have a harmless vagrant killed?' Tabby asked him. 'While I was waiting for you, the children told me that they first encountered the man some six months ago. Where he came from, they had no idea. There are always vagrants wandering about, so they didn't bother to ask.'

'There's something very odd about this particular vagrant, Tabby.' Foxe held up the beautifully intricate gold chain with its pendant. 'How did he come by this, I wonder?'

'I imagine he must have stolen it, Ash.'

'I disagree. A homeless vagrant would surely have sold it at once for whatever he could get for it. This man was living rough. Yet he wore around his neck a piece of jewellery that would have bought him accommodation in the best local inn for a year or more. I'm not going to let this man receive a pauper's burial in an unmarked grave, Tabby. If I can find the family to whom this coat of arms belongs, they'll probably want the body exhumed and buried elsewhere with greater dignity. In the meantime, I'll pay for a proper burial myself. I'll also find who ever had him killed in this way and see he pays the price for what he has done.'

Tabby bowed her head in acknowledgement. 'I knew I could rely on you, Ashmole dear,' she said. 'I feel very uneasy about this man's death. It doesn't take the second sight to guess he must have proved a serious threat to someone — probably someone important. It's vital that you should get to the bottom of this mystery. I can feel it in my bones. A terrible wrong has been committed. It's crying out for justice and it's up to you to see that the villain who ordered it gets the punishment he deserves.'

All Foxe could do was nod in agreement.

Foxe now sent Charlie to Alderman Halloran's house to tell him they had discovered yet another a murder. The coroner should therefore be sent for at once.

Later, when he returned, the boy reported what Halloran had said. 'The alderman wanted to know if you hadn't got enough on your plate already, Master. He says Viscount Penngrove has been sending his servant daily to pester the mayor about the state of the investigation into his son's murder. He wants that investigation put before anything else.'

'Does he, indeed? We don't always get what we want in this life, Charlie, my boy, as the good alderman knows very well. Back to your work now. I need time to think.'

Later, when Foxe was telling Mrs Crombie about what had taken place that day, he told her he now regretted telling someone in a letter his life was too quiet. He'd even said he needed a good mystery to solve. Now he had three.

'Be careful what you wish for!' Mrs Crombie said. 'Isn't that what they say? Anyway, overworked or not, you seem a great deal more cheerful than you have been of late. What brought about the change? Or should I ask who?'

'You may ask all you like, Mrs Crombie, but I won't tell you, other than to say my opinion of the Welsh has risen a good deal.'

And with that enigmatic remark, he walked to the door leading into his house and disappeared through it.

❧

Foxe devoted most of the next day's efforts to finding out who had killed Viscount Penngrove's son. He didn't give tuppence for the mayor's worries, but Halloran had become a good friend and deserved to be set free from his worship's constant nagging.

In spite of the fresh evidence, Foxe still felt sure he knew, more or less, what had occurred at the masquerade ball. He was less certain of who the killer must be. His faith in his reasoning had been shaken by the almost total lack of evidence to support his original decision. He now had to find the facts which would either convince others he had been correct all along or let him come up with an alternative solution.

The reappearance of Lord Aylestone at the end of the evening was the greatest stumbling block. Most of those present had seen him, if only briefly. All said they knew it was him because his Harlequin costume was distinctive. There were several other people present dressed as a Harlequin, but Aylestone's costume had been especially elaborate. Foxe decided his next step must be to discover where Aylestone had got his costume. If he could find out where he had hired it, it might provide some further clues. It was a long shot, but there were no other ideas worth following up.

Foxe marshalled what he knew about the family. Viscount Penngrove lived in a fine mansion on his vast estate to the west of the city. That is, he did so when he wasn't away visiting or at his house in London's Golden Square. His younger son, not liking the close supervision of his movements when he was under his parent's eyes, had moved elsewhere. Foxe thought he'd heard Lord Aylestone now occupied a suitably sumptuous set of rooms in Colegate.

He went through into the shop and consulted Mrs Crombie. He was correct, she told him. The son lived in a house not far from the Octagon Chapel with a valet, two maids and a cook/housekeeper to see to his needs.

Foxe knew he would never be admitted to the viscount's mansion. Still, he had some hopes that the servants at Lord Aylestone's residence would be more accommodating. Now Lord Aylestone was dead, they would need to find new positions. Foxe couldn't imagine the viscount treating them with compassion. He was most unlikely to be concerned about them at all. He'd probably give his steward a curt instruction to get rid of them and forget about the whole matter. Would he provide them with suitable characters? It was doubtful. Beyond confirming their period of service, the steward was unlikely to know enough about any household servant to be able to add more. In effect, they would be cast onto their own resources with minimal assistance. Surely any loyalty they felt towards their former master would not survive such treatment.

When Foxe arrived at the house in Colegate, gaining entry and talking to Aylestone's valet proved even easier than he expected. The man himself answered the door and proved to be the only one of the servants still in residence. As Foxe had assumed, he'd already been given notice. His final task was to bundle up all his former master's clothes. Viscount Penngrove had ordered they should be burned or otherwise disposed of.

'Burned?' the man said to Foxe indignantly. 'Whoever heard of such waste. Still, that family have got more money than they know what to do with. We've all been thrown out without notice! Just the wages what was due to us! I reckoned we was worth something extra to help tide us over till we found new places. Aye, and more besides, just for putting up with Lord Bible-Basher's moods and tantrums. The clothes will go, sure enough. I intend to take my pick first. Then I'll sell the rest and share the money with all the other folk who worked here. If I've also looked around a bit and found a few other things the family won't ever miss, who's to know? Tell me that, sir.'

'Well I know, now,' Foxe said to himself. 'This fellow's anger has prevented him watching what he says. That's good. I'm probably the first person who's offered him a sympathetic ear. His fellow servants will have been worrying about themselves too much. Still, I've no doubt his anger is fully justified. I'm not about to peach on him and get him sent to prison.'

He turned instead to the matter of the Harlequin costume Lord Aylestone had worn on the evening of his death.

'What can you tell me of the costume your master wore to the masquerade ball?' he said.

'That was a fine kettle of fish, make no mistake, sir,' the valet replied. 'I kept out of it as far as I could, but you can't help hearing what's said, can you? Not when all the parties are screeching at the top of their lah-di-dah voices. My master — 'im as were killed — tried all ways to weasel out of dressing up at all, him being so pious an' all that.' The valet turned his head and spat on the ground. 'At least as he pretended. I could tell you a fair few tales about him and his holiness ...'

'The costume?' Foxe interrupted, not wishing to spend more time than he needed on this task and sensing the valet was dying to spit out as much venom as he could.

'That? Everyone knew Lord Bile-and-Bible Aylestone hated anything to do with entertainment. He'd tried refusing to attend the ball, but that didn't work. Next, he tried to refuse to wear a costume, and his father swept that aside too. Threatened to cut him off without a penny, if he didn't do as he was told. Then even his mother turned on him, declaring he was an ungrateful brat, of no use to himself or anyone else. Told him they'd had enough of him. Since he was too lazy and stupid to find himself some source of income, he could get out of this house and starve in the gutter for all they cared. She and his father weren't going to support him any longer. They were offering him one last chance. Find a rich heiress, whose family were prepared to hand her and her dowry over in return for an alliance with a noble family. That's why he was going to go to the masquerade ball, whether he liked it or not. "Find a wife!" she told him. "There'll be plenty on show. Do that or face the consequences!" She was spittin' mad!'

'Seems they'd both had enough of their son's ways,' Foxe said gently, just to keep the man going on that track.

'By God they had! The names they called him! Reminded him his brother was the heir and there was another son older than he was. He could forget about the family estates. If he didn't do what they wanted, they'd leave him to his own devices — even if that meant living in a hovel and associating with people in trade.'

'Back to that again,' Foxe remarked drily.

'It was the only real weapon they had, sir. Anyhow, when Lord Aylestone tried to whine that he wouldn't have time to find a costume, his mother stopped that avenue of escape as well. She must have guessed what her son would do. The countess told him she'd attended an evening at the theatre soon after she and his father had returned to Norfolk for the summer. The character of a Harlequin appeared in the pantomime and she had been greatly taken with the costume. She'd already spoken with his father and they'd paid the woman who made the costumes for the theatre to make a more or less exact copy. There was no need for fittings. She'd been told to use some of the clothes they'd sent to her that were still in his former room in their house. Everything was arranged, and that was that! All he was required to do was to find his Columbine.'

AFTER THANKING THE FORMER VALET AND SLIPPING A HALF-sovereign into his welcoming hand, Foxe hurried to the theatre as fast as he could. There he sought out Mrs Vickers, the wardrobe mistress. He found her seated comfortably in her little room backstage, heating an iron to use on a set of ruffs for a production of Shakespeare's *Hamlet*. A comfortable, contented little woman, well-liked by everyone who met her and always ready to help an actor who'd managed to tear his costume, or an actress who'd made a mistake and needed to conceal her swelling belly for a while. She knew Foxe very well, as did everyone permanent in the place, so she told him what he wanted right away.

'Yes, Mr Foxe, it's exactly as you said. I did make an almost exact copy of our best Harlequin costume for that Lord Aylestone to wear. Not my best work, I'll admit. Seems he refused to let me take his measurements or go to his place for the fittings. It all had to be done in a terrible hurry as well. All I could work from were some shirts, breeches and jackets a servant brought for me. I wasn't even supposed to take any of them apart neither! I did, of course, then sewed 'em up again, so neat no one would notice.'

'Why didn't he borrow the costume in the theatre's wardrobe, Mrs Vickers?'

'For a start, sir, it would have been too small and too tight. Lord Aylestone lived well. Better than most actors by a long way. He wasn't exactly fat, more well-covered, if you know what I mean. If I'd had to alter it, I'd have had to alter it back afterwards. I wasn't eager to do that, as you can imagine, not even for a peer of the realm. The one I made for him had a larger jacket, longer legs to the breeches and a bigger collar for the shirt. I also had to find him larger stockings and shoes. Aside from that, it was as near identical to the one in the theatre's storeroom as I could make it.'

'Did anything else go with the costume?'

'There was a hat — a new one had to be bought for him — a mask ... oh, and a small dagger, which went on the character's belt. The one in the theatre had a retracting blade — you know what I mean — in case any pantomime called for a mock stabbing. Of course, that wasn't necessary for Lord Aylestone's costume. I believe he was to use some knife he already had, with the hilt changed to make it look like a real dagger. I believe his mother insisted. He thought it was unnecessary.'

'What about the theatre's original costume?' Foxe asked. 'Did anyone ask to borrow that?'

'No one, sir,' Mrs Vickers said. 'We did lend out one or two costumes, but only to people we knew well. Mr Bewell had a shepherd and Miss Marsh a shepherdess. Mr and Mrs Handley borrowed two of the costumes we use for *Othello* ... um ... Oh, yes, that nice Mr Wherwell dressed up as a Roman using things we have here. I think that's all.'

'Did they all return their costumes immediately afterwards? No damage or marks to be washed out?'

'None that I recall, Mr Foxe.'

9

The visit to the theatre satisfied Foxe's sense of duty towards his friend Halloran, so he decided he could justifiably spend a little time on one of his other problems. His choice was the murder of the man the street children called "Uncle". Mistress Tabby had told him that finding a resolution in that case was now his personal responsibility and he wasn't going to let her down.

The first step had to be to identify the family whose coat-of-arms he'd found engraved on the gold pendant the dead vagrant wore. Once again, Foxe crossed the marketplace and headed down the hill towards Tombland. He passed through the entrance to the Close surrounding Norwich's magnificent mediaeval cathedral and there, in the cathedral library, he sought out his friend, the librarian. He was bound to be able to help.

It didn't take him long. Once Foxe had shown the librarian the pendant and its engraved crest, the man soon identified it. It belonged to the Valmar family: a long-established dynasty of gentle, though not noble, birth living at Hutton Hall to the south of the city.

'What can you tell me of the current inhabitants of the hall?' Foxe asked the librarian.

'Little enough, Mr Foxe. Hutton Hall was built in the time of the eighth King Henry, I believe — or it may have been Queen Elizabeth. A substantial house, but not an especially grand one, I think. Sir Samuel Valmar is the present head of the family. Rather a stiff-necked gentleman, as I hear. Very attached to the family's history and what he judges to be its proper position in county society. He's a baronet and quite wealthy. He was also High Sheriff a while ago. Friend of the bishop, of course, and a thorough-going traditionalist and Tory. Not someone I can see you liking. I certainly don't. He's the kind of member of the gentry who looks down on anyone who has to earn his living.'

'He has a large landed estate?'

'Not as large as he'd like you to believe! I'd say it was just enough to live modestly. Not nearly enough to let him make the kind of impression he wants to.'

'You said a moment ago he was wealthy,' Foxe said. 'Where does his money come from, if not his estates?'

'A wealthy wife, where else? Lady Valmar is far better born than her husband. Her family is also much wealthier than the Valmar's were before she brought them a large dowry. To be honest, I can't imagine how he persuaded her family to approve the match. I think her father may have been an earl. He was certainly some kind of aristocrat, but maybe it was only a baron.'

'How old is Sir Samuel?'

'He must be sixty or so,' the librarian said. 'I'm not sure. I've probably seen him about the cathedral a time or two, but I don't recall much about him. His wife I do remember. A tall lady, very much the aristocrat. Her father was what people sometimes call a *nabob*. He came from aristocratic stock but must have been a younger son. As I understand it, he earned his title and made his fortune through serving with the East India Company. By the time he returned to England, he was governor of some Indian kingdom or other. Very able man, by all accounts. His daughter inherited his brains, which is perhaps why she didn't marry until a little later than most. Young men of that class want breeding stock, not someone with more brains than they possess. Anyway, as I said, she brought Sir Samuel a considerable dowry. To be fair to him, I gather he's managed it well and even increased it over the years.'

'Children?'

'Two sons and two daughters, I believe. The daughters married into old Norfolk gentry families like their own. I'm not sure about the sons. Sorry I can't tell you more.'

There was nothing for it; Foxe would have to go to Hutton Hall and ask Sir Samuel and his wife about the pendant. Arriving in his new carriage would help him gain admittance, but it would hardly be enough. Especially if Sir Samuel was as status-conscious as the librarian had suggested. Presenting himself as a mere bookseller would ensure he was turned away on the instant. He set aside the following after-noon for the purpose. In the meantime, he would take the time to run through all he knew so far about all three mysteries before him. He might also award himself another visit to Sally Jones — purely in the cause of relaxation and the cleansing of his mind. A medicinal visit, you might term it.

FOXE DIDN'T GET MUCH SLEEP THAT NIGHT, THOUGH HE COUNTED that as a benefit, not a problem. Thanks to Sally Jones, his mind was refreshed, even if his body was somewhat fatigued. Now, having ascended the heights of passion, he thought the descent into normality should not be too abrupt. He therefore decided to delay his visit to Hutton Hall one more day and first obtain a letter of introduction from the mayor. Thanks to Halloran, this was swiftly accomplished. The letter stated that Mr Ashmole Foxe had been appointed by his worship to enquire into a number of recent crimes in the city, including one which involved an item of jewellery, seemingly associated with the Valmar family. The item bore the Valmar coat of arms and had been discovered in the possession of a vagrant found dead in the city. Sir Samuel Valmar was therefore requested to give Mr Foxe whatever assistance he could.

Whether even that would serve to win Foxe an interview with Sir Samuel and his wife remained to be seen. Foxe could only go to Hutton

Hall the next day and find out. In the meantime, Alfred was sent with Foxe's card to request a meeting. It was all very formal and entirely in accordance with the proper etiquette in such matters. Sir Samuel was known to be a stickler for correctness.

Foxe's care was not wasted, since it served to gain him at least an entry. That it could do no more was soon proved. Sir Samuel and his wife received Foxe with a very ill grace. He'd worn his best and most conservative clothes for the occasion; even put a powdered wig on his head, which he hated doing, since it was hot and itchy. Before he left home, he asked Mrs Crombie to look over him and ensure everything was neat and tidy. She'd said he looked more like a prosperous physician than anything else. He even dressed his coachman in something like a proper livery.

Sir Samuel and his wife received Foxe in their withdrawing room. The house, Hutton Hall, looked exactly as his friend Mr Lavender, the cathedral librarian, had described it. At first glance, it was a substantial place made of red brick, with large windows and tall chimneys, probably built in Tudor times. Only after that did you see that it stood within a moat. The driveway ended in a place where a carriage might turn, but still a short distance away from the entrance to the hall itself. To reach that, the visitor had to walk across a stone bridge over the moat and across a small courtyard. The hall's restricted site may have also accounted for its odd arrangement. It had two uneven wings either side of a massive porch. All three of them then extended upwards in an arrangement of pillars and windows. Finally, despite the height of the building and a steep roof, it was topped off with clumps of spindly chimneys, shaped like Grecian columns in brick and finished with elaborate decoration. To add to this eccentric arrangement, some of the central part of the house was constructed of stone. It also had the sort of windows Foxe associated with a church. Maybe that part was older than the rest?

The couple themselves proved to be more or less as Foxe had expected. Sir Samuel was dressed, as you might expect of a Tory squire, in a sober suit of good cloth without frills or embroideries. Lady Valmar wore similarly austere and somewhat old-fashioned clothes, though enlivened by a fine petticoat of gold brocade. Sir Samuel regarded Foxe with evident distaste.

'We can spare you no more than five minutes, sir,' the baronet barked. 'Only doing that out of courtesy to the lord mayor. It is not our habit to answer questions from persons not known to us — especially not persons engaged in commerce. State your piece, sir, and let's have done with it.'

Foxe explained how the pendant had been found. That almost had him ejected at once. Both denied the possibility that any vagrant could have anything to do with them. No one in the house was missing; certainly no one who might be living as a vagrant.

After that, Foxe produced the pendant and showed it to them. He was observing them carefully as he did so and felt convinced that both recognised it, the wife especially. As it was handed to her, she gave a sudden start, before resuming her mask of aristocratic boredom. Sir Samuel agreed the coat of arms did indeed belong to their family, but that was as far as he was prepared to go.

'Thing must've been stolen from a family member sometime in the past,' he said, handing it back to Foxe. 'Can't imagine who that might be.'

Foxe turned to Lady Valmar, but she simply shook her head.

'My wife and I have no knowledge of this pendant or the person who was found wearing it, sir. That's all there is to it. I'll bid you good day. The footman will see you out.'

Foxe was sure both had been lying to him.

❧

BROCK AND MRS CROMBIE, BETWEEN THEM, PROVED TO BE excellent sources of information on the Valmar family. Foxe learned that Sir Samuel was a member of a small group of local gentry who exhibited strong Tory leanings in an otherwise solidly Whig county. Twice before, Sir Samuel had stood for parliament. Both times his Whig opponent had beaten him easily, due to support from Norfolk's many wealthy merchants. After the second defeat, Sir Samuel had abandoned the idea of a political career. He was heard blaming what he termed, "a rabble of tradespeople and attorneys with no breeding whatsoever" for his drubbing at the polls. The notion that voters might need to be won over had clearly never occurred to him.

To add to his discomfort, it was at around the time of his second trouncing that his eldest son and heir, George, left. George had grown into an independent-minded young man with almost the opposite outlook on life to his father. It was merely a matter of time before the two came into a head-on conflict. What provoked the final breach, both Brock and Mrs Crombie believed, was the son declaring he intended to enter parliament. Worse still, he would present himself to the voters as a member of the Whig faction associated with the notorious young radical, John Wilkes. He also, according to Mrs Crombie, refused to marry the young woman his father had chosen for him from amongst his Tory cronies.

As a result of this clash, George Valmar was ejected from the family home and disinherited. Everyone knew that was what actually happened. His father, however, put it about that his eldest son had gone on a journey overseas, where he had unfortunately died. The second son was therefore treated as the heir to the family's wealth and title. He was the spitting image of his father, both in looks and in character. A hard-hearted, stony-faced, pompous old-style country squire lacking refinement or imagination. Father and son were interested mostly in the hunt and the shoot. To this the father added extracting as much money from the family estate as he possibly could. Sir Samuel, as the local magistrate, was the terror of anyone caught poaching game on his estate. As a landlord, he was well known to be grasping and merciless with those who fell into arrears with their rents. His remaining son, Frederick, was reputed to be as relentless in his pursuit of women as his father was in seeking out poachers. Aside from that, he was simply idle.

After his supposed disappearance and subsequent death, the eldest son was never spoken of again in the Valmar household. No memorial to his memory was erected in the parish church amongst the tombs and monuments to other members of the family. As far as he could, his father simply wiped George's name from all family records.

'What of Lady Valmar?' Foxe asked. 'His mother.'

It seemed she was never consulted on anything. Her sole role was to look after the house — and do as she was told, naturally.

'If this George Valmar wasn't dead, what happened to him?' Foxe asked next. 'Did he really go abroad?'

No one knew for certain, it appeared. There had been rumours for a while, some more fantastic than others. People claimed he had left for the American colonies, where he had made a fortune as a fur trader. Others said he had thrown his lot in with a notorious privateer and was roaming the Caribbean in search of Spanish treasure ships. The most likely answer was the least romantic. He had struggled to survive and finally become a fencing-master in London, using the only skill he had been taught.

Mulling this over, Foxe became even more convinced that the pendant he and Mistress Tabby had found was a genuine keepsake of the Valmar family. How the dead vagrant had come by it was far more difficult to determine. It could hardly be the missing son himself. Whether he had become a colonial fur-trader, a privateer or a fencing-master, he wouldn't have ended up homeless on the streets of Norwich. Perhaps it was as that pompous old fool, Sir Samuel, had claimed. The vagrant had simply stolen it. Yet, if he had, why not sell it? If you were so poor that you had to sleep in a filthy alley and beg for food, why keep a piece of solid gold jewellery which could end your poverty for months or even years?

Another thing, Lady Eleanor Valmar had definitely recognised the pendant. Foxe was sure of that. When he produced it and handed it to her husband, Foxe had noticed how she jumped and let out a small gasp — before she mastered her feelings again and denied any knowledge of the thing. If only he could manage in some way to speak to her on her own, without that bullying husband around. Sadly, that seemed impossible. There would be no point in returning to Hutton Hall. Foxe was convinced Sir Samuel would have instructed the servants to turn Foxe away at once, should he have the temerity to return.

Another dead end.

❧ 10 ❧

A more compliant person than Foxe would have abandoned any
interest in the vagrant with the expensive pendant by this
time. He would also have set the mystery of Dr Danson's
death aside as of lesser importance. In their place, he would have
devoted all his attention to discovering who murdered Lord Aylestone.

Foxe was not such a man. The killing of Lord Aylestone mostly
bored him. Not only was he already convinced he knew the identity of
the murderer, after a whole day spent in thought he was even confident
he knew in broad outlines how the killing had been done. All he lacked
was enough proof to present the mayor and Viscount Penngrove with a
sound basis for a prosecution. Doing that was a mechanical process,
requiring nothing but determination and attention to detail. The kind
of thing any competent clerk might undertake. Besides, the mechanics
of trial and conviction were of little importance to Foxe — especially
when he couldn't help feeling a certain sympathy for the perpetrator of
a particular crime. He could not condone murder, of course. He knew
he would have to complete the case eventually and send the poor
fellow to the gallows. Nonetheless, that could wait a little, while he
satisfied his curiosity concerning other, more interesting problems.

Now, for example, it was high time for him to seek another meeting with the delightful and comely Mrs Danson.

Foxe was welcomed by Katherine Danson with the all the courtesy and elegance which had been so sorely lacking in his reception at Hutton Hall. He revelled in it. At the same time, he would, of course, have denied that his fascination with her husband's death had anything to do with the lovely widow herself. No one who knew him would have believed this for an instant. When it came to attractive and capable women, Foxe was like a moth drawn to a flame.

After they were both seated, and normal polite preliminaries were over, Foxe asked Mrs Danson what she knew of the letter which the butler had mentioned. The one that had arrived a few days before her husband's murder. The letter which had made him so excited that he set aside his normal reclusive habits and prepared to receive a visitor. A visitor who was to be admitted to his innermost sanctum, his library.

Unfortunately, she told Foxe she recalled nothing about it herself. Her late husband never mentioned it in her hearing. Seeing Foxe so cast down by this response, she hastened to add a rider. He might, she said, have kept the letter. He kept almost everything sent to him personally. If so, it would be in his desk — most likely in the top left-hand drawer. That was where he kept all his personal papers. Mundane letters or accounts to do with the household he left to her to deal with. Indeed, he allowed her to take care of all such things without reference to him. She then rose, took a set of keys from a drawer, and handed them to Foxe.

'You may look for yourself,' she said. 'If I may, I will leave you to do that without me. Gunton will take you to the library and leave you to it. I'm sure you'll manage better on your own.'

Back in Danson's splendid library, Foxe was like a child in a sweet-shop, tasting one delight after another. He could not restrain himself from wandering about and feasting his eyes on shelf after shelf of neatly bound volumes. Here a volume on the history of Norfolk, there a series of essays on the layout of Solomon's temple in Jerusalem. Placed on its own lectern he found a copy of *"Fragments of Ancient Poetry, collected in the Highlands of Scotland, and translated from the Gaelic or Erse Language"*. That ponderous title, as Foxe knew, covered the epic poems of the ancient bard, Ossian. The ones so recently discovered and translated by Mr James Macpherson. Foxe leafed through several pages, marvelling at the tales of Ossian and his father Fingal, his son Oscar and beautiful lover, Malvina. For a while, he stood transfixed, lost in that twilight world of the ancient inhabitants of these islands of Britain. Only after some minutes could he pull himself away and resume his search for anything which might throw light on Dr Danson's life and death.

A small book on the desk now caught his eye. Opening it, he found it filled with entries in a neat, though spidery hand. It appeared Dr Danson was methodical about his books, in the way of a good many obsessive collectors. On these pages he had noted down the title and author of each volume, together with details of where and when he purchased the book and the price he paid. After that came a cryptic entry like "Upper E, middle, number 6". It took little deduction to work out this indicated where the book was to be found on the shelves. Danson had clearly developed a simple system which would serve to let him find any book in an instant. Indeed, now that he took notice of such things, Foxe found neat pottery labels at the top of every stack of shelves. They were arranged from A, on the wall nearest the door through which he had entered, to P, on the door opposite. Danson had set out his treasures according to his own system, noting in the ledger the exact shelf where each was to be found and its place there, numbered from left to right.

It was entirely due to Danson's methodical arrangement that Foxe made the most important discovery of the day.

His eye had been caught by the entry in the ledger for the book Mr Anthony Smith was so eager to obtain. Danson had bought it from a person referred to as "Kendall" some twelve months before, paying the princely sum of three pounds and fifteen shillings for it. The idea at once crossed Foxe's mind that, if Mrs Danson would be willing to sell it to him, he could sell it on to Smith and make a handsome profit in the process.

However, when he went to the place indicated in the record, the book was missing. Had Danson taken it down to read it and left it somewhere else in the room? Foxe made a lengthy and careful search of the library but failed to find it. Had Danson lent it to someone? There were indications that he did, very occasionally, lend someone a book. Foxe found careful notes of the few such loans on slips of paper between the relevant pages of his catalogue. Each contained the date of the loan, the name of the person who had borrowed the volume and, later, the date of its return. After that, the completed slip had been pasted into a second ledger, which Foxe found in the top drawer of the desk. He wasn't surprised so few loans had been recorded. Danson was possessive of his books, as well as being a natural recluse. Would he have lent out a rare volume for which he had paid so much? Foxe could find no mention of him ever doing so.

Foxe leaned back in the chair Danson had used at his desk and pondered the situation. Another mystery — perhaps a significant one. Mr Smith had been most eager to get a copy of the self-same volume. Had he also visited Danson on the day he came to see Foxe, found him willing to sell for a handsome profit, and taken the book away with him? Foxe couldn't believe it. Danson had been obsessive in everything connected with his library. Surely he would have noted down the details of the sale? He leafed through all the pages of the register of books. Nothing.

Finally, Foxe remembered why he had asked permission to return to the library in the first place. He should be looking for the letter Danson had received. The one which made him both excited and willing to entertain a visitor in this, his innermost sanctum.

He began a systematic search of the desk drawers. He unlocked each in turn, turned out its contents, then put them back and re-locked the drawer. Finally, he found what he assumed to be the correct letter. It was a brief note, roughly sealed and signed with the name the butler had told him the stranger had given, Mr Cornelius Wake. For the rest, the signature proved to be all that was readable. The letter itself consisted of groups of four letters of the alphabet, none making recognisable words. A cipher! Despite going back through all the other papers which he had found so far, Foxe failed to unearth anything to help him decipher it. He'd have to try to work it out for himself.

Fortunately, for his peace of mind, Mrs Danson agreed he could take it home to study it further and he returned home in a thoughtful mood. After taking his dinner, he therefore retired to his own library to try to make sense of what he had discovered.

Questions crowded into his mind. How had the visitor known about Dr Danson and his collection? He didn't believe the huge collection of rare books he had built up over the years was a matter of common knowledge, even among scholars. Foxe himself was engaged in buying and selling such books — had been for more than a decade. His father had arranged the sale and purchase of books long before then. Surely some whisper of the man's collection must have reached them. Yet it had taken the man's murder to bring his library to light.

Foxe didn't believe either that the strange Mr Cornelius Wake had come upon Danson by chance. The note, probably making arrangements for his visit, proved that. He came on purpose, most likely to try to acquire one or more books.

But that only raised another question. From what he had discovered about Danson, Foxe was certain he would have been very unlikely to want to sell any of his collection. Especially one which was extremely rare and which he had paid such an amazing price to obtain for himself. Maybe the visitor offered an even more preposterously high price. No, that would only have confirmed its desirability in Danson's mind and prompted a more definite refusal?

Was this Mr Wake's visit coincidental then, with no bearing on Danson's murder? Foxe dismissed that thought at once. Somehow, Wake knew about Dr Danson's interests and his fabulous book collection. Danson's books must also have covered topics in which Wake took a keen interest himself. Where he had obtained that knowledge was totally obscure, as was the purpose of his letter and subsequent visit. There was also the mystery of the letter Foxe had found. Why write in cipher if all he wished to convey was his interest in the collection and a desire to buy one or more books?

Of course! Foxe grinned. Wake had used code for several reasons. First, of course, to conceal the true purpose of his visit from prying eyes and the second reason must be because doing so would have excited Danson's curiosity. It might also have been a way of establishing Wake's bona fides as a scholar of the occult. He would have expressed his interest in the subjects Danson studied. No mention of buying anything. Writing in cipher not only added a sense of mystery, but it did so in a way likely to appeal to a man who devoted himself to uncovering hidden meanings. That must be it.

A moment later, Foxe's elation had ceased as swiftly as it had begun. He took up the letter and scanned it carefully to make sure. It was as he recalled. All save the signature was written in cipher. The question now was what was the cipher? Without knowing that, it might as well have been written in Egyptian hieroglyphics.

Think, Ashmole! Think!

Mr Gunton, the butler, had been clear that his late master had been expecting a visit on a specific day and at a specific time. His master had given him instructions to admit the man without question and take him to the library, where Dr Danson would be waiting. Unless he had been able to unlock the cipher, how could he have known when his visitor would arrive?

But how? Where in all that mass of books was the one containing the key needed for deciphering what it contained?

Foxe groaned, pulled the candle closer and bent his head over the wretched letter once again.

AFTER TWO HOURS, FOXE ABANDONED ALL EFFORTS AT DECRYPTION. He'd tried every cipher he knew or could find amongst his own books. Nothing helped. Yet he couldn't shake free from the conviction that the answer must be simple. He'd found no notes or scribblings, no pieces of paper anywhere in Danson's library, which he might have used while deciphering this message. He must therefore have been able to do it in his head. He had probably written down the decrypted version on a single sheet of paper and destroyed it afterwards.

Another thought struck him. Danson had been a student of ancient writings. What if the decrypted message were in Gaelic or some other obscure tongue? Easy enough for Danson, impossible for him even to see when a decryption had been successful. Foxe was no linguist. He'd had a better-than-average education, thanks to his father, but one which focused on things of practical use, such as book-keeping. Over the years, he'd picked up a smattering of Latin, enough to read and understand book titles, but nothing more.

Of course! He knew a man who might be able to help him — the cathedral librarian. He'd been to university. He'd take the letter to him the very next morning. It would probably amuse him to pit his wits against it.

Time to turn your mind to other things, Foxe told himself. He'd found another ledger in Danson's desk, in addition to the one listing the man's books in such detail. No cipher was involved this time, but he'd still asked Mrs Danson if he might borrow it to study more fully. Now he took it up and bent his head once again.

Damn it! It was filled with such tiny, spidery handwriting he couldn't see to read it by the light of a single candle. He'd either have to call Molly to bring him more light or leave it to the morning. Then there would be enough daylight to make it out properly.

Foxe was tired, so he opted for the latter course and called Alfred to help him get ready for bed.

Next morning, he rose promptly, took a brisk walk in the garden to clear his head, and told Molly he would have his breakfast early. While he was eating, his carriage was to be prepared. He would have himself driven down to the small house in Cathedral Close where the librarian lived. He'd walked a great deal the day before and felt he'd earned the right to take things easy. It was, of course, much too early to be calling on anyone according to normal standards of politeness. Foxe knew that very well. He simply had to hope the man would be sufficiently interested in the task he was going to ask of him to overlook this gross breach of etiquette.

Such proved to be the case, so Foxe left the letter with him and hastened home to his library to start on the ledger he had left unread the night before.

It proved to contain lists of amounts of money loaned by Danson to a certain apothecary in the city, all at unusually high rates of interest. Foxe knew this particular apothecary, Mr Simon Craswall, was also a heartless money-lender and oppressor of the poor. So, this was how the man was financing all his lending. The interest Danson was charging him looked substantial enough, but the apothecary was doubtless charging double and treble that amount to the poor unfortunates who went to him for help.

All this told a very different story about The Rev. Dr Danson than had appeared in his outward behaviour. He had been living a double life. On the outside, a respectable, if boring, scholar and recluse. Behind closed doors, he had become obsessed with the occult and similar matters. To further his studies, he needed material that was not to be found on the shelves of any normal bookshop. Not in any of the city's libraries either. He had therefore set about collecting the necessary books himself. Unfortunately, they would be both rare and expensive to obtain. That sort of collection could only be built up and sustained by someone of considerable wealth. Someone who was prepared to spend freely. Someone able to keep replenishing his coffers from a suitable source.

On the first occasion that Foxe had been to the man's house and into the library, his attention had been concentrated on the man's body which had been found there. He had not had the time to make any close inspection of the books themselves. Nevertheless, he could not have avoided noting the amazing number of books it contained. Now that he was able to make a full examination, he realised how many rare and valuable volumes stood on those shelves. As a bookseller, one with an interest in rare and valuable items, Foxe could make a rough estimate of what it must have cost to create a collection of that nature. It would have stretched the resources of even the wealthiest men in the kingdom, let alone an obscure local scholar. Danson would have needed to lay his hands on hundreds, even thousands, of pounds on a regular basis. His "pact with the devil" — the loans he made to Craswall to finance the man's predatory money-lending — provided the answer.

How and when had the two first come into contact? That was completely obscure, especially given the second of Mrs Danson's statements that her husband despised modern medicines. It must have been a considerable time ago. That would have been when Danson's first wife was still alive.

Foxe shook his head in frustration. There was no way now of finding out. Still, that was a side issue. What mattered more was how knowing of the source of Danson's wealth could help him unravel the mystery of his murder. Had Danson been aware of the true nature of the apothecary's other business? He must have known. Borrowing such large amounts at ruinous rates of interest would have brought any legitimate business to bankruptcy in no time at all. Craswall's pharmacy was large and prosperous. No sign of business problems affecting it in any way. The loans Craswall negotiated with Danson must have been just to support his activities as a moneylender. The ledger revealed how he had taken out and repaid loans multiple times — and for increasing amounts — so he was making profits there as well.

What in the dealings between him and the apothecary could have caused Danson to be murdered? Had one of Norwich's criminal gangs found out about it and tried to blackmail both of them? That's exactly what they would do, given the chance.

If they had, there was no sign of it. The amounts passing between Danson and Craswall increased steadily. If someone else had been intercepting much of the profit, they would have fallen. Nor had Danson given any sign of buying fewer books, at least according to his wife.

What if Danson and Craswall had refused to pay? Unlikely, but possible. In such an event, a typical gang response would be to apply pressure. In the case of the apothecary, they'd turn to arson. There had been no fire at his shop or his home, to the best of Foxe's knowledge. Nor had Danson's home suffered an attack. They'd either paid or Foxe was on the wrong track entirely.

What about Mrs Danson's brother? Had he found out? How?

Another thought. George Stubbings had worked for Jack Beeston as a thug and enforcer. If he'd now returned to Norwich, it must be because he knew he could get money there. A man who had committed several murders either tried to lose himself in London or fled abroad. Stubbings was well known amongst the criminal classes in Norwich. The only reason to return would be because he knew he could quickly get enough money there to finance a fresh start somewhere else.

Craswall had been a loan-shark in Beeston's time, so Stubbings probably knew all about him. His sister was now married to the source of Craswall's extra funds. What better than to insert himself into that cosy arrangement and milk it for all he could get? Get a job with Craswall as one of those who enforced payment of interest. Get in touch with his sister at the same time. Then blackmail all three: his sister, Danson and Craswall. Pay him and he would go away. Hand him over to the authorities and he would tell all he knew.

A mighty dangerous game, Foxe told himself. Danson and his sister might feel powerless to remove the threat any other way. But Craswall? Surely the wretched Stubbings would have known how dangerous an enemy the apothecary would be.

Of course, he might simply be working for Craswall under a new name. He'd left Norwich as a fresh-faced seventeen-year-old. His time in prison must have marked him, as must his various fights and the wounds he would have received. He might have felt sure he would not be recognised. Some scars, the loss of a few teeth, perhaps a dose of pox might have produced a radical change in his appearance.

What if the clerk in the city treasury, thought to be embezzling money, had got into gambling, encountered Stubbings in his second-favourite role as a card-sharper, lost heavily and been directed to Craswall? Stubbings might have recruited new victims for Craswall in such a way, rather than acting as a thug. Dressed up in good clothes, no one would link him to the violent boy who'd been sentenced to trans-portation.

Foxe came down to earth with a bump. All this was no more than fantasy. There was no sign George Stubbings had played any part in Danson's death. Not unless he'd disguised himself as Cornelius Wake and sent the cipher letter. Nothing he'd been told about the fellow — nothing in his past history — indicated he had enough brain for that.

Had he contacted his sister and offered to help her do away with her husband? Foxe refused to believe she had been involved in her husband's killing in any way. It would take a superlative actress to hide her involvement and the knowledge that her brother was the culprit in a murder in her own household.

What if Craswall, the apothecary, had tired of paying interest to Dr Danson and decided to wipe out the loans instead? Possible, but unlikely, given how long their relationship had been in place. There was no logical reason for Craswall to have Danson killed. Given the calamitous amounts of interest moneylenders like him charged their victims, the interest he paid to Danson wouldn't have been onerous enough. It had to have been someone else. Wake was the only credible suspect, even if he did prove to be untraceable.

Foxe's mood had gone from bad to worse as the morning progressed. He'd felt quite cheerful when he got back from talking with his friend, the cathedral librarian. At that point, he was convinced he was well on his way to solving two of the mysteries confronting him. First the murder of Lord Aylestone and then the death of Dr Danson. That would only leave the unexplained death and doubtful identity of the vagrant found by the street children.

Since his return, it had been all downhill into despondency and gloom. Reading Danson's ledger had further muddied the water. It made his death more difficult to unravel, if that were possible, not easier. Now Foxe had the added complication of a man continually in need of money who had turned to financing a crooked moneylender. What else might he have become involved with? What other illicit activities had he used to meet his constant need for cash?

As for Aylestone's death, Foxe could still see no means of discovering the proof he needed to allow Viscount Penngrove to bring a successful prosecution against his son's killer. To cap it all, he'd risen early, eaten his breakfast in haste — something he abhorred — and given up his normal visit to the coffeehouse. All for nothing! It was enough to darken any man's mood.

If he had but known it, the tide was about to turn in his favour and sweep in a rich harvest of clues and ideas.

⚜ 11 ⚜

Foxe's gloomy reveries were interrupted by Molly, his maid. Alderman Halloran's man had arrived, she told her master. He was asking if he might talk with Mr Foxe at once, since he brought an urgent message from his master.

Foxe had guessed what it must be before Molly had even returned with the fellow. Halloran wanted to know what progress he had made in discovering who was responsible for Lord Aylestone's death.

'The alderman asks if you would attend on him at your earliest convenience, sir. He tells me to say His Worship the Mayor is becoming most insistent in the matter of Lord Aylestone's death, sir.'

'Let him,' Foxe snapped. 'If he's so worried, why doesn't he get up off his fat, municipal backside and find the murderer himself, instead of sending me foolish messages? Does our worthy mayor imagine I am as lazy as he is?'

The manservant was appalled. 'Oh sir,' he bleated in anguish. 'I cannot take such a message back to my master! It would cost me my position.'

'Forgive me,' Foxe said. It was silly to take his bad temper out on the messenger. 'Tell your master the matter is progressing quickly towards a conclusion but cannot be hurried any more than it will go.

Give him my compliments but say that I beg to be excused from attending on him for a day or so. To do so would prevent me from undertaking the actions I have planned and, since they are to secure sufficient evidence to support a successful prosecution, I'm sure he'll understand. As soon as I know more, I will inform him immediately.'

The manservant left, cheered to be taking back a more emollient message, even if it was not what his master wanted. The fact that Foxe's words were no more than a mixture of wishful thinking and soft soap escaped him.

Poor Foxe was tired of sitting in his library alone, cudgelling his tired mind. He'd given up hope of extracting something — anything — from the confusing mass of truths, half-truths and irrelevancies which were all he knew about Aylestone, Danson and the dead vagrant. He needed to set his mind to something else.

'Go for a walk,' Mrs Crombie advised him, when he sought her out in the shop. 'Call on Captain Brock.'

'It's too late in the day for that,' Foxe said. 'Besides, he'll probably be out about his own business.'

'I could explain to you what I am planning for the next steps in young Charlie's education. You hardly seem to talk much with the boy these days, beyond sending him on various errands. And they have nothing to do with becoming a bookseller.'

'I agreed to take him on as an apprentice, Mrs Crombie, only because I knew you would look after him. I am far too erratic a person in my habits to bring up any child. This shop is as successful as it is purely because of your careful dedication. The same will be true of Charlie Dillon's future. It would be wrong of me to interfere in either matter.'

'I asked you to listen, Mr Foxe,' was Mrs Crombie's sharp reply, 'not interfere, as you put it. But if you are determined to find fault with every suggestion I offer ...'

Really! The man was infuriating at times!

Foxe changed the subject at once. Mrs Crombie rarely lost her temper with him, but it did not do to provoke her. 'If you believed a person who had been at the masquerade ball earlier in the evening had left, changed into a different costume and returned later — say just as the ball was breaking up — how would you go about proving it?'

The sudden question took Mrs Crombie by surprise. For a moment she stared at Foxe in silence, open-mouthed.

'Is that what happened?' she said.

'I am sure of it,' Foxe replied. 'Nothing else makes sense.'

At once Mrs Crombie forgot her anger and began to feel excited. 'But you have no proof?' she said. 'Nothing to back up your belief?'

'Not a shred.'

'What of the captain or sergeant or whatever he was? The one who stole Lord Aylestone's love? Didn't he say he'd seen him at the ball and was going to give him a good hiding? Might that man not have killed him in fighting back?'

'I suppose it's still possible,' Foxe admitted grudgingly, 'but it's all too vague for me. No one admits to seeing this person. Nor did anyone hear any argument or fight. Surely some kind of struggle would have taken place. At the very least, they must have shouted at one another. You don't confront someone and start a quarrel which ends in the death of one of you, while keeping your voices down and making no noise. No, I'm sure it had to be as I said. Aylestone was killed by someone who was present that evening, then went away and returned later.'

'And no one saw this man. Was it a man?'

'Undoubtedly. A man and alone. I'm sure someone must have seen him. The most likely reason no one has spoken of it is that they have not been asked. That and the likelihood they would have been convinced it was someone else. The murderer, you see, relied on convincing everyone he'd either left long before or never left at all.'

'Which of those do you think is true?' Mrs Crombie asked. She was struggling to follow Foxe's reasoning. He had been thinking about this for many days. She had only just been presented with the possibility.

'I favour the idea that the killer had been seen leaving earlier. No one would suspect him, since all believed he was long gone. In fact, if I'm right, he came back.'

'Why don't you question the servants who might have been about the entrance at the time?' Mrs Crombie said. 'If anyone returned, they would surely think it was odd at such a late stage in the evening.'

'Not necessarily. They might have thought it was a servant coming to fetch their master in the coach. There are few places to leave coaches about the door to the Assembly House. Most people send them away and tell the coachman to return at a certain hour to collect them again.'

'So, this man came in, killed Lord Aylestone, and left again. All without drawing attention to himself.'

'Possibly. That must be the case, so long as you accept Aylestone was seen alive when everyone says they saw him.'

'How could so many people be mistaken?' Mrs Crombie protested. 'They knew what they saw and will be willing to swear to it.'

'They knew what they *thought* they saw, Mrs Crombie. What if our man crept in, dressed to impersonate Aylestone? The person so many saw peering into the hall would then have been him, not Aylestone. The murder could have taken place earlier, just as the unknown doctor who first saw the body said.'

'But Lord Aylestone's costume was distinctive,' she protested. 'Everyone said that.'

'Distinctive, yes. Unique — no. You see, it was made as an exact copy of one held in the storeroom of the theatre. I've spoken to the person who made it.'

'I am bemused,' Mrs Crombie said. 'This man killed Lord Aylestone earlier that evening, hid the body and left. Somewhere, he got hold of a costume matching the one worn by Lord Aylestone ...'

'Not somewhere,' Foxe interrupted. 'From the theatre. The original on which Aylestone's costume was based.'

'Very well, but I thought you told me the place was locked up.'

'It was. Never mind that for the moment. Go on with your reconstruction.'

'The killer returns in the Harlequin costume ... no, stop. Anyone at the door would have seen him wearing it and wondered, when Lord Aylestone had already left, why he was returning.'

'Our man would have hidden the costume under his cloak. If it was noticed, at a swift glance, a costume under a cloak might be mistaken for livery. Servants are invisible on such occasions. All eyes are on their masters and mistresses. The lateness of the hour practically guaranteed much coming and going of servants and coachmen. Those at the door might easily have failed to notice anything.'

'The man's mask?'

'Kept out of sight under his cloak and assumed once inside. Plenty of corners and unused rooms in the place where it could be done.'

'He would have been cloaked, you say?'

'Assuredly. He needed to conceal the costume until it was needed.'

'The hat, then!' Mrs Crombie said in triumph. She was not going to let Foxe's wild idea carry her away without a struggle. 'Wasn't the hat for the costume also distinctive? You couldn't hide that so easily.'

'Why not? Much can be hidden under a cloak — including a suitable weapon!'

'I can't believe no one would have noticed if a man came in wearing a sword,' Mrs Crombie said. 'No servant wears a sword.'

'I agree,' Foxe said. 'He couldn't have brought a sword, nor was one used. The weapon which killed Lord Aylestone was under him when he was found. A dagger . . . a very oddly shaped dagger . . . large hilt, small, insignificant blade . . . more like a penknife. Yes . . . Why didn't he bring a better weapon?'

Wherever Foxe's mind was now, it was far, far away from the bookshop. Mrs Crombie kept quiet and waited.

'Because it wasn't needed! That's why!' Foxe cried out. 'Surprised at the state of the body . . . our missing physician . . . what did he come back for then? To hide what he had done? Too late for that . . . already done . . . an alibi . . .'

At that point, Charlie burst into the shop, breaking the spell.

'Master! Listen! Two of the street children just called me to the back gate. They say they saw a man wrapped in a cloak coming late to the Assembly Hall on the night that toff was killed.'

'When?' Foxe snapped.

'The clock in St Peter Mancroft 'ad rung out midnight not long afore. That's what they said.'

'They're sure he went to the Assembly House?'

'Quite sure, master. They was 'anging about outside, 'oping to cadge a few coppers off of the drunken gentry as they left.'

Charlie's newly-acquired politeness of speech had deserted him in his excitement.

'Why did they notice this fellow in particular? There must have been several servants arriving about then to collect their masters. He could have been one of those.'

'They says the bloke were trying to keep to the shadows, as if he wanted to avoid being seen. Friggin' furtive, they called 'im.'

'Charlie!' Mrs Crombie scolded. 'Language!'

She was ignored.

'I was right!' Foxe said quietly. 'I knew I had to be.'

He turned back to Charlie and asked another question.

'Can they describe this man, boy? Where are they? I'll go and speak to them on the instant.'

'They've gone, Master. An' the answer to yer question is they couldn't, beyond saying as it were a man.'

'Why not?'

'Too dark, too far away. 'Sides, 'e were keepin' to the shadows as I said. All muffled up an' 'ead down. 'E even had the 'ood o' the cloak pulled up to 'ide 'is face, like.'

'Damn! Damn! Damn!' Foxe pulled himself up sharply. 'My apologies, Mrs Crombie, only it's so frustrating. This proves I was correct in reasoning someone must have returned that night. He was muffling himself up not just to hide his identity — which it seems he did most successfully — but to hide the costume he was wearing until he got inside. Then he would have wanted everyone to see it.'

'Was this costume the one identical to the costume Lord Aylestone was wearing that night?' Mrs Crombie asked. 'Was this murder planned far in advance, knowing what Lord Aylestone would be wearing?'

'I'm certain it was not,' Foxe said, 'Is there a performance at the theatre this evening, do you know?'

'Nobody has talked of such an event. I did hear from several customers that one is to take place there tomorrow,' Mrs Crombie replied, mystified once again by Foxe's sudden change of direction.

'There is also to be a rout at the Assembly House tomorrow evening, I believe. I assumed you were attending.'

'No time,' Foxe said. 'A rout you say? Excellent. The theatre staff will all be present and so will most of the people at the Assembly House. Preparations . . . rehearsals . . . is there time? Yes, just. Charlie, go through to the kitchen and tell the cook I shall be late for dinner tonight.'

Then he vanished to get his coat and was out through the door moments later.

❧

FOXE HAD GONE TO THE THEATRE. AS EXPECTED, THE PLACE WAS A hive of activity. Fresh scenery was being erected for the upcoming production. Men were moving to and fro, carrying parts of painted backdrops and the various other items that would be needed the next day. Those not on stage at the start had to be placed somewhere convenient behind the stage or in the wings, so they could be found swiftly when they were needed. Ropes were being lowered and raised from the flies to lift unwanted backdrops out of the way and lower others. The air was full of dust. The noise was appalling. Shouting, cursing, the squeaking of pulleys and stamping of feet; to say nothing of the din made by the hammering and sawing of the theatre carpenters as parts of the scenery were adjusted. Visiting companies usually provided their own scenery and costumes. This was to be a local production by the Norwich Company of Comedians. A good deal of scenery was stored and brought out when needed, but it was always having to be adjusted to suit the many different programs the public demanded.

In the midst of all the noise and chaos, some of the company were on stage. This was their last chance to run through those parts of the production that were proving especially difficult for them to get right. Now they were being shouted at by the actor-manager of the troupe when someone stumbled over a line or moved to the wrong part of the stage.

Foxe retreated swiftly backstage, away from the noise, where he sought out Mrs Vickers, the wardrobe mistress.

Her small workroom was a good deal quieter but a little less cluttered. Piles of costumes lay on all sides. She and her assistants were checking them to see if they needed any last-minute repairs. There might also be stains which needed to be cleaned away.

'I won't interrupt you for long,' Foxe assured her. 'I just need to see the theatre's version of the Harlequin costume you made for Lord Aylestone. I've heard a great deal about it from others, but I'll feel easier in my mind if I can compare what I've been told with the original thing.'

Several of the woman's assistants looked up hopefully, doubtless hoping to escape the drudgery of stitching up torn hems and gaping seams for a few minutes. They were disappointed.

'I'll get it for you myself, Mr Foxe. I know where it is. These lazy girls would make going an excuse to linger and make eyes at the lads they met along the way. Then they'd come back and claim they couldn't find what they were seeking, just to be sent a second time.'

However, it was Mrs Vickers who took some time to return. Foxe was starting to wonder if she too had a sweetheart amongst the other theatre servants whose company she preferred to his. Eventually, after some fifteen minutes, she came bustling back, her face red and angry.

'It wasn't where it ought to have been, Mr Foxe. Someone must have moved it. Messing with my arrangements! I'll have the hide off the back of whoever meddles with the costumes in such a way!'

She glared furiously at the girls about her, so that they all bent over their work in haste. 'It wasn't hung up properly either.'

'It's not been out of the theatre since you saw it last?' Foxe said.

'It better not have been! Anyone who dares to take one of the costumes without my permission will be on the street faster than they can speak my name!'

Another ferocious glare at the girls about her.

'Remember that!'

'I'm sure you take care of the costumes with every attention, Mrs Vickers,' Foxe said in his most soothing tones. He'd already discovered what he needed to know, but he'd better make certain.

'Do any of the theatre's patrons know about the range of costumes kept here? Anyone asked to see one or more of them recently?'

'No one, save yourself, Mr Foxe. Though I'm sure anybody who's knowledgeable about theatre matters would know we keep many costumes here, certainly anyone who's a member of the board of directors. Not so many would know where to find them or which particular costumes are in storage. Only myself, these worthless girls, the dressers and the actors, of course. They would know exactly which costumes the theatre owned and kept. Most of the visiting troupes bring their own costumes. They're always kept separate from ours and taken away when the visiting troupe leaves. Sometimes we borrow costumes from another theatre on the circuit and they from us, but I always keep a careful tally. It's expensive to replace costumes, Mr Foxe. The manager would soon be at my door if I couldn't account for every penny I spend.'

Foxe inspected the costume carefully but could find nothing wrong with it. No stains, rips or tears. If it had been worn to commit Aylestone's murder, there was a good chance it would have been stained with blood, yet he could find none. Wanting to be certain, he once again asked the wardrobe mistress to confirm that Mr Bewell had borrowed a costume for the masquerade ball.

'Lord bless you, sir! Both he and Miss Marsh did. I dressed them up as shepherd and shepherdess. Very handsome they looked too. Miss Marsh is a pretty lady, Mr Foxe. She has just the face for a country maiden. You know, the kind who doesn't realise how lovely she is until the hero has her dressed up in fine clothes, instead of rags. Good costumes they were too. We use them quite often for characters in bucolic dramas.'

'Those costumes were returned in good order?' Foxe said.

'Yes, sir. Miss Marsh returned her costume the very next morning. Most upset she was too about the way she'd been abused by that Lord Whatever-His-Name. Mr Bewell forgot his, he said. In fact, he didn't return it for several days. It was all an excuse, as I very well knew at the time. When he did bring it back, I looked it over and, sure enough, he'd got something on the sleeve of the shirt and tried to clean it off himself. When I asked him, he said it was wine, but that weren't true.

Blood it was. Not so much, but it was there. I soon got it off, off course. Cold water you need for bloodstains, Mr Foxe. Soaking in cold water.'

'You didn't mention this when I asked you about the return of costumes before.'

The woman hung her head. 'I forgot,' she said.

'Is Mr Bewell in the theatre now do you know?'

'He is right enough, Mr Foxe. Probably on stage, trying to run through his part. He's to play the leading role in tomorrow's production. First time in the lead! The dear young man's so proud!'

Foxe smiled. 'He'll not want to be bothered with me then,' he said. 'Not today. He's part of the company, I believe?'

'Yes, sir.'

'Then I can find him at another, more convenient time. Oh, just one more thing. This dagger and sheath are part of the costume?'

'Just for the look of it, Mr Foxe. Harlequins don't usually kill anyone on stage. Still, to be on the safe side, I always put a trick dagger in that sheath. You know. One with a short, wooden blade that fits up into the handle. Paint it silver and it looks like the real thing from far enough away. The sheath's too long for the blade in it, just to make it look as if it's holding a real dagger.'

Foxe had no more questions. As he left the theatre he was torn between satisfaction and regret. The case was just about sound enough, he supposed. Only circumstantial evidence, but it would have to do. Still, he'd let Bewell have his moment of glory on stage the next night. He deserved that.

In the meantime, it was time to turn his attention once more to the other two deaths. Halloran and the mayor would have to wait another day for relief from being pestered by Viscount Penngrove.

12

There days had passed since Foxe left the encrypted letter from Danson's library in the custody of Mr Lavender, the cathedral librarian. It was high time to discover if his friend had been able to make any progress with deciphering its contents.

With this intention, Foxe set out immediately after breakfast to walk to Cathedral Close and visit the man again. It was a fine morning, though with a stiff breeze blowing as so often is the case in Norwich. Just the time for a brisk walk down through the market to Tombland and the cathedral. Foxe always enjoyed the sights and sounds of the stallholders, many of whom would have been up since dawn getting their stalls ready for what they hoped would be a busy day. Not the smells, though. Fortunately, the wind was blowing much of the reek from the fish market in the other direction. The stench of blood, offal and dung from the beasts in the meat market could not be avoided so easily. Nor could the frantic bellowing of cattle and the squealing of pigs as they saw others falling before the poleaxes of the slaughterers.

Thankfully, he was soon past the market and heading down the hill towards the quietness of the precincts of the cathedral. Much of Tombland was occupied by substantial houses, set either side of the road from the north. Good, solid buildings mostly occupied by families of whom the same things could be said. Then he was into the Close itself; a world within a world, one tied more to the rhythms of the ecclesiastical year than the secular one outside its gates.

He found Mr Lavender busy repairing a book, which looked as if it had been violently attacked by some deranged critic of its contents. The covers had been torn away from the spine. The title page was torn nearly in half, and two at least of the signatures within the page block itself had been wrenched from their proper places. The librarian was close to tearing his hair out.

'I can hardly deny the Archdeacon the facility to borrow books, however much I'd like to,' he said to Foxe. 'Unfortunately, he's becoming increasingly vague and absent-minded in his habits. He also has several large dogs, whom he treats more like sons than animals. He even allows them to wander where they will in his house! Look what they have done to this volume! Bite-marks on the covers, pages torn, several of the groups of pages — the signatures, which are bound together to make up the text part as a whole — ripped from the spine. It's going to take me days to make good the damage. Days!'

'If it would help you,' Foxe said, 'I can take the book away with me and let my apprentice work on it for you. The lad loves book binding and repair. My own shop and circulating library rarely provide him with more of a challenge than the occasional broken spine or cover stained with wine or coffee. He'd relish working on a book in a state like this, I'm sure.'

'Might it not be too much for him to undertake, Mr Foxe? I'm not a skilled bookbinder, but I've repaired hundreds of damaged books in my time. This one is going to challenge me to the uttermost.'

'He has young, deft hands, Mr Lavender. More to the point, he has abundant time and needs to be kept from wasting it. Why not let him try? I'm sure he'll make an excellent job of it. He has all the tools and I've sent him to two of the finest book binders in Norwich to increase his skill and knowledge of the art.'

Mr Lavender wavered. 'There's no doubt it would be a godsend to me at this point, Mr Foxe. How much would you charge? As you know, the funds available to me are extremely limited; even to repair damage inflicted by senior members of the cathedral chapter — and their dogs.'

'There will be no charge, I assure you. Look on it as a charitable act. You will be allowing a young man to practice a skill which will serve him for the rest of his life. Besides, you have, I hope, been able to undertake a time-consuming task for me and bring it to a successful conclusion. The encrypted letter, Mr Lavender. Has it yielded any of its secrets?'

'You may take this book to your apprentice, Mr Foxe, and my thanks along with it. Now, the letter. In view of your most generous offer today, I'm delighted to be able to tell you that I have indeed met with success. I can tell you exactly what it contains. Whether it will make more sense to you than it does to me, I cannot say.'

Lavender stepped out of his tiny workroom and went to a desk set against one wall of the library.

'Here it is, Mr Foxe,' he said. 'It proved less of a challenge than I feared. The cipher used was nought but a simple letter substitution. One of the kinds anyone might use in a confidential journal. Two things made it appear more challenging. First, writing down the enciphered version into groups of four letters; that was designed to conceal the varying lengths of the words behind them, of course. Then the fact that the original text was in Latin. Rather poor Latin, I must say. Still, once decrypted and split into words in the proper way, it read easily enough. You were correct in thinking it had to have been enciphered in a way that would allow the decryption process to be swift — at least for anyone knowing what to expect. You were, however, quite in error in suspecting the message was written in any language as obscure as Gaelic.'

'Latin is obscure enough to me, Mr Lavender. I lack the depth of your education.'

'Deep perhaps, but not nearly as useful in practical matters as yours, Mr Foxe. Yet in this case it did indeed prove useful, as you say.'

'What does the letter say?'

'Here, I have written you a translation in full. The gist of it is that the bearer is operating on behalf of a secret society of scholars, one which extends throughout Europe and includes contacts in Egypt, Mesopotamia, India and China. This society, he says, is devoted to seeking out hidden sources of spiritual knowledge and understanding. Having heard about Dr Danson's own interest in such matters — and the library of rare books which he has amassed — the society wished to consult certain books they believe he is holding. In return, they offer a copy of a privately printed monograph containing information gleaned from — let me get this right — "a papyrus scroll in Coptic, recently discovered in a tomb in the deserts of Egypt, containing hitherto unknown revelations by the greatest of occult philosophers, the great Hermes Trismegistus"'.

'Good Lord!' Foxe cried, forgetting he was within the cathedral precincts and thus probably on consecrated ground. 'No wonder Dr Danson was at home to such a visitor! The fellow set out his bait with great cunning and the fish must have swallowed it whole. No mention of any particular book though? No suggestion this society wished to purchase anything?'

'No on both counts. Only the seeking of permission to consult certain volumes in the library.'

'Very odd, Mr Lavender, and somewhat vexing. I was convinced Dr Danson was murdered because he refused to sell a volume to his visitor; a volume the mystery man then stole.'

'Why would any man go to such lengths over a book, Mr Foxe? I know avid collectors are prepared to pay a great deal of money to get what they want. I have never heard of any resorting to murder to do so.'

'You are probably correct, Mr Lavender, and I have let my imagination run away with me. I have been known to do as much on numerous occasions. My thinking has also been coloured by a visit from another mysterious fellow. He asked me about a title which would have been exactly the kind of thing to excite Dr Danson, probably the man who wrote this letter as well. I made an immediate linkage which may not exist outside my head. This meddling in matters of the occult is entirely foreign to me.'

'To me as well, Mr Foxe. I'm sure I don't need to tell you the church regards all such interests as sinful. None but fools deluded by Satan look into such matters. They do so at the peril of their immortal souls. Superstitious and blasphemous rubbish, all of it.'

'What bothers me most at this moment is that understanding the contents of this letter doesn't take me any further forwards. I had hoped it would aid in discovering who the man was, and whether his visit had anything to do with Dr Danson's death. Now, it seems, that notion too was no more than another case of putting two and two together and making five.'

'Why, if I may ask? A connection seems to me most unlikely.'

'Again, I must now accept your doubts as valid. Perhaps it was no more than a coincidence that the book Mr Smith wished me to find for him was one I have found to be missing from Dr Danson's library. I jumped to the conclusion it had to be connected somehow with his murder.'

'Is it not more likely that Mr Smith went to see Dr Danson after he visited you, found the book he wanted and concluded the sale? It would have been courteous to inform you of his success, but not obligatory.'

'No one at Dr Danson's house mentioned such a visit.'

'Did you ask?'

Foxe shook his head in disbelief. How could he have been so stupid?

'No,' he said sadly. 'The instant I discovered the book was not in its place on the shelf, I linked it to the murder. I did ask if anyone knew if Danson had loaned it to someone. I didn't pose the question of purchase. In fact, if I am being honest with myself, the answer I received even to the question of a loan was ambiguous. His wife merely said she took no interest in her husband's obsessive collecting and rarely ventured into the library. It was I who interpreted that to constitute a definite "no". I can see now that I had formed a hypothesis and was unconsciously making the evidence fit it. Unforgivable!'

'Merely human, Mr Foxe. We all do it at times. Don't be too hard on yourself.'

Foxe wasn't comforted by this remark, though knew it was kindly meant. Feeling angry at his own failings, he thanked Mr Lavender profusely for his help, picked up the poor, wrecked book for Charlie to try to restore, and took his leave.

⚜

FOXE RETURNED HOME FEELING CONSIDERABLY DISHEARTENED. THE walk down to the cathedral had been easy going all the way. The walk back uphill now seemed to symbolise the state of his various investigations. What had before seemed on the brink of a full elucidation, now offered little but further effort. There was nothing for it but to work through everything he knew yet again.

Only the uncovering of Lord Aylestone's killer was on the point of final resolution. Not that he relished what lay before him. The task of confronting the actor, Adam Bewell, then having him arrested by the constables on the charge of murdering Lord Aylestone, was certain to be distasteful. Foxe enjoyed the intellectual challenge of his 'mysteries', the business of sorting through the evidence and finding a solution. Bringing the perpetrator to justice was necessary, but nearly always unpleasant. He had few qualms about seizing some ruffian or a person of truly evil intent. In this case, something told him Adam Bewell was basically a good man caught up in a series of emotions he was unable to control. Worse still, the victim had been a member of the aristocracy. It was unlikely the actor would be treated mercifully when finally convicted.

Still, there was nothing else to be done. He had at least allowed the poor young fellow his moment in the limelight as the lead actor. He hoped that at least would go well.

Turning over the best way to deal with what lay before him the next day, Foxe had an idea. It would be demeaning to go to the theatre or Bewell's lodgings with a pair of constables and haul him away like a common criminal. Why not find a way to lure the man to Foxe's own house? Give him the chance to explain himself, if he was willing to do so? There was still an outside possibility he could discover something in the way of mitigating circumstances to let the two of them formulate a successful plea for mercy and avoid the gallows.

Comforted at least a little by this idea, Foxe turned to the other case where he felt he might be closest to finding a solution. He would occupy the evening by examining all the evidence again. Perhaps sitting quietly in his library after a good dinner, washed down with wine from his excellent cellar and a glass or two of fine port, would bring him inspiration. He would tell Molly to set a decanter of vintage brandy beside to aid things along. Then he would review all he knew again. With luck, some fresh idea would come to him on how best to proceed. It had happened that way many times before.

Despite all he had said to Mr Lavender, Foxe was still hopeful he was getting close to a solution to the mystery of the killing in Dr Danson's library. He still didn't know who the killer was, of course, nor why Danson had been done to death. Yet, something in his gut told him another burst of effort would produce the answer. He would make a start by sifting again through all he knew, or could deduce, so far.

What if Mrs Danson had lied to him, if only by omission? The visit of Mr Cornelius Wake was real enough, and the man's purpose was now clear. She had led him to believe that mysterious figure was the only visitor on the day of her husband's death. What if there had been another? What if the theft of the book and the murder of her husband were two separate incidents?

It was most likely Wake who had stolen the book. Who else would be knowledgeable enough to seek out that single volume amongst all the rest? Who had a better reason to make off with it? He would have needed to silence or incapacitate Danson first, of course. Danson was an elderly man. It would be easy enough for someone young and vigorous to render him unconscious. All it would take would be a hard blow to the head, or some drug slipped into the wine if the two were drinking. Then Wake could find the book, thanks to Danson's meticulous arrangement of volumes on the shelves and make off with it before anyone in the house noticed.

If that were true, why was there any need for murder? That was the point at which this pattern of reasoning must falter. Why kill, when you had no need to do so?

Suppose someone else had visited the house that day. Someone with a far better and stronger motive for ending Dr Danson's life. Foxe felt certain the butler, Gunton, would have told him at once if he had known of an extra visitor. Either this person had crept in unobserved, or Mrs Danson had let him in. Who would Mrs Danson be willing to shield by lying? The obvious answer must be her brother, George Stubbings.

❦ 13 ❦

Early the next morning, Foxe received a note from Mistress Tabby. She had written to tell him of the discovery of the body of a man floating in the river. The dead man, she wrote, had been about twenty years of age, with a badly scarred face and hands roughened from heavy work. His throat had been cut.

He sighed loudly and put the note on his desk. Yet another murder. There had been several such killings recently, all connected with the rivalry between "Smiler" Hayes and "Growler" Spetchley. It was what you had to do to take over the position of premier gang boss. You killed your rival's men. There was supposed to be a truce, but violence between gangs might break out again at any time. The truce — if it existed — would still be a fragile thing. A single, small incident would bring it to an end. Still, this new murder was probably a coincidence; not something which concerned him.

'Hold on!' Foxe told himself. Unbidden, a thought had popped into his head and was now claiming his attention. 'What if the dead man in the river was actually Stubbings, Mrs Danson's brother? Not coincidence and not a man linked to either gang. What if George Stubbings was the man who had ended his days in the River Wensum, like so many others before him? That really would interest me. Could it be the truth? Could it?'

Thinking about it further, Foxe now saw a believable series of events emerging. Stubbings had managed to escape from prison. That was certain. He might well have returned to Norwich after that, exactly as the gossip suggested. Foxe had already considered the possibility of the man finding work as a bully-boy, employed by the apothecary, Craswall, who had been operating as a loan shark. So much had been proved by Dr Danson's ledger. That sort of person always needed bullies to inspire fear and enforce their demands for payment.

Yes, it was making a pattern!

The little Foxe knew about Stubbings suggested he was reckless with money and thus always greedy for more. His type had few, if any, scruples and little loyalty to anyone save themselves. If he had indeed been working for Craswall, he must have been privy to many of his employer's criminal secrets. Maybe the temptation to engage in a little blackmail had got too much for him? It would be easy enough to get money for himself by raising the amount of payment demanded and pocketing the extra. If so, he had not stopped to think that the apothecary was a good deal cleverer than he was. Far more ruthless too.

Very well, Foxe said to himself. Take this further.

How would Craswall respond? Men like him hated to be cheated themselves, however willing they were to cheat others. He would also be alert for any signs made by his hired ruffians that they were considering blackmailing their master. If his activities as a money-lender became public, the apothecary's legitimate business — and his standing in the city — would have been ruined. Would he pay for their silence? Hardly! The moment he encountered an attempt at blackmail, his response would be swift — and fatal. Suppose one of his victims had been killed while trying to stand up to his bully-boy, perhaps through desperation? The money-lender himself would face the gallows. The actual killer might be tempted to turn to blackmail in an attempt to save himself. Pay me to go away, or I'll hand myself in and turn King's Evidence against you.

George Stubbings had killed a prison guard trying to help Jack

Beeston escape. That almost earned him a visit to the gallows. He had killed again to escape the prison hulks. Two death sentences would be hanging over him. Those who killed even once found killing easier the second time. A man who had killed twice would be hardened enough to kill a third time without a qualm. George Stubbings would also be in urgent need of money, especially if he intended to try to start a new life somewhere or escape overseas.

Someone in need of money made Foxe think again of the embezzlement of money from the city treasury which Halloran had mentioned. What if one of the clerks had got into debt, perhaps through gambling or to pay for medicines for some sick member of his family? What if he'd taken money from his place of work, intending to pay it back later, before he was discovered? Suppose his thefts had been spotted too soon? Such a man might well have turned to Craswall for a loan to let him replace the money before the trail led to his door.

Foxe's mind raced ahead. A person like the clerk, someone who had been respectable all his life, would probably never dream of what would happen next. The way the interest would pile up. The need for new loans to meet those payments, on top of the original loan. Then on and on in the same way, until meeting the continual demands for money became a crippling burden. Next, if the prey tried to escape by refusing to hand over more, one of the bully-boys would come around to make sure he changed his mind. Suppose on that day the bully-boy had been George Stubbings, a proven killer with nothing to lose . . .

'Slow down, Foxe! Slow down!' he now told himself. 'You haven't a shred of actual evidence for any of this.'

Still, add all those together and a likely scenario emerged at once. Mrs Danson's brother could well have become over-enthusiastic in dealing with the clerk, to the extent that the man died. Desperate to escape a third charge of murder, and therefore in urgent need of money to pay someone to take him abroad, Stubbings might have tried to wring some from his employer, using the threat of exposing him and turning King's Evidence. It was the kind of stupid, half-brained idea a reckless bruiser might come up with. If he had, it would certainly account for him having had his throat cut and ending up in the river.

So what? None of that had anything to do with Danson's murder.

Forget Craswall for a moment. Why should George Stubbings have murdered his sister's husband?

Another idea then. George Stubbings returns to Norwich needing money and starts working for Craswall. At the same time, he thinks he'll find out what his sister is doing. He assumes she's still working in the bordello. He'll approach her and force her to hand over something as well. If he went to the bordello, he'd find out at once what had become of her. She's married a rich man. Better and better. He goes at once to seek her out in the hope of extracting some cash. She either refuses or he thinks she hasn't given him enough.

He returns on the day of Wake's visit. Finds the front door has been left open by Wake as he slips away. He goes in to indulge in a little burglary and enters the library hoping to discover something of value to steal. Instead, he finds Dr Danson groggy or unconscious. Even such a dullard as Stubbings would realise killing him would make his sister a wealthy woman. He could then blackmail her, claiming she'd asked him to do it. The madam at the bordello had told him the brother had tried to sponge off his sister before. Why not do it again?

Evidence! He needed evidence!

He could start by enquiring of Halloran if any of the treasury clerks was not at his post. Probably one who had given no reason for being absent. If the answer was yes, he would send one or two of the street children to where the clerk lived to find out more.

Stop!

He would also need to confront Mrs Danson and demand to know why she had been lying to him.

Foxe groaned loudly. He'd made the mistake of allowing his admiration for the young woman to slip over into something like affection. Now he was going to hurt her badly; maybe even prove she'd had a hand in her husband's murder. If she had, this action would send her to the gallows — and he would be responsible.

He had no sleep that night.

❦ 14 ❦

Foxe was glad to leave his bed the next morning. He had spent a
wretched night with his mind running over what he knew
again and again, like a jungle creature trapped in a cage in
some miserable touring menagerie. Either that or an animal caught in a
trap; constantly seeking some way out and finding none. Very well. If
he had to ruin two peoples' lives in the cause of justice, he'd best get it
over as quickly as possible.

Since trying to eat any breakfast would have made him sick, Foxe
went into his library the moment he left his bedroom, telling Molly to
bring him a pot of good, strong coffee and nothing else. Next, he sent a
message to the manager of the theatre, via Alfred, his manservant,
asking Mr Bewell to visit him at noon. He would have liked it to be
earlier, but actors, he knew, tended to be late risers. Getting Bewell out
of bed to answer an urgent summons would alert him at once that
something serious was afoot. The last thing Foxe wanted now was to
cause the man to try to make a run for it.

After delivering the message, Alfred should then enquire, as casu-
ally as possible, how the previous night's performance had turned out.
If well — especially if Bewell's performance had been praised — he
should say that his master wished to offer his congratulations in

person. If poorly, he should offer no explanation of the reason for Foxe's request. Foxe's reputation at the theatre was high and the manager would be eager to please a wealthy patron. Bewell would doubtless come as requested whether Alfred had explained the reason or not.

Confronting Adam Bewell and charging him with the killing of Lord Aylestone was risky. There was no doubt of that. He had thought over the alternatives during that long, painful night, and decided there was no other way forward. Halloran had lately been sending Foxe almost daily messages asking for firm information to give to the mayor. Viscount Penngrove was ranting and raving about lack of progress, harassing the mayor to such an extent he had taken to his bed. He'd even told his servants not to admit any more messengers from the viscount whatever the circumstances. There would be no peace until Foxe presented them with Lord Aylestone's murderer. Did he believe he had enough evidence for a trial and conviction anyway, even without a confession? It was far from watertight, but it might just do.

Charlie Dillon had also been sent early on a mission. His was to collect a suitable number of the street children for Foxe to question again about the man with the gold pendant, the one they called "Uncle". Rather than go on fretting while he waited for Bewell to arrive, Foxe went to the far end of his garden. There, by the stables where Charlie had his room, he found a gaggle of children already clustered about Charlie.

There was about a dozen of them, most standing, but a few seated on the ground. Foxe judged their ages to range from around five or six up to fifteen or sixteen. Even that early in the morning, the older girls were already dressed in the tawdry finery which marked them out as prostitutes. The boys, whatever their ages, merely looked what most of them were: thieves and pickpockets. The very youngest girls simply looked wretched. Every time he saw these children, it pained Foxe to know the vast bulk of the people of the city thought of them as vermin; on a par with the rats which ran everywhere. Their only desire was to see the city authorities round them up, confine them to orphanages and there put them to work. In the public's mind, the poor wretches deserved punishment for being what they were. Only a few people like Foxe knew what they really needed was love, help and compassion.

Foxe told Charlie to bring him a seat from the stable and he sat himself down amongst them. The group were all dirty and half-starved. They almost certainly all had fleas and lice. Foxe didn't care. Nor did he fear to come close amongst them. For many years now, Foxe had done what he could for such children, distributing money and making sure his servants provided what food they could to the neediest. On that day too, he sent Charlie at once to the kitchen to ask Mrs Whitbread, his cook, to send out whatever food she could get together.

He came back with two plates heaped with bread and crusts spread with meat dripping and a half-finished cake. Only when everything had disappeared into hungry bellies did Foxe begin his questions.

'Which of you has agreed to speak for the others?' he said. A girl of maybe fourteen years, taller than the rest and clothed in an especially gaudy costume, raised a hand.

'I'm Daisy,' she said shyly. 'I'll speak for them.'

'Thank you, Daisy,' Foxe replied. 'The rest of you stay quiet until Daisy has answered each question I put to her. Then you'll have your chance to add anything you wish. If you all talk at once, I'll not be able to listen to any of you properly. If you do wish to say something, raise your hand and wait until I point to you. Behave properly and there'll be more food and pennies for everyone. Do you agree?'

All nodded eagerly. Some even crossed their hearts in token of making a solemn promise.

'Good. Now, Daisy. What sort of a man was the person you called "Uncle" — the one whose body some of you found a few days ago?'

'A lovely man,' the girl replied. 'Kind an' soft-spoken like you, Mr Foxe. Spoke like a rich man too, for all that 'e 'ad no more than the rest of us. The scraps 'e could get were scarce enough to keep 'im alive, but 'e were always ready to share 'em wi' us.'

A number of heads nodded in earnest agreement to show she was speaking for all of them in what she said.

'Did he tell you anything about himself?' Foxe said. 'Did he ever explain how he came to be begging to survive?'

'Uncle were a wunnerful teller o' stories, weren't 'e?' Daisy replied.

More nodding heads. 'Liked to gather some of us about 'im at night and spin us yarns.'

'What about?'

'We thought 'is mind were wanderin' see? Almost all 'is tales was about a man like 'himself 'oo lived in this 'maginary world. A place where 'e 'ad servants, a grand house and a stable full of 'orses. That was allus what 'e told us stories about. 'e also warned us to be careful about 'ow we chose to live in the future. No more thievin' and whorin' than we 'ad to do to live. What 'e said was it were 'is own fault as 'e had bin brought so low. Aye, an 'e longed to see 'is family again, only that weren't possible.'

One of the others raised a hand to speak. 'Folks is allus tellin' us things like that, they is. Only angry like. 'E sounded sad when 'e said it. Even cried a bit once.'

Another raised a hand to speak, a girl this time. 'You've forgot that other story what 'e came out with that made 'im cry. 'E said 'e had once 'ad a wife an' a child, but 'is wife 'ad died. It were grief what made 'im go a-beggin'. It were true, if you asks me, an' all.'

The other children start to mock her at that, saying she had a head full of romantic ideas and nobody else would have believed such a tale.

Foxe called for quiet, then asked the girl if she could remember any more.

'All as I can call to me mind is that Uncle said 'e'd started to live rough after 'is wife died cos 'e couldn't bear to stay in the 'ouse wi'out 'er.'

Their spokesman, Daisy, now stepped in. 'That's right enough, Mr Foxe,' she said. 'That's what 'e did say an' all. I 'eard 'im meself. I believed 'im too.'

'Did he say where the child was now?' Foxe said. 'Or whether it was a boy or a girl?'

'A boy, as I remembers,' Daisy said. 'What else? Yes, 'e also said once as what the child was living with 'is dead wife's parents. Said as 'ow the lad were better off wi'out 'im, since 'e couldn't provide for 'im as a father should.'

Other children added one or two details after that, but it was clear they knew very little more. Still, Foxe was well content with what he had. He sent them away with pennies and food as he had promised. Finally, he told them he was willing to pay a significant reward for information on where this child might be. They were to find out as soon as they could and send back word to him through Charlie.

⚜

WHEN ADAM BEWELL CAME INTO THE ROOM, FOXE THOUGHT THE young man looked as if he had an ague. His face was pale, there was sweat on his forehead and his hands shook.

Foxe had decided to talk with the actor in his library and alone. The constable he'd summoned was in the servants' part of the house awaiting a call. Probably in the kitchen eating Mrs Whitbread's cake and washing it down with a small beer. Foxe hoped talking with Bewell wouldn't take long. He felt wretched enough as it was. Prolonging the agony wouldn't help him or his visitor.

Before he could say anything, the actor spoke. His voice was shaking. It sounded totally different from the firm, carrying tones Foxe had heard him use during the rehearsal when he visited the theatre.

'I know this is a trick, Mr Foxe,' the actor began. 'I debated with myself whether or not to come at all; but, if I run away now, I'll be running for the rest of my life. Why did you lie in your message? You weren't in the theatre last night. I looked for you, as I have been looking for you ever since I heard you were taking an interest in Lord Aylestone's death. I didn't mean to kill him, you know. That's God's truth, I swear it. If you hadn't become involved, I might have even got away with it. You've taken away my sleep for the past week, Mr Foxe. Now you're going to take away my life as well.'

Foxe sighed, cursing himself inwardly for his involvement. He should have left it to Viscount Penngrove to do his own dirty work. Too late now. He couldn't ignore what he knew, nor turn a blind eye to a man's death, however unpleasant the fellow had been.

'Tell me what happened,' he said, as gently as he could. 'I know you and Lord Aylestone quarrelled at the ball. Then the manager asked you and your companion to leave and you escorted Miss Marsh home. I also know you lied to me when you said you went home afterwards.

You'd recognised Lord Aylestone's costume as a duplicate of the Harlequin outfit in the theatre's wardrobe, hadn't you? Maybe the wardrobe mistress even told you about what she'd been asked to do. Either way, you went to the theatre instead. There you put on the duplicate Harlequin costume to replace the one you were wearing. After that, you returned to the Assembly House.'

'How did you know?' Bewell asked. 'I thought I'd been so careful.'

'No one but a person connected with the theatre would have known where to find the costume in the dark, Mr Bewell. I was suspicious simply because of that. Mrs Vickers told me something later which made me certain. When you took the costume back afterwards, you had forgotten exactly where it had been. As a result, you misplaced it on the racks in the theatre's wardrobe. You also botched the attempt to clean the evidence off the original costume you'd worn, even though you kept it for some time after it should have been returned. Lastly, I have the evidence of eye-witnesses. They told me someone returned to the Assembly House late in the proceedings and only just before Aylestone's body was found.'

'I feared you, Mr Foxe. Now I see I also underestimated you. Everything you've said is correct. You might have been there yourself.'

'You weren't careless in most respects,' Foxe said. 'I know the theatre well and was able to seek out the people I needed, then stitch their evidence together. You did make one mistake, though.'

'What was that?'

'You killed Lord Aylestone with his own dagger, then left it under the body. An intruder would have either used his own weapon or taken what he had used away with him. The final piece in the puzzle was supplied by a remark the physician, who first examined the corpse, made to those about him. He said he was surprised at how quickly the body had begun to cool and stiffen. At that time, you see, everyone thought Aylestone had been killed just before he was found. In fact, Mr Bewell, his death had taken place before you and Miss Marsh left. Am I not right?'

'You are, sir. But it wasn't murder. It was an accident.'

'Tell me what happened then,' Foxe said.

'As you know, sir, Lord Aylestone had made a spectacle before all the guests that evening. The moment he noticed us, he started shouting and raving. He demanded that such scum — that's what he called us, the scum of the earth — should at once be ejected. He didn't stop there, either. He wanted to have us horse-whipped for having the effrontery to attend in the first place. He called Miss Marsh a "painted whore" to her face. Said she used the theatre only to solicit wealthy clients to "wallow in beds of lust and defile themselves with debauchery". All this with hundreds of people within ear-shot. He didn't moderate his voice either. No, he shouted and roared like the worst kind of hell-and-damnation preacher.'

'He'd had plenty of practice,' Foxe said quietly. 'Go on.'

'As you can imagine, poor Catherine Marsh was reduced to tears. Even before the manger spoke to us, she begged me to take her home. By ill-luck, as it turned out, in fetching our outdoor clothing, I encountered Lord Aylestone a second time. We had arrived late, you see, and the servant who took our cloaks said the usual place for them was already full. He would have to put them on a table in that unused room behind the ballroom.'

'Which was where Viscount Penngrove took his son to rebuke him for his behaviour,' Foxe said.

'Exactly. Everyone knew they were in there. The viscount was yelling at his son by this time, threatening him with dire consequences if he didn't curb his temper and return to the ball, as he had been ordered. While that was going on, I couldn't get our cloaks.'

'You waited.'

'I did. I had no choice. It was a chilly night, Mr Foxe. Miss Marsh needed her cloak to avoid taking a chill on top of all else. All actors are mindful of their health. To be ill is to miss your place on stage and lose your wages. Fortunately, the row between father and son was soon over and the viscount strode from the room and returned to the ballroom. Everyone assumed his son would do the same. Naturally, I moved away at that point, not wishing even to lay eyes on the fellow, in case he returned to heap further insults on me. I waited out of sight, then returned to get the cloaks. By the time I ventured into the room, I was sure he must have gone.'

'But he was still there.'

'Yes. Striding up and down, waving his arms and muttering to himself. I tried to dart in, retrieve what I wanted and get away, but he saw me almost the moment I stepped through the door. As I feared he would, he began his insults and threats again. This time, his voice alone terrified me, that and the staring eyes and flushed cheeks. He spat out his words at me, Mr Foxe, keeping his voice low and waving his fists to emphasise his fury. Called me "the spawn of Satan" and "an abomination on the face of the earth". Said I should be treated "as God had treated the evildoers who dwelt in Sodom and Gomorrah". Then he pulled the dagger from the sheath at the belt of his costume and started jabbing it in my direction. I thought he had lost his mind.'

'He probably had at that point, Mr Bewell. Please go on.'

'In the end, he rushed at me, Mr Foxe, waving that little dagger and shouting something about "the avenging sword of the Lord of Hosts". I thought he was going to kill me.'

'What did you do then?'

'I backed away as far as I could, but the door was shut behind me. I knew that, if I turned my back, he would strike me in an instant. In the end, I tried to grapple with him and get the weapon from his hand. That was when it happened. Somehow, as we struggled, he managed to stab himself in the chest with that little blade he'd been brandishing at me. One moment we were locked in a desperate struggle, the next he'd slumped in my arms. I knew he was dead at once. All I could think of then was how to get away.'

'You didn't call for help?'

'The man was already dead. Don't ask me how I knew it, but I was quite sure I was right. What would have happened if I'd gone to call someone and admitted I'd been with him in that room? Just the two of us alone? I was dishevelled, out of breath, and I'd got blood on the sleeve of my costume. Who would have believed my story? Certainly not the viscount! He would have had me taken away at once, already branded in the eyes of all as a murderer.'

'You're probably right,' Foxe said. 'So, you took up the cloaks and went back to take Miss Marsh home.'

'I did, but first I thought to hide the body to prevent anyone finding it until I was clear of the place. There's a sort of large alcove in that room, Mr Foxe. You probably know that. It's usually covered by a curtain. I dragged Lord Aylestone's body behind the curtain, tidied myself up as best I could and left. If I still appeared shaken and upset, no one would be surprised. After the treatment that disgrace to the nobility had subjected me to before everyone else, I was bound to look flustered. To my relief, Miss Marsh was almost silent as I escorted her to her lodgings. All the way, my mind was working at a feverish pace, trying to see how I might escape the noose. After all, it had been self-defence, even if I couldn't prove it. That's when the idea came to me, Mr Foxe. If I could impersonate Lord Aylestone and convince all he had been alive and well long after Miss Marsh and I had gone, no one would think I had any hand in his killing. Except you, and I knew you weren't in attendance that evening.'

'I dislike masquerade balls,' Foxe said. 'Always have. Tell me how you managed to get into the theatre. The manager assured me the place is locked up firmly whenever it's not in use.'

'It is, Mr Foxe. The weak point is old Garnet, the keeper of the stage door. The man's something of a soak, never happier that when he has a flask of gin in his hand. Several times in recent years he's rolled home after a performance or a rehearsal and lost the key. Then no one could get back in the next day. In the end, the manager threatened to dismiss him, if he did it again. Garnet was in despair until someone came up with an idea. They got a locksmith to cut a duplicate key, attached it to a length of tarred twine and hung the thing where it could be reached from outside. It's there, but it can't be seen. All who work in the theatre know where to find it.'

'How did you find your way to the place where the costumes were hung and select the right one? Surely it was pitch-dark inside.'

'That it was, sir. However, there are a few windows in the parts where I needed to go, and no houses overlook that side. It was a small risk, but worth taking. I had an end of a candle in my pocket and my flint to light it. It gave a poor light, but it served.'

'So, I was right. As soon as you'd left Miss Marsh, you returned to the theatre,' Foxe said.

'Not quite. I went to a tavern first and took a drink to steady my nerves. Then I did as I told you. When I got back to the Assembly

House, I was wearing the duplicate costume. I also had the hat which went with it hidden under my cloak. Those keeping the door were distracted by various servants and footmen leaving and coming back. Some went to summon coaches and others returned to tell their masters all was ready outside. I slipped inside, went again to the room where I'd hidden Lord Aylestone's body and left my own cloak there. Then I donned hat and mask and walked back into the main hall. I chose a place close to the dais where the musicians were seated and made sure I was in plain sight for several moments. To make all look natural, I peered about the ballroom as if I was seeking someone. I needed to make sure enough of those present saw me in my disguise to report that the noble lord was fit and well long after I was supposed to have left.'

'What then?' Foxe asked.

'To make doubly certain, I went back to the area by the door. There I accosted one of the hall's servants. As Lord Aylestone, I demanded my cloak and that of a mythical companion — describing to him exactly where I had just left my own cloak after I entered. I'm a good mimic, Mr Foxe. I flatter myself I would have sounded enough like the man himself to fool most people. When he returned, I put Lord Aylestone's cloak on and hung the other over my arm. Then I told the servant to inform my supposed companion that I had his cloak and would wait for him outside. After that, I walked out and strode away, never pausing until I reached the theatre again and safety.'

'What did you do with Lord Aylestone's cloak?'

'Once I was clear of the Assembly House, I slipped into the mouth of a dark alleyway, put my own cloak back on and threw the other on the ground. I reasoned it would soon be found by some beggar or sneak-thief. He'd take it up and sell it for whatever he could get. It was a good cloak.'

'Then you let yourself back into the theatre and replaced the Harlequin costume. Only you put it in the wrong place.'

'By that time, sir, I was desperate to be back in my lodgings. I thought I had put it where I had taken it from.'

For a few moments, both men were silent. The actor was doubtless afraid of what was going happen to him. Foxe was marvelling at the young man's quickness of mind in finding such a solution to his problem. It was Bewell who eventually broke the silence.

'What will happen now, Mr Foxe? Will I have to face the gallows for what I did?'

'I doubt it, Mr Bewell. There was a strong element of self-defence in your action. Everyone in Norwich is well aware of the late Lord Aylestone's descent into some kind of religious mania. His family also have a well-deserved reputation for being hot-tempered. I believe one uncle killed a man in a duel not twenty years ago. Another close relative was arraigned for the murder of someone he believed to be his wife's lover. He only escaped by fleeing abroad before facing trial. When they hear your tale, I doubt any jury in this city — even in the county as a whole — will bring in a "guilty" verdict on a charge of murder. Nor, I suspect, would Viscount Penngrove relish hearing a full account of his son's madness proclaimed in open court. No, young sir. If your lawyer is competent, the worst that can happen is to face a charge of involuntary manslaughter. You may go to prison for a few years, but it's quite possible a jury, handled properly, will acquit you of that too.'

'I have no money for lawyers, Mr Foxe.'

'Never fear. I'll find one for you and pay his fee, Mr Bewell. I'll also speak up for you to the judge. I believe your tale and would not see your life totally ruined. You may yet take many leading roles on stage after today. However, right now you must go with the constable, who's waiting for my call in the kitchen or somewhere else amongst my servants. Be of good cheer, Mr Bewell. I'm on your side, whatever happens.'

⚜

ONCE HE HAD SEEN MR BEWELL SAFELY TAKEN INTO THE CUSTODY of the constable, Foxe left the house himself to take news of the arrest to Alderman Halloran. He should have been feeling pleased to have reached a successful conclusion to the case. In reality, he felt only sick at heart. Thanks to him, young Bewell would face a long ordeal, starting with weeks in prison, and culminating in a trial at the next assize. By Foxe's reckoning, he scarcely deserved any of it. Most of what he'd done could be put down to mischance. He was clearly a personable enough fellow, caught up in events he had neither provoked nor could avoid. Certainly not a murderer. Lord Aylestone, on the other hand, was a religious bigot from a family afflicted with a long-standing strain of madness. That madness, in the end, had taken control of him. It had driven him to the point of where he saw himself as God's instrument in cleansing the city of the servants of the Evil One. Men had been put in Bedlam for less. If any man deserved incarceration, even death, it was Lord Aylestone, not the young actor.

Unfortunately, the trials of that day for Mr Ashmole Foxe were not yet at an end. As he turned into Colegate, he almost collided with Lady Valmar, who was standing on the pavement about to ascend into her carriage. The door of one of the grand houses was still open behind her. It looked as if she had been inside taking tea with a friend.

It was too good an opportunity to miss. Foxe knew he would never be admitted to her house to talk with her. Now he darted forward and called out that he must speak with her on a matter of the gravest importance.

'Must speak with me, Mr Foxe? Must? Your impudence astounds me, sir. Stand aside and let me pass into my carriage!'

'Not until you have heard what I have to say, your ladyship. I now have proof that the pendant I showed you belonged to your own son. His was the corpse which was found in the city, the pendant about its neck. You knew that from the moment you saw the pendant.'

'My son, as you term him, has long been dead to me, sir,' Lady Valmar replied. 'Nor was he ever a vagrant, to be found in some filth-ridden alley in our city. If he still lives, which I doubt, he must be far away from here.'

'You are wrong on all counts, Lady Valmar. Your eldest son never left Norwich. Exactly how he found enough money to survive, I do not yet know, but survive he did until very recently. For a time, he definitely lived a poor but honest life amongst artisans. In the end, however, he was reduced to living on the streets and begging to survive. Even so, he never sold the gold about his throat, though it would have brought him enough to live on for a year or more. Finally, he was murdered. By whom, I now believe I know. Exactly why it was done, I do not yet know for certain — though I have a shrewd idea.'

'Does your rudeness and impudence know no bounds, Mr Foxe?' the lady said. 'My husband and I have told you what happened to our son. There is an end of it! Now be on your way, before I have my coachman throw you in the gutter where you belong!'

'The guilt for the man's death lies somewhere in your own household, Lady Valmar. Think on that!'

Provoked into a fury, the woman pulled back her arm and struck Foxe full in the face, causing him to stagger back with the weight of the blow.

'Stand aside, I told you! How dare you insult my family in such a way! I will have you whipped for it!'

As she darted forward to step into the waiting carriage, Foxe fired the last of his ammunition.

'There is a child, Lady Valmar,' he cried. 'Your grandson! A child who is now without a father.'

For a moment, she was checked. Then she stepped into the carriage and signalled angrily for the coachman to drive on. Just the same, Foxe felt sure she was crying.

Alderman Halloran was delighted by Foxe's news about finding the culprit in the death of Lord Aylestone. He made him spell everything out in detail. Then he declared the mayor would forever be in Foxe's debt for what he had achieved.

'That Viscount Penngrove has come near to hounding our poor mayor into an early grave, Foxe,' he said, after all had been explained. 'I will pass on to him your thoughts about the fellow Bewell. For my own part, I feel sure you're correct in assuming no charge of murder will be brought against him. Even to sustain a charge of manslaughter seems unlikely. However, that will be up to the judge who tries the case, not me. But what has happened to you, my friend? Is that the beginning of a black eye I see? Has some rogue attacked you on your way here?'

'No rogue, Alderman, but Lady Valmar. I met her scarce a dozen yards from your door. When I tried to tell her what I had discovered about that vagrant I told you of — the one wearing the gold pendant — she grew so angry she struck me full in the face.'

'What in heaven's name could that have to do with her ladyship, Foxe? You must have provoked her sorely indeed, if she went so far as to strike you. I know you can be an impudent fellow at times, but surely even you would not forget yourself so far as to speak roughly to her or try to seize her arm.'

'Nothing like that, Halloran, I assure you,' Foxe replied. 'I merely told her that I knew the dead man to be her eldest son; the one her husband had driven from the house and supposedly cut off from his inheritance.'

After that, of course, Foxe had to begin at the beginning and tell the alderman all he knew — together with a good deal of what he only suspected as yet. At the end, Halloran stared at him in horror.

'Would his own kith and kin do as much as you suppose, Foxe? How did they find him?'

'I think her ladyship could answer that question, Halloran, though I doubt she will. That poor woman bears a heavy load on her conscience. I saw her crying even as she was driven away. My final revelation that she had a grandson she knew nothing about must have struck her like a bolt of lightning from God himself.'

'By Heaven, Foxe, this is a bad business,' the alderman exclaimed. 'It will never come to court though. Surely you see that. Even you could not bring forward enough evidence. Even if you had it, Sir Samuel Valmar would use all his influence to see it was rendered useless. As it stands, it's you who should fear legal proceedings being taken against you. The moment Lady Valmar tells her husband what you have said and done, he'll be mad for revenge.'

'They will not proceed against me, Halloran, of that I am sure. They will reason that I can do nothing and would prefer silence to having the family's shame discussed throughout the city. To this day, Sir Samuel refuses to admit what actually happened between him and his son. If he's forced to speak on the matter, he comes up with the tale that his son departed overseas and died there. No whiff of scandal must sully the Valmar name. Sir Samuel is a deal too proud for that.'

'Then the truth will remain hidden — unlike the damage to your face.'

'Maybe, Halloran. Maybe. My enquiries are not yet complete. Who knows what may come to the surface in due time? By the way, I think I may have discovered who has been embezzling money from the city treasury and why.'

'What? Who is it? The mayor will see him hanged for it!'

'As to that, the mayor is too late. The man I have in mind fell into the hands of an unscrupulous money-lender. When he could no longer meet his obligations from his own resources, he turned to theft. That also became impossible for him, once the mayor's suspicions had been aroused.'

Foxe had heard all this from the street children just before he set out, but he didn't mention that. They'd told him the man's death had been caused by a visit from George Stubbings.

'I suppose he's now fled from the city,' Halloran said.

'In a manner of speaking. Do you know if any of the treasury clerks have been reported too unwell to work recently?'

'His Worship did mention that one of them had fallen gravely ill from the smallpox, I believe. Has the fellow died?'

'Yes, but not from sickness. Rather from an excess of zeal on the part of a ruffian sent by the money-lender to encourage further payment. That was your man, Halloran. He's already suffered in full the penalty for stealing prescribed by the law. The money, however, is gone for good.'

❧ 15 ❧

When he returned to his shop after his meeting with Halloran, Foxe's mood was still one of deep unhappiness. It was not his treatment by Lady Valmar which upset him. If anything, her fury at hearing the proof of her son's fate only confirmed what was in his mind. He'd felt sure she and her husband had been telling lies from the moment he first showed them the gold pendant. Even if there had been a rift in the family, any normal parents would have reclaimed the pendant immediately. Particularly if they believed it had been stolen. Yet, both had dismissed it with barely a glance and made no protest when Foxe tucked it back into his pocket. It was almost as if they felt such guilt at what had taken place, they could not bear any reminder of their lost son, even after his death.

The trouble was, if they maintained this attitude and the fiction about their son dying abroad, Foxe could see no means of challenging it. Sir Samuel Valmar was a highly influential man, well respected in the city, if not liked by many. Foxe could not launch a prosecution against such a person without bringing forward compelling evidence. Nor could he proceed against the surviving son, Frederick Valmar. His instincts told him that one of those two had paid the assassin to dispose of a threat to the succession to lands and title. Sadly, it had so far failed to tell him which one it was. It might have even been both of them.

Rather than return to his library immediately, where he would only sit and fret further, Foxe went through into his shop. It was not far off the time Mrs Crombie would close for the day. With any luck, there might be no customers present so that he could pour out his woes to her at least.

Mrs Crombie took one glance at Foxe's face and hustled him through into the storeroom, where they might talk in peace. She told Miss Benfield, her cousin and assistant, to shut up shop, then leave for the day. Miss Gravener, the young woman who ran the circulating library, had gone already, since the library closed an hour before the shop itself. Charlie was sent post haste to Mistress Tabby to seek a salve for his master's face and eye.

'That eye's turning a deep shade of purple,' Mrs Crombie said when the two of them were alone. 'The man who did it must possess a strong right arm. Have you at least had someone bathe it for you?'

'No man did this,' Foxe said. 'It was a woman in a fury with me.'

'Not Lady Cockerham, surely? She came into the shop earlier today and mentioned that you hadn't been to visit her for some time. She didn't seem angry then, only somewhat sad.'

'Not Lady Cockerham. Lady Valmar.'

'Lady Valmar? What on earth did you do to make her strike you? Surely you haven't been trying to force your attentions on her. She may still be a most elegant woman, but she must be at least twenty years or more your senior.'

'I told her the truth, that was all.'

'Where did this happen?'

'In the street. Colegate, to be precise.'

Naturally, nothing would suffice after that but to tell Mrs Crombie all.

'Begin at the beginning and tell me all,' she said firmly. 'While you talk, I will see if I can tend to your bruised eye.'

Neither of them had time to get very far with their respective tasks. Charlie hurried in a moment later with a small pot of salve. He told them he'd met Bart in the street coming the other way.

'He'd got this balm in his hand,' the boy said. 'I asked him how he knew to bring it, but he simply said he'd been told to do so. You know Bart. It's nearly impossible to get more than a few words from him.'

'I wish I knew how she did that,' Foxe said. 'There are times when I think she knows what's going to happen to me before it does. What is in this ointment anyway? On the label, she's simply written "Arnica and Solomon's Seal" and the instruction to apply it liberally, but to make sure none of it goes in the eye itself. Do you know what those herbs are used for, Mrs Crombie?'

'If you wait a moment, I'll go back into the shop and find a herbal,' she replied. 'Then we'll both know.'

She was gone some time. When she returned, she was carrying several volumes.

'I found Solomon's Seal easily enough, Mr Foxe. This book has the shortest and simplest description. It says, "It is found wild in woods in some of the northern counties, but is not common. The root is commended very much by divers respectable authors as an outward application for bruises." Arnica was much harder to discover anything about. The best I could do quickly was a note in this other book saying it is a popular remedy in Germany, also for bruises. It seems to be a yellow flower which grows high in the mountains there and also in the Alpine regions of France and Switzerland.'

'That will be sufficient, Mrs Crombie,' Foxe said. 'Thank you for your efforts. Put some on, if you would be so kind, and we'll see if it does any good.'

'There,' she said after a few moments. 'Now, tell me what made Lady Valmar give you these bruises — and leave nothing out.'

It took a long time, but when he had finished his tale, Mrs Crombie couldn't suppress her outrage.

'I had heard Sir Samuel Valmar is a brute of a man, Mr Foxe,' she said, 'as is his son, Mr Frederick. The difference between them, I am told, is that the father is cold and calculating, while the son is the epitome of the old-fashioned country squire: hard-riding, hard-drinking and interested in nothing but chasing foxes and shooting things. Oh, and making free with his hands should any of the younger female servants be foolish enough to come within his reach. Sir Samuel is at least intelligent. One lady who happened to mention the family in this shop told me the workers on the estate at Hutton Hall reckon Mr Frederick has fewer brains than the foxes he persecutes so diligently.'

'I have also discovered Lady Valmar is unusually strong for a woman, Mrs Crombie,' Foxe replied with a wry laugh. 'when she hit me, I had the greatest of difficulty staying on my feet.'

'She would need to be of a most determined nature to survive being married to Sir Samuel. He's a tyrant in all his dealings and cannot bear to be crossed, even in the slightest matter. Even so, I find it hard to believe a mother would so completely repudiate her firstborn. To maintain those feelings, even when presented with proof of the depths to which the family's behaviour had reduced the poor man, is almost beyond believing. As for colluding with husband or son to have him murdered, that really is beyond belief! Either she is totally unnatural, or she is too afraid of her husband to act in any other way than she has. If the latter, all any of us can do is pray for her. I can scarcely imagine the agony she must be feeling at this moment.'

They were both silent for a while after that, locked in their own thoughts about the families and the misery they can bring to their members in place of what should be love and support.

Foxe would have left then and returned to his library, but Mrs Crombie put her hand on his arm and indicated he should remain.

'Since we are dealing with sombre matters, Mr Foxe, tell me what you have done to upset Lady Cockerham. I thought you and she had become good friends. I know you were . . . very close, shall we say . . . to her maid, Maria not so long ago. Maria was with her mistress when they came here today. My! How that young lady has changed! She was always a pretty girl, Mr Foxe — none know that better than you. Now she walks and talks like a lady, wears fine clothes and I swear has grown several inches taller. You would not call her pretty now. Beautiful is the only suitable word. Seeing the two together would take any man's breath away. I would find it impossible to say which is the more lovely, the dark-haired mistress or the fairer servant. Poor Charlie came into the shop while they were here and was struck dumb by what he saw. Indeed, I feared for a moment he would fall down in a faint!'

Mrs Crombie grinned. 'You know the old saying, "like father, like son"?' she continued. 'It just struck me that today we have been treated to something akin to "like master, like apprentice". I swear Maria winked at the boy behind her mistress's back, for he turned red as a beetroot and hurried off into the workroom. I suspect he must have gone through into your kitchen soon after, Mr Foxe. When he finally deigned to return to ask me if I had anything he should be doing, his cheek too was reddened as if he had received a sound slap on it. Young Florence may lack the power in her arm to match Lady Valmar, but I dare say she has enough to make it clear that any enthusiastic descriptions of Maria Worden in her presence will bring swift retribution. That young woman regards Charlie as her personal property.'

'Does he feel the same way, Mrs Crombie?'

'I doubt it. Like most boys of his age, he is developing a roving eye — something certain men never grow out of, I believe. However, enough of that matter. You have still not answered my question.' She stopped and put her hand to her mouth in alarm. 'Oh, no, Mr Foxe! You haven't asked her to marry you? Surely you couldn't be so foolish!'

'What if I did?' Foxe said. He was on his dignity now. 'It is an honourable question to put to a lady.'

'Honourable but foolish, in your case. She turned you down, of course. Then you behaved like a naughty child rebuked by his mother and went away to sulk. You have been sulking ever since.'

'I have not been sulking! Nor is it natural that she should have refused my proposal. I am handsome enough, I believe. Also well-respected and more than wealthy enough for most women to think I would be a sound catch.'

'Only those who didn't know you, Mr Foxe. Do I have to explain? I see that I do, though you may not like what I tell you. There was a time once when I feared you might propose marriage to me, Mr Foxe. I am far beneath Lady Cockerham in status or wealth, but I flatter myself I am not without physical charms. Had you done so, I would have refused you as well.'

'Why? Do I treat you so badly?'

'Quite the reverse! I have never made any secret of my undying gratitude for your kindness and generosity towards me. Nor do I believe you would treat a wife in any other way than as a model husband should. You would probably even try hard to discipline yourself to be faithful. In fact, within a short time you would cease to be the Mr Foxe of whom I and others are so fond. Instead, you would become both boring and dull, even respectable; the very qualities which would lead a woman to be eager to accept you as a husband would disappear within a year at the most.'

'Why should that be? I would be the same man.'

'Not at all! Today's Mr Foxe is eager to exercise his brain against the most intractable puzzles. He takes risks and cares little for what others think of him for doing so. If need be, he flouts convention with almost total disregard. He may be a bit of a rogue, but that only adds to his attractiveness. Why does he do these things? It is in his nature, of course. Nothing could change that. What makes the difference at present is that he is free to do as he pleases. If he makes a mistake, incurs someone's disapproval, finds society shuns him, it is of little account. He can provoke the highest placed people — like Sir Samuel and Lady Valmar — and snap his fingers if they persuade their influential friends to frown on him and polite society to shun him. If he had a wife to consider — or even worse, children — he could do none of this without involving them in his disgrace and its consequences. Would he do that? Of course, he wouldn't! He is too honourable a man to see others suffer because of him. No, he would trim and moderate his behaviour, try to curb his curiosity and tread warily where once he stepped forward without a care in the world. Boredom would soon follow, then dullness of mind and forgetfulness of what had once made his life what it is today. I would not have brought you to such a pass for all the wealth in the world, Mr Foxe, and nor would Lady Cockerham I'm sure. She turned you down because she values your happiness and future more than anything you could offer her as your wife.'

After that, Foxe could find nothing to say.

❦ 16 ❧

If Foxe had been discomfited by what Mrs Crombie had said, the introspection it caused him was soon overtaken by severe pangs of conscience. He knew he should go to confront Mrs Danson before doing anything else. With one mystery solved and hopes of proceeding further with the business of the gold pendant seemingly out of his reach, there was no excuse for more procrastination. Her testimony might well provide the final clues needed to solve the murder of her elderly husband. He also owed it to her to inform her of the death of the man he felt certain must have been her brother. What held him back was simple dread of finding she was either directly involved in the death or, at the very least, complicit.

Thanks to these gloomy reflections, his breakfast the next morning was again a miserable affair. Mrs Whitbread's excellent bread rolls, still warm from the oven, stuck in his throat. Molly's attempts at cheerfulness drew such fearsome grunts and scowls that she fled back to the kitchen in tears. There she told Mrs Whitbread she must have done something dreadful to upset the master and must soon be dismissed from his service. Even Alfred, Foxe's devoted manservant, confided to Mrs Dobbins, the housekeeper, that he had never before seen his master so morose. Being down-to-earth in his judgements, he attributed Foxe's poor spirits to an excess of brandy the evening before. Together with the lack of night-time female company, of course.

After eating little and scalding his mouth on a bowl of coffee, Foxe could bear it no longer. He rose from his table, demanded his hat and second-best coat on the instant, and swept from the house. He left his servants who were relieved to see the back of him.

Hardly had Foxe reached the edge of the marketplace when an excited group of street children stopped him. They had found Uncle's child, they told him. The boy, now aged about nine or ten, they estimated, was living in the home of his grandfather: a certain Mr Meyrick. He had recently begun an apprenticeship with his grandfather, who was a cabinetmaker. The boy's name was Harry, they told him; Harry Valmar.

Here was a heaven-sent opportunity! He could avoid seeing Mrs Danson for even longer, while dealing with something no one could deny was relevant. Foxe seized it with both hands. He turned aside from his intended destination on the instant and let the children lead him to the cabinetmaker's modest house and workshop.

They took him to a small street off Timberhill. There they pointed out a house still in the old-fashioned, timber-framed style of many of the city's older buildings. The house stood four-square to the street. It had three stories with a place to one side from which issued the sound of sawing and hammering. It wasn't the finest house in the street, but it wasn't the meanest by a long way and it seemed to be kept in good order. The cabinetmaker's business must be a prosperous one.

Foxe's arrival at the workshop caused a great stir. Mr Meyrick was not used to entertaining persons of quality. Should he need to deal with such a one, they always expected him to wait on them, not the other way around. As soon as he laid eyes on his visitor, he started to excuse the state of his workshop. He apologised for the wood dust which lay everywhere and told his men to stop their work in case the din should offend his visitor's ears.

The cabinetmaker was far from being an old man, despite his bald head and the beard about his face now containing more white hairs than grey ones. Foxe judged him to be close to sixty years in age. For all that, he was a sturdy-built fellow; not tall, but strong. That would be thanks to many decades of working with hands and arms and lifting balks of timber. There was something kindly about his face. Foxe judged him to be an honest tradesman of the kind which made up the backbone of the city's wealth. He liked him instinctively.

Foxe told the men they should continue with their work while he talked to their master. Then he asked the cabinetmaker whether there was a quiet corner of the workshop where they might be private. Mr Meyrick would have none of it. He would have nothing save to conduct Foxe outside again and take him to the front door of the house itself. Once there, the turmoil began again, as Mrs Meyrick flew into a panic at the sight of a gentleman in her parlour. While her husband hurried off to wash his face and hands and tidy himself, she fussed about, apologising for their poor accommodation and sending a maid away in haste to fetch the best china coffee pot and cups. That done, she flapped her hand frantically at the seat and back of the best chair and invited Foxe to seat himself. Foxe might have been the king himself, arriving unexpectedly on some tour of his kingdom.

'I am merely a bookseller, a shopkeeper and tradesman like yourself,' Foxe protested. 'Please calm yourselves. I can assure you I have visited many houses that were much less tidy and clean than this one.'

'Bookseller you may be,' Meyrick protested, 'but all in this city know you to be a wealthy man, sir. One who mixes with the gentry on easy terms, to say nothing of men like our mayor and other leading citizens. You should have sent word for me to come to you.'

'Nonsense,' Foxe said. 'There are merely a few questions I wish to ask you. I would not drag you away from your own business for so paltry a matter. You are a cabinetmaker, I believe?'

'I am, sir, and generally held to be a good, skilled craftsman. Though I says it myself, I can fit together a table or a chair as well as any in this kingdom — save for the true masters in London, of course. I've made pieces fit to grace any gentleman's home, though I must own that the majority of my customers are local shopkeepers and tradesmen like me. For them I supply sound pieces of good quality. Not the finest inlaid and carved furniture such as you must own. I work in oak, elm, mahogany and sometimes walnut. Lovely wood walnut, but becoming scarce and expensive nowadays, even for veneers.'

'You have a grandson, I believe, who is now apprenticed to you.'

'Aye, Mr Foxe, and a good lad he is. 'Tis early days, but I reckon he has the makings of as able a worker in wood as I am — and that's saying a good deal.' You could hear the pride in the man's voice.

'What of his father, Mr Meyrick. Does he work here as well, or in some other trade?'

The other man's face darkened and his pride in his grandson was swiftly converted into the most profound sadness. 'That's a sad story, Mr Foxe, and I'll not burden you with the hearing of it. The boy's an orphan now — near enough anyway — must make his way in this world with only the help and guidance my wife and I can offer him.'

Foxe had, of course, expected this response. He'd only asked the question to make sure he was in the right place before probing further into matters which could only arouse painful memories.

'The story of that lad and his father is what I have come to you to seek out, Mr Meyrick,' he replied softly.

'Why's that, Mr Foxe, if I may ask?'

'Of course, you may, Mr Meyrick. First, though, please answer me on one point. Did the boy's father wear a small gold pendant about his neck; one engraved with a coat of arms?'

'You bring me bad news I fear, sir,' Meyrick said. 'My wife and I have long expected it, though we kept hoping we might yet be proved wrong. George did wear such a pendant as you mention. Not openly, you understand. Always hidden away behind a scarf or cravat about his neck. He told us it was the arms of the Valmar family. That was his name, you see. George Valmar.'

'From Hutton Hall?'

'No. He said he had nothing to do with those grand folks. He was only the younger son of some distant part of the family — a second or third cousin, or something like that. He shared the same name, but nought else. I don't know whether he'd ever tried to make contact with the family there and been turned away, but he rarely spoke of them. When he was forced to do so — perhaps by some questioner who noted the similarity of his name — it was never in kind or friendly terms.'

'How did he come to be here?' This was the crux. Foxe might make a guess as to what had happened, but he needed to be certain.

The tale the old craftsman now told him was the stuff of one of the new novels Mrs Crombie kept in their circulating library. The sort which were borrowed and read avidly by many the ladies of the city.

It began with George Valmar turning up one day and seeking to rent a room.

'I used to let a room or two to suitable people, Mr Foxe,' Meyrick said. 'This is a large house and my wife and I were never blessed with a big family. Only a single child, sir. A daughter, whom we named Lottie — Charlotte, that is. Mr Valmar spoke politely enough and was well-dressed too. Not quite as finely as you, Mr Foxe, but well enough to show he was not a mere labourer or some low-grade artisan.'

'What did he do for a living?' Foxe asked.

'He said he'd come from London, where he'd practiced as a fencing master. Called himself "Monsewer Georges Val d'Isère" by way of trade, on account of the French and Italians being accounted the best fencing masters.'

'Could he have passed as a Frenchman?'

'Well enough for folks in this city, he told us. Unless he should be unlucky enough to encounter the genuine thing of course. Said he'd enough of their lingo to pass muster. He'd found the competition in London too great to make more than a poor living, mostly on account of the number of foreigners living there. Knowing Norwich to be the second city in the land, he thought to try his luck here.'

The Meyricks had let Valmar have a room and he had soon settled in. Before long, the inevitable happened. He and Charlotte Meyrick grew fond of each other and married.

'The most devoted couple you ever did see, Mr Foxe,' Meyrick said, surreptitiously wiping his eyes with a dust-stained handkerchief. 'George did well as a fencing master, certainly more than well enough to provide for his wife and their child, when it came. Henry, they called him, after his grandfather. We calls him Harry. Two Henrys in one house gets confusing.'

'They married in a church?'

'Aye, they did. Proper marriage and all. All Saints' parish we're in and to All Saints' Church they went. Vicar wrote it down, fair and square, in the church register. George Valmar and Charlotte Meyrick, bachelor and spinster of the parish.'

'They had only the one child?'

'Just the one, Mr Foxe. Young Harry. Spitting image of his father.'

'For some eight years, all went well' Meyrick continued. 'Then the boy's mother, Lottie, fell ill with a severe tertian fever. George called a physician and my wife nursed her as only a mother can, but 'twas no use. The poor girl went into convulsions and died, leaving her child motherless and poor George near mad with grief.'

'What did he do after that?' Foxe asked.

'I reckon he was truly driven mad, Mr Foxe. Stark mad. Nothing else could explain what it was happened next.'

'What was that, Mr Meyrick?'

'He upped and disappeared. Attended her funeral, then walked away. Said he needed to be by himself for a while. At first, we thought no more than his grief was to blame. My wife and I both spent time on our own after our daughter died, thinking of her and praying for her soul. Then the days passed, and George didn't return. I sent men out looking for him. I even went myself two or three times. 'Twere no good. We've never set eyes on him from that day to this. Must be more than two years now.' Meyrick stopped and looked steadily at his visitor. 'I suspects you've come to tell me he's dead, Mr Foxe. That right?'

'It is, Mr Meyrick, and very sad I am to do so. His body was found more than a week ago. At first, of course, no one knew who he was. He'd been living rough, you see. What put me onto his true identity was the gold pendant. I discovered the meaning of the engraving. First, I tried at Hutton Hall, but they denied all knowledge of such a person.'

'Aye, they would, as I told you. He wasn't connected with that lot.'

'That isn't true,' Foxe said gently. 'If he told you as much, it was to conceal his true identity. It was true he had nothing to do with Sir Samuel Valmar and his wife by the time he came here. He must have also believed that he never would have again. He probably thought it best to invent a tale of being a distant cousin to explain his name and prevent awkward questions.'

'Who was he, then?'

'George Valmar, exactly as he told you. Only the George Valmar who was Sir Samuel's eldest son and heir to the baronetcy.'

'Good God alive! Begging your pardon for swearing, sir, but you've fair taken my breath away. Are you sure?'

'Sure enough. They denied it when I went there. That was because he and his father had quarrelled many times. The last time their disagreement was bad enough for his father to deny him the house and try to disinherit him. Sir Samuel has a nasty temper, Mr Meyrick. He cannot bear to be crossed. After I'd tried to get him to acknowledge the gold pendant taken from George's body, he became furious. Told me to leave on the instant and instructed his servants — in my hearing — to deny me entry, should I come to the house in the future. I happened to come upon Lady Valmar in the street and challenged her to acknowledge the dead man was her son. It was she who struck me, Mr Meyrick, giving me the black eye you can see I still have.'

'I wondered about that, Mr Foxe, and where you got it. I never believed a lady of quality might stoop to actual violence. To deny your own flesh and blood! A mother too! I cannot imagine how any woman could fall so low as to do that. Are they both lost to all decent human feeling? Wickedness, that's what it is. Pure wickedness. To behave in such a way! The devil truly walks amongst us, Mr Foxe, seeking whom he may corrupt.'

Mr Meyrick fell silent for several minutes while the enormity of what Foxe reported sank in. Then, all of a sudden, he started up and turned again to Foxe, his eyes blazing with anger.

'Was my poor son-in-law buried in a pauper's grave? Was he? Me and my wife couldn't abide such a thing as that. He was a good husband to our Lottie and a fine man, sir. For him to have been buried in such a way would fair break my heart. Tell me where he lies, Mr Foxe, so that I can make things right.'

'He's not in a pauper's grave, Mr Meyrick. I saw to that. He was placed in a proper coffin and laid to rest in the churchyard of St Peter Mancoft, my own parish. I hoped one day to restore him to the bosom of his family, should I be able to find them. The Valmar family vault should rightly be his last resting place. Nevertheless, I'm sure the churchyard here, close to the family whom he chose for himself and who loved him to the last, would be better. You may ask to have the coffin moved and reburied, Mr Meyrick, or leave him where he is. I have already arranged for a stonemason to carve a proper headstone. I don't care a whit if Sir Samuel objects.'

'May God bless you for your kindness, Mr Foxe! 'Twill be hard enough to tell my wife what has happened. If she thought he lay in a pauper's grave, she'd never get over it to her dying day. We'll see as he lies next to his wife, as is only fit and proper. That is, if you agrees to it.'

'I shall see it is done as soon as possible, Mr Meyrick. I shall also instruct that both their names are carved on the headstone. No, you need not offer to pay for it yourself. I have already determined to do so and can afford it far better than you. There is one condition, however.'

'Anything, Mr Foxe, so be it's lawful and seemly.'

'Both, Mr Meyrick. I want you to say nothing of this to young Harry — at least, nothing until I say you may. There are matters I need to attend to first. You may tell him his father has died, but no more than that. I dare say it will be enough for the present anyway. Let us wait until what I plan to do has been accomplished. Then I will return and tell you what further news you may give him. Please say nothing to your wife either, beyond telling her George has been found dead and given a decent funeral and burial place. Please, I beg you, say nought about his true identity. Not yet.'

Mr Meyrick promised to do as Foxe asked and Foxe left, leaving the stricken cabinetmaker to break the sad tidings to his wife and grandson. For himself, Foxe had rarely in his life been so angry; nor so determined to do all in his power to right so manifest a wrong. Let Sir Samuel rage and threaten all he wished. He would take no more notice of his noise than he would of the barking of a lady's lapdog.

FOXE TOOK HIS TIME WALKING HOME. AFTER SEVERAL DAYS OF COLD

and damp, the weather had turned warmer and the sun had come out. He always enjoyed walking through the city on fine days. He would stroll along, nodding left and right to various acquaintances. It was often a good time to work out new ideas about whichever puzzle was then occupying his thoughts.

On this occasion, he certainly had plenty to mull over. For his own peace of mind, he had to try to find a way to proceed further in the matter of George Valmar. That poor fellow might indeed be dead, but there was now his son to consider. The boy's future should not lie in a cabinetmaker's workshop. He should be learning how to run the household and estates which would one day be his by right.

But were they? Sir Samuel Valmar claimed his son George had died somewhere overseas. He had also told other people that he'd disinherited the young man after their final quarrel. Were either of these statements true? Foxe didn't think so — indeed, he was sure the first one was a blatant lie. Could he be certain? Had George Valmar truly been deprived of his inheritance? If he had, any son of his, legitimate or not, could make no claim on the Hutton Hall estates.

At once, Foxe turned aside, to make his way to where his own lawyer, Mr Samuel Morphew, lived. If the man was at home, it would be simple to ask him. All these grand estates tended to be entailed. Inheritance was then legally restricted to direct male heirs. It was not in the gift of the person currently in occupation and could not be taken away without obtaining legal permission to do so. Foxe had heard of such entails being removed — 'broken' the correct term was — but thought it was exceedingly rare and difficult to achieve. Yet without breaking the entail, Sir Samuel Valmar would be unable to prevent his eldest son inheriting so long as he were alive. Any direct, legitimate, male descendant of that son would automatically become the heir after his father's death.

He was out of luck and the lawyer was not at home. Still, Foxe was able to make an appointment to see the man the next morning. He always enjoyed visiting Samuel Morphew. Not only was the man a pleasant, cheerful fellow and a good friend, but he possessed elegant taste, furnishing his rooms in a way Foxe found especially pleasing.

Next morning found the two of them sitting in the room Mr

Morphew used for his business, drinking fine coffee. All the while Foxe looked around him, admiring the mahogany furniture, the gilded mirrors on the walls, and the magnificent display of Chinese porcelain vases along the mantelpiece.

'Where d'you find these fine Chinese pieces?' Foxe asked Morphew. 'Surely there is nowhere in this city where a man might buy such splendid items.'

'I'm lucky enough to have a relative who works for the East India Company,' Morphew told him. 'Senior members of the company like him are allowed to import small amounts of porcelain for their own use or to sell to chosen friends.'

'I wish I had a relative like that,' Foxe said ruefully.

'You have a friend who does,' Morphew replied. 'Tell me what you would like, Foxe, and I'll see what I can do for you. But be warned! Such pieces cost a good deal of money.'

'I'm sure they do. Still, I would be willing to pay a substantial amount to own one or two items of a similar nature.'

'I doubt that you've come here to discuss purchases of porcelain,' Mr Morphew said. 'Shall we get down to business? I have a good deal to do today, even if you are at leisure.'

'I want to discuss the law surrounding entailment of an estate,' Foxe began. 'Let's say you wished to disinherit your eldest son and the estate was entailed on the next, legitimate, male heir. Could you do it? If you could, how would you go about it and break the entail?'

Morphew stared at Foxe in amazement. 'But you don't have a son, legitimate or otherwise — at least, as far as I know,' he said. 'Besides, the business I have done for you in the past makes me certain that your own inheritance is not subject to any entail either. What on earth is this all about? Another one of your puzzles?'

Foxe nodded his assent. 'It could be of vital importance, Morphew,' he said. 'If I'm right, it was an entail of this nature which led to a most brutal and wicked murder.'

'I'm intrigued,' Morphew said. 'Can you tell me anymore?'

'I would prefer not to go into any detail, unless it's essential for you to be able to answer the question I just posed to you,' Foxe said. 'Is it?'

'Not if you only wish to know the basics of the law on the matter. If you wish to explore a specific case, I would need to see the precise wording of the original Will in which the entail was established. Most of them follow a standard approach, but it's possible to imagine certain variations in specific cases.'

'The basics of the law will be more than good enough,' Foxe said.

'In that case, Foxe, my answer is that you could break such an entail, but it wouldn't be easy. When an estate is entailed, all main beneficiaries under the terms of the original Will have only a life interest in its income. They don't own the land or the mansion in their own right. That means they can't sell it, or any portion of it. They can usually raise money through a mortgage, using the estate as security, but no more. All subsequent inheritance is also governed by the terms of the original Will. That includes who may properly be accounted as the heir. In ninety-nine cases from a hundred, such Wills require that the estate should pass strictly to the next, legitimate, direct male heir in each generation. If that fails, the next closest person in descent from the one who made the Will — the next legitimate male, I mean — will inherit. The purpose, as I'm sure you will grasp, is to make sure the lands and wealth are retained within the family.'

'Tell me how I would go about breaking such an entail,' Foxe said.

'Very well. As I mentioned, it is a difficult and lengthy business. You would first need to gain the agreement of the executors and trustees for the original Will — or their successors. If you could do that, the next step would be to apply to the relevant court. That may be the consistory court of the local diocese or the appropriate archdiocese. If the Will had been proven in Norfolk, for example, that means the Archdiocese of Canterbury. It's more likely to be the Court of Chancery in London — a fearsome place, believe me. In either case, you would make an application to set the terms of the original Will aside, thus transferring outright ownership of the land to the current possessor; or to vary those terms in the way you wished. The courts are nearly always extremely unwilling to do something like this, unless you can offer them a compelling reason. It would definitely be expensive and probably very, very slow. In the Court of Chancery, it could take years. Such cases have been known to last over several generations. It's not unknown for the money to run out long before any resolution has been reached. Besides, the courts are nearly always extremely unwilling to do something like this, unless you can offer them a compelling reason.'

'They wouldn't agree to what you wanted simply to allow you to punish your eldest son after a quarrel?'

'I imagine the court would be most unwilling to disinherit any existing legitimate heir, save on the most pressing grounds. In basic terms, my answer is that they would not agree.'

'And if that eldest son had a son of his own?'

'Then they would be even less willing, since that would mean disinheriting a second legitimate heir as well.'

'Thank you,' Foxe said. 'You have been most helpful and told me all I need to know at this stage. One final point. Would it be possible to lay hands on the original Will to check its specific terms?'

'Unfortunately, a Will is not a public document. The executors or trustees would never divulge such information, save on the death of the current beneficiary. Certainly not to anyone outside the immediate family. I'm sorry.'

There Foxe had to be content. Another dead end, it appeared. Still, you never knew what time would change.

BY RIGHTS, FOXE SHOULD NOW HAVE SET THE MYSTERY OF GEORGE Valmar's aside and turned his attention once again to bringing someone to justice for the killing of Dr Danson. He was already as certain as he could be about the identity of Danson's killer. Since the man Foxe suspected was dead, that left only two puzzles about the affair. Who sent him to steal the book from Danson's library, and why?

Foxe was convinced such a man had either been sent to steal on behalf of someone else or knew someone to whom he thought he could sell the book. Neither seemed likely to apply to George Stubbings. From all he had heard, the said Stubbings was almost certainly illiterate. None who sent him could have been certain he would know which book to take from the shelves. He would not have been able to read the titles for a start. He certainly wouldn't have stolen for himself;

nor did Foxe believe book theft would have occurred to Stubbings as a way to earn money.

It was while Foxe was trying to work out what this might tell him that he had another idea. This one had the further advantage of allowing him to continue to procrastinate about confronting Mrs Danson. On his way home from Mr Morphew's house, he therefore looked around for some of the street children. He usually sent Charlie to find them when he wanted them or dispatched the lad to give them a message. Still, several could usually be found hanging around the marketplace. There they begged or stole from the stallholders, looked for opportunities to pick pockets, or, in case of the older girls, solicited for trade.

Soon enough, Foxe found a girl whom he recognised from the last group which he had talked with. He called her over and gave her some pennies for herself and to distribute amongst the others. Then he set her the fresh task: to find out whether any stranger had been asking for the man they called Uncle during the past few weeks. If there had been such a one, he would like as good a description of the man as they could give him. He was probably rough looking, Foxe told the girl, but not necessarily. It could be a servant, even one from a great household.

Once again, the street children did him proud. Before the end of that day, he already had his answer. A man, probably a servant from the way he dressed, had questioned several stallholders and even a few of the older tarts. He said he was looking for a man he described as being aged around thirty years and well spoken. One somewhat above the average height with fair hair and sturdy limbs. The only other thing he could tell them was that the fellow was said to have been living rough and sleeping on the streets. He wanted a detailed description — and a name, if possible — and offered to pay for anything he was told.

None of the street children would have helped him, naturally, but he hadn't asked them. Still, he must have found what he was looking for, because he hadn't been seen now for two weeks or more. Then another man had appeared. This one already knew that the man they called Uncle was the person he sought. All he wished to know was where he slept at night.

Foxe asked if they could describe this second man. They said he was dark skinned and had black hair. There was also something about him which scared them — and not just because he spoke with a foreign accent.

Brunetti for sure, Foxe said to himself. It had to be. The first man would have been a servant sent to locate George Valmar and make sure it was the right person. After that, the second man, Brunetti, was instructed to find and eliminate him. The question was, who sent the assassin? The father or the younger son? It had to be one or the other. They were the only two people who would be desperate to prevent poor George claiming his proper position as the legitimate heir.

❦ 17 ❦

By this time, Foxe had exhausted all excuses and could no
longer postpone talking with Mrs Danson. A man going to the
funeral of his dearest friend could not have set out more reluctantly than Foxe that morning. He walked with his head down and his
eyes on the ground before him. He looked neither to the right nor the
left. If anyone greeted him, he ignored them. All the while his mind
was in a turmoil of conflicting emotions. He hated himself, hated the
notion of the task before him, coming close to hating Mrs Danson for
causing him to become fond of her. All the while, he rehearsed
different words and questions in his head.

Should he tackle her directly or try to introduce his concerns
slowly and subtly? What would he do if she refused to tell him
anymore or ordered him out of her house? That would be not the
worst problem either. What would he do if she confessed to arranging
for her husband to be murdered? The law said he must hand her to the
constables to face trial and probable death by hanging. His heart said
he should beg her to reconsider her words and save herself.

When Foxe finally entered her house, Mrs Danson received him
quietly and graciously, as was her habit. They sat once more in her
drawing room, drinking tea and exchanging polite conversation in the

approved manner. Poor Foxe was still looking for ways to postpone the inevitable. He looked around him and complimented his hostess on the taste with which she had furnished and decorated the room. He admired the walls, painted a pale lavender colour to set off the natural whiteness of the plaster mouldings. He remarked on the long mirrors set opposite the windows to reflect the light. He praised the carefully-chosen paintings: a mixture of portraits and landscapes in the Dutch style. He noted that there was a distinctly feminine feel to the room, enhanced by the display of fine Chinese vases and bowls. He asked if all this was due to the first Mrs Danson or the present one. All in all, Foxe declared himself delighted with almost everything he saw.

What he kept secret was that his delight extended to the lady before him. Mrs Danson was wearing mourning dress, as would be expected. The sombre colour set off to perfection the delicate shades in her skin and her lustrous hair where it escaped from under a simple lace cap. Foxe wished — oh, how he wished! — that she was less beautiful and less amiable in her manner. It was going to be bad enough, without the attraction he couldn't help himself feeling towards her.

Eventually, the proper preliminaries had been exhausted and the moment had come for him to say what he needed to say. Much of the night before, all through breakfast and at every step of his walk to her house, Foxe had cudgelled his brain to find a gentle way of doing it. It was all to no avail. Everything he could think of sounded false or insincere. Now, in desperation, he abandoned all such attempts and plunged ahead.

'Why did you lie to me, Mrs Danson?' he began. 'There was another visitor to this house on the day your husband died, wasn't there? A person who came after Mr Wake, or whatever his name was, had left. It was your brother, George Stubbings, wasn't it?'

'I didn't lie to you, Mr Foxe,' she said calmly. 'No one else came here on that particular day. My brother came the day before. Would to God he had not done so! I hadn't seen him for more than two years. I devoutly hoped never to set eyes on him again. Then there he was, grinning all over his face and asking for money, as ever. He told me he'd heard that I had married a wealthy man and expected me to share my wealth with him. He even held out his hand. If I had had a weapon at that moment — and he were not almost twice my size — I would have struck him down where he stood. Instead, I explained that my husband handled everything to do with money. All I had was what little pin money I had saved. He was welcome to that, if only he would go away and leave me alone.'

'What did he say?'

'Little enough. He took my money of course. He also cursed me for being what he called "a vengeful unnatural hag who forgot her kin when she had at last lifted herself out of the gutter, which was where I truly belonged". A delightful way for a brother to address his only sister, wasn't it? Then he left, vowing to return very soon for more.'

'Did he?'

'Once more. That was on the day after my husband had been killed. I assumed he'd heard about it somewhere. He came in, gloating, saying I was a rich widow now and could give him all the money he needed. When I asked him what for, he said it was to allow him to get away from this city and go somewhere people couldn't find him. Why did he want to do that, Mr Foxe? He'd already been away from Norwich for years. Why come back only to talk about leaving again as soon as he could?'

'Wherever your brother had been living – probably King's Lynn or Cambridge, I would guess — he'd taken to thieving to support himself. Before long, he was taken and brought before the magistrate, who sent him for trial at the assizes. There he was condemned to death, as the law demands. That sentence was swiftly commuted to transportation for seven years, probably because of his age. How old was he, by the way?'

'George is five years younger than I am,' she replied. 'That makes him nineteen now.'

'Then he would have been seventeen at the time he was sentenced. Unless the crime is very serious, no judge wishes to send a person of that age to the gallows. Instead, he was sent to a prison hulk at Portsmouth to await a suitable ship to take him to America. Unfortunately, he managed to escape along with two others, killing a guard while doing so. Both the others were soon recaptured. Both swore your brother had been the killer. Whether that was to save themselves or the plain truth hardly matters. In the eyes of the authorities, young George Stubbings was now a murderer. When he was caught, there would be no reprieve this time. He would be sent to the gallows.'

By now, Mrs Danson's face had lost all its colour and Foxe could see tears on her cheek.

'Georgie always was headstrong and violent, even as a boy,' she said, 'but I never thought that he would sink so low as to kill a man. He is the only kin I have, Mr Foxe. Even if I'd known what you've just told me, I don't think I could have handed him over to the magistrate — not to be hanged.'

'I fear that wasn't the only murder on his hands,' Foxe replied. 'He must have laid low somewhere until the hue and cry after him had died down. Then he came back to Norwich, he began to work for an apothecary who also acted as the most unscrupulous kind of money-lender. A certain Mr Craswall.'

'Mr Craswall! But I know him! He came here often to talk with my husband. I thought it was to discuss my husband's health.'

'I'm afraid it's clear from some papers I found in your husband's library that wasn't the case. Dr Danson had been lending Mr Craswall large amounts of money on a regular basis and at high rates of interest.'

'It must have been to pay for more and more purchases of his beloved books,' Mrs Danson said. 'I could never work out how he could go on finding the large sums he spent on them. However many he possessed, he never felt he had enough. It wouldn't have been so bad if the library he put together was something to be proud of; something he could show to visitors and share with his friends. Instead, it's full of books about his other obsession. His belief in some kind of hidden knowledge to explain the world about us and open the way to understanding all the mysteries of this life. When we were first married, he tried to explain it to me, for it obsessed him even then. To my mind, it was all so much silly superstition, blended with large doses of imagination, supposed magic and a good deal of heresy. What do you think of it, Mr Foxe? Is it as some men say? That a woman's mind is too feeble to be able to grasp such serious subjects?'

'I have met many women whom I would rate as being at least as clever as I am, Mrs Danson, several of them more so. As for the rest of it, even as a man, I heartily endorse your view. It was all nonsense. Yet, as a bookseller, I know there are people willing to pay large amounts of money for such books.'

'Then I will ask you to sell them for me as soon as I am granted probate. However, that is for another time and another meeting. What bothers me now is whether my husband knew what Mr Craswall was using the money for.'

'I believe he must have known,' Foxe said. 'It couldn't have taken him long to realise that no legitimate small business would have needed such regular inputs of capital. Nor could any have generated enough profit to cover the high rates of interest he was charging — let alone generate an adequate return on top of it.'

Mrs Danson shook her head as if by doing so she might drive away the pain and misery she was feeling. Inwardly, Foxe cursed the malevolent fate which had caused him to be the one to inflict such misery upon this woman. Of course, she would have to know sometime. Better that she should hear in this way than through the sideways looks, malicious hints and exaggerated gossip. Better than in open court. He had to hope so.

'Let me be clear on this,' she said after a moment. 'My brother was working for Mr Craswall in his activities as a moneylender, and my husband was involved as well.'

'I'm sorry to have to tell you that your brother was one of this man's paid ruffians,' Foxe said. 'He went around threatening or doing harm to those who didn't pay what they owed on time.'

'Curse him! I'll never give him another penny, however much he bullies me. As I told you, he threatened the second time he came here to keep returning with fresh demands. If I tried to escape by informing on him to the magistrates, he said he would swear I had asked him to kill my husband to set me free to marry another. I knew many would think as much anyway. When you came here today, that thought was upper most in your mind also. I could see it in your face.

'I didn't love my husband, Mr Foxe, but I was happy with him and he looked after me well. Why should I want him dead? Certainly not to marry another, younger man. I've had many, many young lovers in my time. Most were nothing more than fumbling wretches, no more able to give a woman pleasure than they were of learning Arabic. Few even tried. They used me for their own pleasure and set me aside, to use me again or not, as and when they pleased.'

That remark cut Foxe to the quick. Was he a man such as that? He would find it more than hard to deny the charge.

'You won't have to fear your brother ever again, Mrs Danson,' he said. 'He's dead.'

Foxe hadn't meant it to come out so baldly, even brutally, but he could see no other way of putting it. For several moments, Mrs Danson was silent, her eyes shut, and her hands clasped into fists. Then she gave a great sigh and opened her eyes once more. He could see the tears staining her cheeks and longed to take her in his arms to comfort her.

'Poor Georgie!' she sighed. 'I wish he'd had a better life. Now you tell me it's past almost before it had properly begun. Until this news, I suppose I was clinging to the hope that one day he might reform. Now even that has ended. How did he die?'

Here was the question Foxe had been dreading most. To know her brother was dead was bad enough. To know how he had died would be many times worse. He would have avoided giving an answer, had it been possible. Now the look she fixed upon him through her tears denied him the chance of any further evasions.

'So far as I can make out, he was sent to persuade a clerk — one who worked for the city treasury — to pay the money he owed to Mr Craswall. The clerk had become involved in gambling for high stakes. In time, his losses far outstripped his ability to make them good. Then he must have fallen into the hands of Mr Craswall and asked to borrow to pay his gambling debts. That was bad enough, given the enormous rate of interest Craswall would have demanded. Sadly, he then made things worse by continuing his habit and losing still more. He even stole money from the place where he worked. I do not know whether that was to settle some of his debts or make further wagers. Like many another before him, he soon reached the point where he could neither repay what he had borrowed nor meet the interest demanded.'

'George went to extract whatever he could from the man — by force if necessary?'

'Exactly. It was something he must have done many times before. However, this time he went too far and killed the poor fellow. Not only would that make Craswall furious, he might even hand your brother over to the magistrate to avoid coming under suspicion himself.'

Mrs Danson raised her hands to her face in horror. 'Please don't tell me he killed Mr Craswall as well.'

'No, not that. Something even more stupid. He tried to blackmail the man, just as he threatened to blackmail you, and probably for the same reason. He knew he'd never be safe now until he was far away from here. He needed the money to make his escape. If he'd thought about it at all, he would have realised that Craswall would never pay. He should also have known the moneylender was more ruthless and more cunning than he was himself. The man simply used some of his other ruffians to make sure your troublesome brother wouldn't bother him again. Your brother's body was found in the river. His throat had been cut.'

'God forgive me! I told him he would come to a bad end, Mr Foxe. Now I have been proved correct. I never dreamt that would be what actually happened. Nor that it would happen so quickly.'

'Your brother was a petty criminal, who was foolish enough to take on hardened rogues, Mrs Danson. He should have realised how dangerous that was.'

'He was only nineteen, Mr Foxe. We all make foolish mistakes at that age.'

Foxe hesitated. He had already caused this woman so much pain. If he continued, he must inflict still more. Should he leave and return on another occasion? Should he get it over with here and now, so he could assure her there would be nothing worse yet come? Both paths were equally repellent to him at that moment. In the end, he chose the latter, as much to save himself further anguish as to avoid inflicting it on her.

While he was making up his mind, Mrs Danson spoke again. 'You have brought me a great deal of bad news today, Mr Foxe. First you tell me that my younger brother — my only living kin — is a thief and murderer. Now it seems my husband was no better than a rogue and a criminal himself. Worse! I have seen what such moneylenders can do and the misery they bring to all who fall into their hands. You tell me my brother was working for such a man and my husband was providing him with the means to continue his filthy business. Even now, your face tells me that there is more to come. Tell me at once, I pray you. Don't leave the threat hanging over me. I couldn't bear that.'

'From all that I have learned, Mrs Danson, I fear there is another murder to be set to his account.'

'Not my husband? Not that! Oh God, not that! To think I let George leave this house and didn't report to anyone that he had been here. I thought he was only trying to get money from me, as he had done many times before.'

Foxe reminded her that the medical examiner gave evidence her husband had died from a heart attack. Even if it was George Stubbings who had stabbed him, he would not have been the cause of the man's death. Foxe had been certain of events in his own mind before today. All he'd lacked was firm evidence that Stubbings had been to the house on the day Dr Danson died. Mrs Danson had now admitted he'd been there the day before and the day after her husband's death. She was adamant that no one else had visited on the fateful day other than Mr Wake. If what she said was true — and Foxe felt certain it was — Stubbings could not have been responsible for Dr Danson's death. He now searched in his mind for another way forward.

'Did anything else unusual happen on the day your husband died, Mrs Danson?' he asked. As so often, it proved to be the most seemingly random shot which went straight to the mark.

She thought for a moment.

'Nothing important. Wait,' she said. 'There was one thing. Someone left the front door open. Gunton told me he found the door ajar just before he went into the library and discovered my husband's body. That's why he went into the library, even after my husband had expressly told him not to. He thought his master or his visitor had gone out without telling him.'

'Had Mr Wake gone by that time?'

'I believe so. Why not ask Gunton yourself, Mr Foxe? I'll call him.'

When he came, the butler confirmed all his mistress had said. After he had shown the visitor into the library, his master told him they were not to be disturbed on any account. He would call when he needed him again.

'What did you do after that?' Foxe asked.

'I went on my way, sir, first to the kitchen, then to my own room. There I spent some time polishing the knives and silver labels. You know, sir. The ones which hang around the necks of the port and sherry bottles. After I had finished, I took a cup of tea with the house-keeper. That is something we usually do at some time during the morning. It helps us to stay in touch with whatever the other one is doing. After that, I went back into the hall to make sure the visitor's coat and hat were ready for him when he left. I found both gone and the front door ajar. It wasn't like the master to let someone out without telling me, sir, but he could be unpredictable at times. To make sure his visitor had indeed left, I went to the library and listened outside the door. Finding no sound of voices from within, I opened the door and looked inside.'

'That was when you found your master dead,' Foxe said.

'Indeed so, sir. The moment I looked into the room, I could see him slumped in his chair. At first, I thought he must be ill, only when I got closer could I see the blood on his chest and stomach. He'd fallen over to one side and his head was thrown back. That must have been why his wig was lying on the floor. He must have struggled against his killer. When I looked closer, I could see his hands were clenched into fists. I thought there were signs of a blow to his head as well. The thought went through my mind that he and Mr Wake had quarrelled in some way and Mr Wake had struck him. Then, horrified at what he had done, the man went back to the hall, snatched up his coat and left.'

Yes, thought Foxe, that's the most plausible answer. He could never be certain until he could track down this mysterious visitor and ques-tion him.

'Did you find a strange knife or a dagger?' he asked the butler. 'Or anything else that might have been used as a weapon to kill your master.'

'No, sir. Nothing of that kind. At the inquest, the medical person said he thought the master might have been stabbed with a paperknife from his desk.'

'Did you agree with that observation?'

The butler shook his head. 'I did not, sir. When I saw the blood, I thought immediately of the paper knife myself. There was no blood on it, sir, I'm sure of that. Nor was there any blood on the desk. The paperknife was on the floor, lying beside the wig. That was why I looked at it. To my reckoning, it must've fallen to the floor some time earlier. The master had been slitting the pages of the book he'd just received when I took Mr Wake into the library. He could easily have knocked it to the floor, when he jumped up to welcome his visitor.'

'You told your mistress you found the front door wide open?'

'More ajar,' the butler told Foxe. 'Definitely not fully open. I thought at the time someone had gone out and left it like that to avoid making any noise when he closed it.'

After the butler had left, Mrs Danson asked Foxe what he made of what he'd been told. Did it confirm his suspicion that her brother had been involved?

'You must realise that this is all guesswork, Mrs Danson. It could be that the mysterious Mr Wake killed your husband, then left as quietly as he could. I hope for your sake that proves to be the case.'

'Yet you still don't believe that is what happened, do you?' she replied.

'It bothers me,' Foxe admitted. 'Someone stole a rare book from your husband's library. It was a book of the type that, in the letter he had written asking for an appointment, Mr Wake claimed was of great interest to him and the people who had sent him. Let's assume it was Mr Wake. He maybe asks your husband to sell him the book. Your husband naturally refuses. He's a collector, not a dealer, and this book is especially rare. I saw from his records he'd paid more than three pounds for his copy.'

Mrs Danson gasped. 'As much as that? No wonder he needed to make more and more money all the time. What a waste!'

'Not to him, Mrs Danson. He would have seen it as an investment in knowledge. To return to my story. Dr Danson refuses to sell, so Wake decides to take it anyway. He's young and strong and your husband is an old man. I imagine he thought it would be easy to get his way. First, he threatens your husband. When that doesn't work, he strikes him, leaving him stunned. He then looks for the book he wants, finds it, thanks to the systematic way your husband shelved his collection, and prepares to leave. Then, to make sure Dr Danson can't say what has happened, he takes out a dagger he is carrying and kills him.'

'A convincing reconstruction of events, Mr Foxe. Why don't you believe it?'

'I do believe most of it, Mrs Danson. Up to the point where Mr Wake kills your husband, that is. That part makes little or no sense. Wake almost certainly did strike your husband on the head to stun him. I'm equally sure he then snatched up the book up and left, taking care to do so as quietly as he could. To kill him after that seemed so unnecessary. Dangerous too, since his visit — and his name — was well known. He could have given a false name, I suppose, but to come here determined to kill to have that book argues for premeditation. Your husband was a secretive man. It's most unlikely he would have allowed details of specific books in his library to become known to others.'

'Most unlikely, I agree,' Mrs Danson said. 'He rarely let anybody even go into the library. I cannot believe he would have broadcast abroad the details of any book in there. If we exclude Mr Wake, why do you believe my brother would have returned with the intention to commit murder?'

'Nothing else is possible,' Foxe replied. 'As I see it, your brother had come back that day hoping he'd frightened you enough to make you willing to give him more money. He must, by this time, have been desperate to get away. Whatever he'd managed to steal or extort from others, still wasn't enough. When he got here, I think he saw the front door either open, or at least not properly closed. A person with his record of theft would have seen that as an open opportunity to creep inside and find something of value to steal. You've already told me he'd been here before. That may have been enough for him to have worked out where the principal rooms were.'

'I told him where the library was, Mr Foxe. The first time he came here, the day before my husband's death, he'd become furious with me when I could give him no more than a few shillings. I'd spent much of my pin money earlier that week, buying myself a new hat. I gave him all I had left, but it couldn't have amounted to more than four or five shillings. He started shouting at me, demanding I sell something so that I could give him more. That made me very frightened, as you can imagine. The last thing I wanted was a confrontation between him and my husband. I begged him to be quiet, in case my husband heard all the noise and came to see what was going on. I even told him my husband was upstairs in his library, which lay directly above this room. Oh, good heavens! I recall now that I told him that was where my husband kept what he treasured most. What I didn't say was that I meant books.'

'He must have thought you meant valuable items like silver or porcelain, Mrs Danson. If so, he would have headed straight there when he came back the next day — if he did.'

'Wouldn't my husband have called out if a stranger had come into his room? Especially if it was a rough-looking fellow like my brother.'

'I thought that too, until your butler reminded me your husband had suffered a blow to the head sufficient to knock his wig to the floor. Your husband was probably still insensible at the time your brother went into the room. There's just one point. Even allowing for your husband's careful arrangement of his books, Mr Wake wouldn't have wanted to take the time to search around a library of that size. Not looking for a single book. Is it possible your husband, knowing that this was an especially rare volume, might have taken it from the shelves himself to show it to his visitor? Maybe it was then Mr Wake asked to buy it and your husband refused. Overcome with the desire to possess what he couldn't buy on a legitimate basis, Wake then struck your husband, snatched up the book and departed on the instant.'

'My husband would certainly have refused to sell anything, Mr Foxe. You said that yourself. He bought books all the time, but I never knew him sell any.'

'Very well. Let's assume that's what happened. Later, your brother looked into the room and thought Dr Danson was sleeping. He took a quick look around and reached the conclusion there was nothing there which he could sell, even if he took it. Would you say your brother was a cunning man, Mrs Danson?'

'Cunning, yes. Quick to see anything that he could turn to his advantage, even though in other respects I would have doubted his intelligence. My parents sent us both to the local school. I learned to read and write — to be precise, I learned to read fairly easily and enough writing to be able to sign my name and make simple notes. Proper spelling always eluded me, Mr Foxe. I dare say that if I showed you anything I had written, the way I wrote the words would make you burst out laughing. My brother couldn't even read, let alone write. Most days, he played truant. When our mother died, and our father soon after, he gave up any attempt at learning. But he was always cunning, even devious.'

'In that case,' Foxe said, 'he would have realised that, if your husband was dead, you would be a rich widow, in full control of your wealth ...'

'As I am told I will, Mr Foxe. I inherit all my husband owned. I have already spoken to the lawyer who drew up his Will. He left it to me, since he had no other living relatives, just as I have none now. This is indeed a more likely explanation of what happened than the other one. I can only hope that it proves in the end to be untrue. Especially because it makes me the cause of my husband's death.'

'You mustn't think that,' Foxe said quickly. 'If your brother had behaved towards you the way he should have done, with love and affection, he would have not become involved in your husband's death in any way. If your husband had not been so greedy for money to fund his book purchases, he too would be living today. Each is to blame for his own death, not you.'

'What a wretched world we live in!' Mrs Danson replied. She had stopped weeping, but her face clearly revealed the misery and grief Foxe's news had brought her. He longed even more to take her in his arms and comfort her. Since propriety would admit of no such action on his behalf, he could do no more than murmur indistinctly and hope that his face too spoke eloquently of his own pity and remorse.

'Wait!' she cried. 'Gunton said he felt sure my husband was not killed with the dagger he kept on his desk, Mr Foxe. There was no blood on it, he said. Yet the medical examiner at the inquest was sure it was the murder weapon. How did he make such an error?'

'Your husband was stabbed and there was a dagger found by him. I expect he simply assumed at first that was what had killed him. Later, he became sure your husband was already dead when he was stabbed. The lack of blood would not have bothered him. His finding also explained why your brother could assume Dr Danson was asleep. I doubt he would have guessed the man was dead. He may have stabbed your husband with the dagger from his desk, but I doubt it. A man like George Stubbings would have been carrying his own.'

'I shall leave this house as soon I can,' Mrs Danson said, 'and this city as well. There is nothing but sadness for me in this place; that and bitter memories. Will you help me dispose of my husband's books, Mr Foxe? His obsession with this so-called secret knowledge and these books he believed might reveal it to him are the reason why he came to such a sad end.'

'I will if you wish it,' Foxe said.

'I do, most ardently. They are of no use to me. I hate the very sight of them. I suppose all the money my husband lent to Mr Craswall will have been lost?'

'Most of it, I imagine.'

Dr Danson had kept careful records of each sum the apothecary had borrowed, together with signed documents acknowledging the debts. Even so, Foxe knew they would be worthless. The business of a moneylender like Mr Craswall pretty much ensured that must be the case. Men like him lent money in the expectation that little, if any, of the principal would ever be paid back. Their business was to extract interest payments from their victims for years. They hoped to continue doing so until the wretches were drained of every penny and farthing they could scrape together.

'I expect the executors of your husband's Will to do all they are able to retrieve as much of the money held by Craswall as possible,' Foxe continued. 'I shall give them the papers I found to assist them in that task. Even so, I fear they will have little enough success. I doubt very much that Craswall will be able to pay much of what he owes to your husband's estate.'

'I shall not worry too much about that money, Mr Foxe. The value of this house and its contents will give me ample to live on. My wants are modest. What I desire most now is to be able to live a quiet, respectable life, free from other people's demands.'

'I wish you well in that, Mrs Danson,' Foxe said, his voice shaking. 'You deserve it, if anyone does.'

With his final visit to Mrs Danson over, the case of the dead man in the library should have been complete. To Foxe's mind, however, two burning questions yet remained. Who precisely was Mr Wake? Why had he been so desperate to get his hands on that particular book that he was willing to steal it? Otherwise, what faced Foxe now was the task of conveying yet more bad news. This time it would be to Alderman Halloran and the mayor. The money stolen from the city treasury was gone for good.

MUCH LATER — LONG AFTER MRS DANSON HAD LEFT NORWICH AND the painful memories of her were at last fading a little in Foxe's mind — all he had prophesied came to pass. The executors of Danson's Will pursued Mr Craswall diligently, demanding the return of the sums owed. He delayed and promised all he could but now found himself ruined. When his secret business as a moneylender became general knowledge, his business as an apothecary collapsed. His house and shop were seized and sold, together with all his stock. He himself was thrown into the debtor's prison. There he suffered the punishment so many believed he deserved. Since he had sent so many of its inmates there himself, they took their revenge. Within less than a day, he had died a violent and painful death.

✣ 18 ✣

'Poor, Foxe!' Alderman Halloran said to Foxe, towards the end of that same day. The two of them were sitting in the alderman's library drinking glass after glass of fine claret. 'You've solved two most puzzling mysteries, yet neither accomplishment has brought you any pleasure. Don't worry about the money from the city treasury. The mayor and I agreed some while ago that it would never be seen again. It wasn't that large an amount either. Annoying, of course. No one likes to discover they have been employing a thief. Still, nothing that can't be coped with easily enough.'

He raised his third glass — or was it the fourth? — to Foxe and drank deeply. Foxe did the same, toasting the alderman.

'Now, let me give you some good news,' Halloran continued. 'The man Brunetti, the one you believed was responsible for the death of the vagrant with the gold pendant, has been taken alive. I heard the news scarce two hours ago. Last night, he and some other ruffians got into a brawl and the Italian wielded that damn stiletto knife of his to deadly effect. The dead ruffian's friends then pursued Brunetti and trapped him in an old shed. They would have killed him in turn, but all the noise attracted the attention of the night-watchman. He wielded his rattle to good effect and thus summoned two of the constables. Together they held back the crowd and overpowered the killer.

'Brunetti spent last night in the lock-up, knowing it would not be long before he faced the hangman. Bullies of that kind are always cowards when it comes to their own hurt or death. By morning, he was desperate to try to save himself. He wants to turn King's Evidence against a man whose name will be very familiar to you: Sir Samuel Valmar. Brunetti has not only confessed to the murder of your vagrant, that's the man you say was actually Sir Samuel's lost eldest son and heir, but he also claims the said baronet spoke to him in person and paid him five pounds to do the deed.'

'Would his evidence be enough to bring the baronet to court, do you think?' Foxe asked eagerly.

'To my mind, it would not,' Halloran replied. 'I'm sorry to disappoint you, Foxe. Having heard your story about George Valmar, I feel as eager to see his father in the dock as you do. This evidence, however, will not suffice. Can you imagine any judge or jury accepting the word of an admitted murderer — a foreigner from the lowest class of society as well — against the testimony of a man of such eminence in the county as Sir Samuel? All the baronet would need to do to escape is to deny everything. Indeed, I cannot imagine such a case even being brought before the court. Can you?'

Foxe shook his head sadly. 'I cannot,' he said. 'No magistrate would sanction it, nor would it pass a grand jury. Yet to see that arrogant bastard escape justice sticks and burns in my throat. You will tell me it is the way of the world, Halloran, and I will agree with what you say. Yet, as Mrs Danson said to me scarcely an hour ago, does that not prove what a wretched world it is that we live in?'

'Don't despair, my friend. Something may yet turn up which will tilt the scales in the direction of justice. Now, about this boy you say is George Valmar's son. Can that be proved, together with his legitimacy?'

'It can. I spoke with the vicar of the parish church myself and he allowed me to see the church records. The marriage of George Valmar, bachelor of the parish, and Charlotte Meyrick, spinster of the same, is duly recorded there. As is the baptism of their child, Henry Meyrick

Valmar. The vicar remembered both events and is willing to swear to the accuracy of his entries.'

'And you say the boy is healthy and being looked after well by his grandparents?'

'He is. I have also taken care to ensure that he is beyond Sir Samuel's reach. That's in case he learns of his existence and tries to deal with him as he dealt with his father. Young Henry is being watched with great care, both day and night.' Foxe had given money lavishly to the street children to ensure this was so. Their sharp eyes and quick reactions would, he knew, be of greater use than hiring a dozen men to do the same job.

'Now you have told me of the boy and explained who he is, I will pass on that knowledge to the mayor. I'm sure he will agree with me that nothing can be done directly at this stage. However, should any attempt be made on the boy's life, the reason for it will be known in the right quarters. Try as he may, Sir Samuel will find himself unable to take action to break the entail and frustrate the proper succession to his lands. Not without the whole sorry business becoming public knowledge. Until then, I will ensure that the mayor, like myself, will stay silent on the matter. The boy's life may not then be in quite such danger as it would be if gossip spreads about his identity. Let us hope it stays that way until he is of age and can claim what is his due.'

If Foxe thought that the surprises at least for that day were complete, he was soon proved wrong. When he returned to his home, he found a letter waiting for him, summoning him to visit Lady Valmar on the next day at three o'clock in the afternoon. No reason was offered. Needless to say, there was never any doubt that he would go.

⁂

As soon as Foxe's carriage turned to pass through the splendid wrought-iron gates at the entry to Hutton Hall, the gate-keeper stepped out and brought them to a halt. At the same time, a woman, middle-aged and dressed like a superior servant, left the gate-house and went up to speak to Foxe's coachman. After a few moments in conversation with him, she came to where Foxe was waiting. He had already opened the door of the carriage, ready to step out to discover what the matter might be. Instead, the woman signalled to him to step back inside, then climbed into the carriage herself and sat opposite him.

'My mistress is waiting for you, Mr Foxe, but not at the hall. I'm to take you to her. I have already given your coachman the necessary instructions. If you will allow me to do so, I will ride with you there. It's a longish way and my legs are not as young as they used to be.'

She offered no further explanation but sat silently as the carriage ran on down the driveway. After perhaps a quarter of a mile, it turned off to the left. After that, it followed a narrow track which led to a small cottage built of flint and brick with a thatched roof. The thatch was rotting, weighed down with moss where the trees overhung. The window and door frames had not seen a touch of paint for many years. There had once been a neat garden around the place. Now it was overgrown: a tangled mass of weeds and brambles. Both house and garden had seen better days.

'This is the old gamekeeper's cottage, Mr Foxe,' the woman said at that point. 'The poor man was killed recently in a fight with a gang of poachers. He wasn't married and was getting old too old to manage his job and keep this place in any kind of good order. His replacement has not yet arrived. When he does, I find it hard to believe he'll relish living here. The master begrudges any money spent on estate houses — save only the lodges and any other properties which may be seen from the road. He is absent on business today, thank goodness. Even so, my mistress wishes to speak to you in private, well away from prying servants listening behind doors. This cottage is both empty and remote from the house itself. You will not be disturbed. I will wait in another room until you have finished and then escort my mistress back to the house. We often take long walks in the gardens and grounds on a fine day. No one will suspect she has been meeting you here.'

With that, she leant forward, opened the carriage door and stepped out, leaving a surprised Mr Foxe to follow her. Together, she in front and Foxe behind, they went up to the door of the cottage. The maidservant knocked three times before opening it and signalling Foxe to enter in front of her.

Lady Valmar was waiting for him in what must once have served as the gamekeeper's parlour. Now cobwebs hung from the ceiling, the floor was marked by drifts of dust, and leaves had blown in from somewhere to settle about the hearth. Lady Valmar stood stiff and upright, just as he remembered her from their last meeting in Colgate. This time, however, her face bore the signs of sleepless nights and recent tears.

As soon as Foxe had entered the room and without any preliminaries, she spoke, her voice weak and shaking a little.

'Tell me about my son, Mr Foxe. My poor, darling, wronged George.'

'You recognised the pendant,' Foxe said. 'I knew you had. I saw you start as I laid it before you.'

'He loved that pendant. I gave it to him on his twelfth birthday and he wore it always. Am I right in assuming that he is dead?'

Foxe nodded.

'I dared say nothing before. My husband had threatened me with terrible consequences if I spoke as much as a word,' Lady Valmar continued. 'He's beaten me many times, Mr Foxe, so I know what to expect if I dare to disobey him. He's not really a bad man. Not wicked. It's mostly that he can't bear to be disobeyed or thwarted. That was why he threw George out of the house and said he would disinherit him. My other son, Frederick, knows to avoid anything that would upset his father. It's easy for him. He's only interested in hunting and drinking with his friends. George wanted to do more. To get involved in things; to improve the estate. He was all for introducing new farming methods and rotations and improving the lives of those who work here.'

'Your husband wouldn't hear of it?' Foxe said. 'But surely, it would have been to his advantage?'

'Even if it did, he would have rejected it. He hadn't thought of it first, you see. He also cares nothing for his servants, his workers. No, nor even for his wife. All he cares about is some outworn concept of family honour and status. He thinks being a Valmar gives him the right to do anything he wishes, so long as he can maintain things as he claims they have been for hundreds of years. Frederick goes along with him because he's too lazy to do anything else. Now, tell me about George. Do you know what he had been doing all these years?'

'So far as I can discover,' Foxe replied, 'living first in London. Then he returned to live in Norwich in the house of a cabinetmaker. In both cities, he earned his living as a fencing master under the name of Georges Val d'Isère.'

Lady Valmar smiled. It was a weak smile, but the best she could manage.

'That is the name of a village in the French Alpine regions, Mr Foxe,' she said. 'I had a French maid; one who was with me when George was a small child. She came from that part of France. She loved my son and spent a great deal of time with him. She even taught him something of the French language. He had a natural ear for languages, Mr Foxe, and picked it up in no time. Later, his tutors improved it still further, but she gave him a flying start. How typical of him that he remembered her!'

'The cabinetmaker he lodged with had only one child, your ladyship,' Foxe said. 'A daughter. Naturally enough perhaps, she and your son fell in love and then married. After that, George found the two of them a house nearby.'

'What has happened to her?' Lady Valmar asked eagerly. 'Does she live there still? I thought you said the man from whom you took the pendant was living as some kind of vagrant?'

'He was,' Foxe replied. 'Your son's wife died about two years ago. According to her parents, her death caused him such grief that he acted as if he had lost his mind. After that he disappeared. No one knew where he had gone. It was only after his body was found that I discovered he'd been living on the streets as a vagrant. Whether he still knew who he was and what he had been, I cannot tell you. All I know is that he entertained the street children with tales of life as a child in a grand mansion. They thought he made them up to amuse them.'

'How did my son die?'

Foxe had been dreading this question. Should he tell her the truth, or try to sidestep an answer by saying he'd not seen the body himself and was not sure? No, that would be lying. She deserved better than that.

'A professional assassin killed him, Lady Valmar. Probably when he was sleeping. A professional who kills for payment. Your son was murdered.'

Lady Valmar let out a deep groan. Then she put her hands up to cover her face and hide her tears. Between sobs, she gasped out how much she had loved her firstborn. How proud she had been of him as he grew up. How much his father's cruelty in banning him from the house had affected her, ruining her life and happiness ever since.

'He even struck the boy, Mr Foxe. Struck him in the face and called him a disgrace to the family name. Told him to get out and never return. Yet, throughout this whole tirade, my son said nothing. He stood like Christ before his accusers. At the end of my husband's tirade, he turned on his heel and walked out of the house. I never saw him again. My husband wouldn't even let me go to him to say goodbye. At that moment, sir, I hated my husband from the very depths of my soul.'

Foxe waited. It would have been unthinkable for him to do anything else. Lady Valmar was somewhere else, remembering that terrible day; clenching and unclenching her fingers and shaking from the emotions which ripped through her body and mind. When at length she grew calmer, Foxe tried to apologise for upsetting her. She waved his words aside.

'Do you know who sent the assassin?' she asked him.

'I have some ideas, your ladyship, but I cannot yet be certain.'

There was no way he could cause this woman even more pain by sharing all he knew. Especially the certainty that the man who had caused this deed to be done was a member of her close family. Instead, he tried to send the conversation down a different track.

'Your son, George, had a son of his own. I've seen him. A fine boy, whom I'm told is the image of his father.'

Lady Valmar stepped forward and took hold of Foxe's arm, as if by doing so she could wring information out of him.

'Who is he? Who? Where is he? How old is he? Please tell me at once, Mr Foxe, I beg of you. I have a grandson! A grandson! Is he well?'

All the time she was speaking, she was shaking Foxe.

'I believe he is some ten years old, your ladyship,' Foxe replied, gently disentangling himself from her grip. 'A strapping young lad, as I said, full of life. He lives with his other grandparents, who have looked after him tenderly since his father left. I gather your son never told them his past history or true identity. They assumed the boy had no other family and intended to bring him up to follow in his grandfather's trade.'

'Praise God! May He bless them for their kindness!' She paused, as another thought came to her. 'Have you told my husband any of this?'

'I have not, your ladyship,' Foxe said. 'Not yet.'

'Then do not, Mr Foxe, I beg of you. The boy will be happier without him having anything to do with my husband. How I wish I could go and see him! The image of his father! I don't know whether to laugh or cry.'

'I will do as you ask me, Lady Valmar,' Foxe said. 'Your second son will of course need to know at some point of the boy's existence. I know this estate is most likely entailed, almost certainly on the next, legitimate male descendant of the original owner. Am I right in thinking that?'

'You are. For all his bluster, my husband could not interfere with that. After my son left, he told everyone he had gone abroad; then that he had died there. Both lies, of course, but both things he devoutly hoped might yet become true.'

'Then Frederick's hopes will one day be dashed. Your son, George, may indeed be dead, but this lad I told you of — Henry, they call him — is the true and legitimate heir to this estate and the baronetcy. Not Frederick.'

'My husband will never accept that, Mr Foxe! Never! The child of a cabinetmaker's daughter? He would rather die! He will certainly put every obstacle possible in the boy's way if he finds out.'

'That is what I thought,' Foxe said. 'Even so, my lady, there are other matters about which I must speak with him. Matters he will certainly not wish to hear about either. I'm sure he will put every obstacle in my way too. He told the butler, in my presence, that I was not to be admitted should I return at any time.' Foxe glowered at the thought. 'He will find I am not so easily kept away. There is nothing he can do to me. I do not fear your husband, Lady Valmar. Both I and my wealth in business are beyond his reach. He may rant and rave all he wishes, but I will find some way of telling him to his face what I am sure he most dreads to hear.'

'But surely, Mr Foxe, to hear of his son's death, whether in Norwich or anywhere else, will be no more than he has wished for all these years?'

She paused, wrinkling her brow in thought. What could it be that her husband would be afraid to hear, if he allowed Mr Foxe to speak with him again?

'He knew about our son before this, didn't he?' Lady Valmar hissed. 'He knew! He knew George was alive! Did he also know where he was?'

'I am quite certain he did not know all, your ladyship. Yes, I think your husband knew his eldest son was alive and well. That, and probably no more. At least until recently.'

Lady Valmar seem to have missed Foxe's caveat.

'Then may God curse him to hell!' she cried. 'I didn't think I could hate him any more than I did, Mr Foxe, but this news has proved me wrong. I have changed my mind, Mr Foxe. Tell him he has a legitimate grandson. Tell him about the new heir. Only don't tell him how to find the boy. Then, when you tell him, I hope the poisonous bastard chokes on the news! May it be like a burning coal lodged in his guts! A mortal wound from which that evil spawn of a pox-ridden whore can never recover! I hope he dies in agony and spends eternity in torment!' A life of employing ladylike language was overturned in a moment by the depth of her fury.

Once again, Foxe was forced to wait until Lady Valmar could gain control of her emotions. When she did, she was able to speak to him more calmly again.

'Will you be my messenger to the boy, Mr Foxe? I dare not meet you again in person, but Agnes, my personal maid, who brought you here, is entirely trustworthy. May I send her to you with a message for the boy? Better still, I will write — Do you know if he can read?'

'I'm told he reads very well, your ladyship. His father taught him much and his grandparents have been sending him to a school nearby.'

'Very well. Then I will write to him. Wait a moment! Does he know his real identity and that of his father? Have you told him?'

'I thought to spare him the pain, at least for a few years yet, Lady Valmar. Until today, I was forced to assume that both you and your husband would reject him. There was no point in filling his head with dreams which might very well not come true — at least until your husband died. By then, he will be old enough to fight his own struggle to receive all that is due to him. Now, if you wish it, I will tell him at least part of the truth. Let him understand that he has a grandmother who cares about him. By all means let him know that much, your ladyship. But, if you will be guided by me, write to him merely as his grandmother. Let all mention of your wealth and status be omitted in any letters you send him. I'm sure you can invent a plausible reason why it is, as yet, impossible for you to meet with him.'

'You are a wise and compassionate young man, Mr Foxe, and I will do as you say. Maybe from time to time I will send him what little money I can. Will those who care for him allow me to do that, do you think?'

'I'm sure they will,' Foxe replied. 'Yes, I'm sure of that — and help him to spend it wisely as well. I will tell them enough of this meeting to understand all they need to at this point. His grandfather and grandmother know the truth of young Henry's breeding but have promised to stay silent. They will say nothing of your name or standing. I will explain to them that you knew nothing of the boy's existence until I told you today. I will also tell them there are certain pressing domestic reasons which must keep you from him for the time being. I believe they trust me enough not to pry any further.'

FOXE WENT HOME FROM THE MEETING WITH LADY VALMAR feeling angry and frustrated. He was also deeply concerned for the woman's well-being. She had told him that her husband had used physical violence towards her before when she had disobeyed him. Heaven knows what he would do to her if he discovered she had been talking secretly to Foxe about the son whose existence he had denied for so long. Before he came away, Foxe had tried to persuade her to leave for her own safety. All she had done was shake her head and tell him she had promised to be Sir Samuel's wife for better or for worse. That it had turned out to be all for worse did not release her from that promise.

Now accepting her eldest son's death at the hands of his father or brother would prove to be part of that bargain. Foxe had not been able to share that knowledge with her; nor would he, until he could not avoid doing so.

In the meantime, he felt more anxious about confronting Sir Samuel than he had before. He could look after himself. What worried him was that he must weigh his words to avoid being the cause of the man finding out any of his knowledge was due to this clandestine meeting with his wife. He had long expected any further meeting with Sir Samuel would be a most unpleasant affair. How do you confront a man — any man — and accuse him of having paid an assassin to murder his eldest son? To accuse the younger son of having done that deed would be almost as bad. Yet, it was the only way he stood any chance of protecting Lady Valmar and bringing the case to an end at the same time.

After dinner that evening, Foxe sat in his library and tried to turn his thoughts to something else. He occupied his mind with the problem, still unsolved, of the book that had been stolen from Dr Danson's library. He was now as certain as he could be that it was not George Stubbings, Mrs Danson's black sheep of a brother, who had murdered his sister's husband. Since the man was dead anyway, to gain further proof was impossible. He found it inconceivable that Stubbings, a fellow whose sister said he was illiterate, would steal any book — let alone one as obscure in its content as that one. A book containing pornographic pictures perhaps. Maybe a book in a rich binding; something which looked valuable, even if you could not read a word of what was written inside. Not a book which, according to the mysterious Mr Smith, was totally unremarkable from the outside. While inside it contained nothing beyond pages of text, interspersed with symbols and magical signs.

But if Stubbings hadn't taken the book, who had? Mr Cornelius Wake? Had he killed Danson by striking him? Had Danson died from the shock and exertion of trying to stop his book being stolen? This

Mr Wake was a man about whom virtually nothing was known. Only the fact that he had written to Danson in Latin, using a relatively simple code to prevent his letter being read by unauthorised eyes. Even that much could not be explained easily. He might have written in Latin to indicate that he was a learned man with a serious purpose in asking for an interview. The use of code seemed entirely superfluous, unless it was meant to be a sign that he was part of some hidden brotherhood already known to Danson.

After more than an hour of turning this over and over in his mind and getting nowhere, Foxe took his candle over to his desk. There he found pen and paper and wrote a letter. Then he folded and sealed it, addressing it to Mr Anthony Smith at St George's College, Cambridge.

In the letter, Foxe wrote that he had found a copy of the book Smith was searching for. Unfortunately, it had been stolen and the owner murdered before he could open negotiations about a possible sale. The book had been in the library of a certain Dr Danson, a reclusive book collector in the city. Whoever it was who had been so desperate to lay their hands on the book, it seems he had been willing to steal it, presumably because Danson refused to sell. Perhaps even kill for it. He, Foxe, would continue trying to find another copy, but he didn't hold out much hope.

That done, he called for Alfred, his manservant, to come to help prepare him for his bed. At the same time, he gave Alfred the letter and asked him to send it off next morning. With luck, it would reach Cambridge in two days at the most.

19

When his carriage drove up to the gates of Hutton Hall the next morning, Foxe was afraid, at first, that he would be denied entry. What he would do then, he wasn't quite sure. He would think of something. Whatever difficulties were put in his way, he was determined one way or another to secure a meeting with Sir Samuel Valmar.

His resolve was destined to remain untested. The same gatekeeper who had been there the previous afternoon stepped forward to open the gates. He even nodded to Foxe's coachman in a friendly manner and then stood aside to allow them to drive onwards towards the house itself.

On the previous occasion, when Foxe had come to the Hutton Hall estate, he had been far too preoccupied with his own thoughts to take much notice of his surroundings. This time was different. Now he looked around on all sides, noting the extent of the land and how it was planted; taking in exactly what young Henry Valmar would one day inherit and committing it to memory. When the time was right, he would be able to give the lad a detailed description of his future inheritance. Besides, the activity might serve to calm his mind before the storm which was sure to come.

Like most driveways to grand country estates, the road up to Hutton Hall was long and gently twisting. The mansion stood in the centre of an extensive area of landscaped parkland. Whoever designed this park must have been determined to conceal the house itself for as long as possible. He had therefore used the natural undulations of the land and carefully-sited stands of mature trees to screen it from view for most of the way. Beyond the gate, the drive ran for perhaps three hundred yards amongst fine trees. Foxe noted sweet chestnut, beech and holly, mingled with many magnificent English oaks, now in their prime. Sandier, heathland areas were marked by clumps of silver birch. As he looked around him, Foxe realised such a wood must represent an asset of considerable value. Although there was no sign of felling, he found it hard to believe that whoever had planted the area had not done so with the eventual value of the timber uppermost in his mind.

As it left the wood, the roadway veered slightly to the left. Then it ran along the bank of an extensive area of water to cross a bridge over the stream feeding into the lake. Finally, it swung back to the right to resume its former course. All this time, a gentle rise on the right-hand side concealed whatever the park might contain in that direction. After another quarter of a mile, the driveway turned for the last time to run up the slope and descend the other side to cross yet another small stream. The trees had thinned now, to be replaced by open grass-land, grazed by the sheep that stood in small groups, their well-grown lambs beside them. It was the very picture of a well-run estate that was being farmed in the modern manner.

Only when they had crossed the stream and breasted a rise on the other side did the house itself come into view. Even then, it was still some three or four hundred yards distant. The entrance drive did not approach the mansion from the front. Instead, it arrived at a right-angle to the principal frontage, first passing the stable yard and exten-sive household offices grouped about a courtyard. Foxe could see servants moving about. He noted a bakehouse, a brewhouse and sundry storage areas, all facing what must be the kitchen range, where a thin column of smoke rose from amongst the chimneys clustered on the roof.

Finally, with a kind of flourish, the drive turned sharply to the left, before swinging back in a half circle. His carriage came to a halt in front of the main entrance to the mansion itself. Everything about Hutton Hall had been designed to express the power and wealth of its owners. There were massive pillars on either side of stone stairs sweeping up to the main door. The grand entrance doorway was framed by a vast portico in the manner of some ancient Grecian temple. On either side of this splendid entrance, there were no fewer than four tall windows. The matching set above them must be for either a library or a series of splendid bedrooms. Above those again, a third row of windows, much smaller now, indicated attic floors where the servants would be housed. In Foxe's eyes, it was a mansion worthy of a marquis or even a duke, not a comparatively lowly baronet. Foxe wondered how he could have missed noticing such ostentation and opulence on his first visit, however much his mind had been distracted.

A footman came forward to hold the door of his carriage open and Foxe stepped down. He could now see the imposing figure of the butler awaiting him at the head of the steps. Far from being turned away, Mr Foxe was being given a full ceremonial welcome. Why should that be? Surely Sir Samuel must be no more pleased to receive him this time than the last?

All was explained when Foxe climbed the right-hand set of stairs and reached the spot where the butler stood waiting for him.

'Good morning, Mr Foxe,' the butler began, after bowing to the visitor in the approved manner. 'Her ladyship instructed that you should be received in the proper manner. If you leave your hat and outer garments with the footman here, I will conduct you to the Great Hall. The master is waiting for you there.'

Naturally, all this affability ended the moment Foxe stepped into the Great Hall itself. Sir Samuel would have used this as the meeting place to impress his influence and social status on all his visitors, and on Mr Foxe most of all. Now he received Foxe standing, his back to a large fireplace with an elaborate alabaster surround. Above him could be seen the coat of arms of the Valmar family. I may be a man like you, all this seemed to proclaim, but I am not just your social superior. I am a Valmar too. Remember that.

The baronet had dressed himself in a suit of fine brown wool embroidered in gold, over a pale cream waistcoat sprigged with tiny flowers. From his leather shoes with their golden buckles and his spotless white silk stockings up to his freshly powdered wig, he was the embodiment of the rich landowner suffering the attentions of some troublesome tenant. He was also in a combative mood. He launched his attack at once and without preliminaries.

'Say what you have to say, sir, then get out!' the baronet barked. 'I am only suffering your presence because my wife begged me to do so. According to her, you have some important information affecting the Valmar family. My family heritage is everything to me. We Valmars came over with the Conqueror and have been here ever since. In all that time, no one has dishonoured the family name. No one ever shall, while I live and breathe. Now, get on with it — and be brief!'

When Foxe had stood before this man the last time, Sir Samuel had affected an air of complete indifference. Now all was different. What he wanted was to send this meddlesome tradesman about his business; preferably with his tail between his legs. By the end of his opening speech, his face was suffused with red and purple from the effort of holding his temper in check. Foxe noted how the other man's breathing was shallow, his fists clenched tight and his eyes narrowed with fury. He had expected some such display of temper, but even he was taken aback by the vehemence of Sir Samuel's attack. Still, he had determined in advance nothing would shake his calmness. He therefore replied in a quiet voice, his words measured and his tone mild and reasonable. To his quiet satisfaction, he observed immediately how much this gentle manner seemed to inflame Sir Samuel even more.

'How long have you known that your eldest son, George, was alive and well and living nearby in the city?' Foxe asked. 'I say was alive, since he has recently met his end, as I'm sure you know very well.'

For a brief moment, Sir Samuel seemed to rear back. It was as if Foxe had landed a heavy and totally unexpected blow, which had come close to knocking him off balance. Then he gathered his strength once again to return to the offensive, his voice as loud and harsh as Foxe's had been quiet and rational.

'By God, sir, I am amazed that you have the impudence to come here and speak of that rebellious cur! I banished him from this place and cut him out of the family more than a decade ago. Alive or dead, it is nothing to me! If that is all you have come to say, sir, I will ask you to leave this instant. George went abroad and died there.'

'You know he did neither.'

'I know nothing of the sort!' Sir Samuel raved. 'I arranged an excellent marriage for my so-called son. One that would have added substantially to this estate and paved the way for the family's entry into the ranks of the nobility. An entry long overdue and more than richly deserved, I maintain. What did he do? Refused so much as to meet the young woman! Said he had seen her once at a ball and that was more than enough. When I asked him what was wrong with her, he said she had a face like a sheep, bad skin, bad teeth, no figure at all that he could discern, and the character of a frightened rabbit. As if any of that mattered against the fifty thousand pounds she would bring to her husband! I told him. If he wanted pretty playthings, there are enough and more to be found on all sides. I should know. What d'you think has kept me sane all these years? Despite a wife who deals with me only as a matter of duty — and that with a poor grace.'

'Are you telling me, Sir Samuel, that was why you drove your son out of this house and tried to deny him his inheritance? Simply because he refused to marry the woman of your choice?'

By now, Foxe had begun to enjoy himself. Acting the part of the man of reason confronted with someone who had long abandoned any pretence at rationality, a man gripped with a blind obsession for an outdated notion of family honour, had given him the advantage. He meant to keep it.

Valmar was incredulous.

'He defied me, sir! Defied me to my face! Told me he would marry whomsoever he chose, and I could go to the devil, for he needed neither my help nor my approval. Is that any way for a son to speak to his father? I knew it then. Bad blood! Can't have bad blood in the Valmar family. It must have come from his mother, of course. Couldn't have been due to me. Of course, I threw him out. Disinherited him as well, damn his eyes! Now you...'

'But you couldn't disinherit him, could you?' Foxe interrupted, his voice steadier and calmer than ever. 'For all your claims to the contrary, that was something you were not able to do. The Will by which you hold this estate does not allow it. Like most such estates, this one is entailed on the eldest, legitimate male descendant of the original owner who had the Will drawn up. You have only a life interest, Sir Samuel. You cannot sell any part of what you have inherited nor interfere in the succession.'

Much of this was bluff, since there had been no way for Foxe to discover the actual terms of the original Will. However, one look at Sir Samuel's face was enough to prove his statement was correct.

By this stage, the roles had been reversed and Foxe held the advantage. He pressed it home relentlessly, never raising his voice or deviating from the proper standards of politeness. Yet all the while allowing the other man neither time nor opportunity to recover himself.

'I have consulted an expert in the law,' Foxe continued. 'He has confirmed that he can find no trace of any attempt to overturn the terms of the original Will, nor to break the entail. Indeed, in his opinion, based on many years of dealing with such matters, no responsible group of executors, no court in the land, would entertain such an idea. Especially on the grounds that your son refused to do your bidding when it came to choosing a wife. The story you put about, your claim your son had gone abroad and died there, did not contain a shred of truth. It merely reflected your most heartfelt hopes. I ask you yet again, when did you first learn that your son, George, was in robust health and living in Norwich?'

'Damn you, Foxe! Damn you, I say! Interfering busybody!'

Sir Samuel's words were still full of aggression. It was his posture which conveyed the truth. His legs were shaking now, and his breath came in uneven gasps. Before Foxe stood a mortally wounded animal, still attempting to stand its ground while knowing its strength was failing fast.

'George had bad blood, I tell you! Bad blood!'

'Rubbish!' Foxe snapped back. 'That bad blood, if any such thing exists, lies in you. It shows itself all too clearly in your pride and uncontrollable temper. Your tantrums have become boring, Sir Samuel.

Now, I am asking you for the last time: When did you know where your son had gone?'

It was over. All the fight had gone out of Sir Samuel Valmar, baronet and one-time domestic tyrant. 'I thought he had gone far away, Foxe,' he replied, his voice uncertain and expressing little, save total weariness. 'I hoped he had, anyway. The years passed and no news of him reached me. I told myself he had either decided never to return or had died somewhere. What else was I to think? I assume you know where he was all those years.'

Here was a man in despair. Someone who had discovered that a fantasy he had concocted to cover his blind arrogance and stupidity had crumpled about him. A cold wave of reality had swept in, brushing aside all his displays of temper. Now it was sweeping away all hope of living his life as he had always done: the unquestioned ruler of family and domain.

'He was living first in London and then in Norwich,' Foxe said. 'Here he took lodgings with a cabinetmaker and his family while earning his living teaching, fencing and giving French lessons. The family with whom he lived knew him as Mr George Valmar. They believed him when he said that his name was due to his descent from a remote and impoverished branch of the family which held Hutton Hall. To the rest of the world, he was a refugee driven from his family's modest estates in France due to their adherence to the Protestant religion. It was during this time that he fell in love with the daughter of the house and married her.'

'Married the child of a common artisan? Are you certain of this?' Valmar shook his head, as if unable to take in the enormity of what Foxe was telling him.

'I have seen the parish records, Sir Samuel. I have also spoken with the vicar, who well recalls joining the two of them in holy matrimony.'

'But why? Why, for God's sake? He turns down an heiress with fifty thousand pounds. Says he wouldn't marry her if she had a hundred thousand or more. Then he takes to marry some common girl from the gutter. A woman of low birth lacking any fortune whatsoever. Why?'

'They loved each other,' Foxe said. 'From all I have heard, it was an idyllic marriage.'

'Wait! Wait! You have the wrong man, Foxe. When they had finally tracked him down, the people I hired told me my son was living as a homeless vagrant.'

'It is the same person, I assure you,' Foxe replied. 'All went well until your son's wife died. Her death seems to have driven him out of his mind with grief. He left his home and disappeared. None knew where he was. The cabinetmaker, his wife and friends searched every-where, but found no trace of him. Some, like you, assumed he had gone far away or had died. Yet, the cabinetmaker and his wife never gave up hope. They kept him in their prayers and thoughts against the day when, they felt certain, he would return to the house where he had been so happy. It was not to be. The people you hired saw to that, didn't they?'

Sir Samuel's response was a half-strangled whimper.

'All along,' Foxe continued, 'poor George wore that gold pendant engraved with his family's coat of arms. The one his mother had given him, I believe. He kept it, even though selling it would have raised more than enough to free him from poverty and set him up again else-where. I knew that you had recognised it when I first came here. I could see your wife recognised it as well. I imagine you guessed what had brought me to talk to you; how I had discovered the dead man was linked to your family. So, you threatened her and forced her to deny any knowledge of the pendant and what it proved. It was that which first made me suspicious of you. How could you have taken steps, before I came, to make her deny her own son? It had to be because you knew in advance that the man who owned the gold pendant was already dead.'

'How could I have known?' Valmar's objection was feeble.

'Because it was you who paid the Italian, Brunetti, to put an end to your son's life, wasn't it, Sir Samuel? I know it was. What's more, Brunetti has now been taken by the constables and has already confessed to the deed. He even described how you were the person who told him to do it. It appears he is impatient to testify against you.'

'Him? Who would take the word of a professional assassin — a damn foreigner as well — against the word of the head of one of the foremost families in the land? This will never result in a legal action,

Foxe. You know that as well as I do.' What ought to have been a triumphant statement of impunity came out instead as a plea for understanding. 'I had to do it. Can't you see that? I had to.'

Foxe brushed his attempt at justification aside. 'Nonsense! Again, you give yourself away. How did you know Brunetti was a professional assassin? All I mentioned was the name.'

Sir Samuel started, then just managed to recover himself. 'I had to do it,' he repeated. 'Listen! If a horse in my stables turns vicious, it's a sign of bad blood. Surely you can see that. Should I keep the beast, in spite of it? Should I allow it to find fresh opportunities to harm those around him? However fond I was of the beast, I would have to tell the head groom to lead him off somewhere and shoot him. Root out the bad blood. It's what is necessary in all such cases. This was the same thing.'

'Your son was not a horse, sir, to be put down when it pleased you. He was a living, breathing human being; one that you had sired yourself. Don't talk to me anymore of bad blood! Try as you might, you will never justify yourself in that way. You caused a man to be murdered, Sir Samuel. For that, I am not afraid to call you a villain and murderer to your face.'

Somehow, Valmar managed to call up a final flicker of pride and defiance. 'Do you dare to stand there, Foxe, and insult me in that way? Do you dare to pour scorn on my concern for my family's name? I'll have the law on you for this, you see if I don't!'

'On what grounds?' Foxe replied calmly. 'For telling the truth? Others may fear your bluster. I do not.'

Sir Samuel's attempt to fight back now ebbed away as quickly as it had arisen. Once again it was replaced by weariness and dejection. 'What does it matter anyway?' he said in a dull voice. 'George is dead. The succession is safe.'

'The succession?' Foxe said. 'Yes, that is certainly safe, Sir Samuel. George Valmar had a son.'

With those five words, all that Sir Samuel Valmar had lived for crashed about him in ruins. Like a once flourishing town devastated by a violent earthquake, his destruction too was complete. All colour drained from his face. He clutched his chest, his breath coming in gasps. He wore the expression of a man who had looked into a pit which had opened at his feet and seen his death waiting at the bottom. Unable to stay on his feet, he slumped into a chair and began to sob.

Even Foxe could not help feeling pity for the fellow, despite all he knew. If he could have done, he would have stopped at that point and given Valmar time to recover himself. What drove him on, against all his natural inclination, was the determination to make sure that this wreck of a man in front of him could not reach out once again to snuff out another life.

'That boy,' he said, 'your grandson, is the legitimate heir to this estate, not your second son, Frederick, as you wished and schemed. He is also beyond the reach of your insane obsession with the purity of Valmar blood. I have seen to that. I have also laid all the evidence I possess relating to his claim before the Lord Mayor of Norwich, who has accepted its validity. Try as you may, Valmar, you will never be able to dispute his claim. Besides, if you even attempt to do so, all that I have told you today will be repeated in public and in open court. Is that what you want? To have your precious family name dragged through the mud? To see it become the butt of open derision by your so-called common folk? Is it? Is it?'

Each sentence struck Sir Samuel another deadly blow. He huddled in his chair, helpless and afraid. In the end, all he could do was to gasp, 'Get out!'

Then he closed his eyes, wrapped his arms about his chest, and did his best to shut out the realisation that the full measure of retribution due had come upon him at last.

Foxe turned on his heel and left.

20

Foxe left Hutton Hall with little sense of achievement and none at all of triumph. Instead, he felt only sick revulsion at the wickedness that had been revealed. That and pity for the wretched creature Sir Samuel had become. The man was caught up in the inevitable collapse of a life based solely on an obsession with family status and honour. Surely it was impossible that Sir Samuel Valmar had been sane when he had ordered the assassination of his eldest son? If he had been, he had descended into an evil greater than most could even conceive. And if he had become a madman, pity was a better response than anger.

It was clear, however, that Mrs Crombie was in no such dilemma about her response to all that Foxe had told her. To her mind, Sir Samuel Valmar had committed dreadful sins. His actions must surely result in an eternity in hell fire.

The two of them were sitting in the workroom behind Foxe's bookshop. By the time Foxe had returned to his own house, he knew it was close to the time when she and her cousin, Eleanor, would be closing up for the day. They would be bustling about, sorting out books left in the wrong places and returning packets and bottles of patent medicines to the correct shelves. Charlie, Foxe's apprentice, would probably have been sent out to deliver packages of books to regular customers. Then, after all the others had left, Mrs Crombie would make sure the shop was secure before going home herself.

At one time, Foxe had made a regular practice of dropping into the shop at around this time. He would draw Mrs Crombie aside from her work and bring her up-to-date with whatever mystery had been engaging his interest. Somehow, those visits had become less frequent of late. On that day though, in need of someone who would listen to him while he cleansed his mind of what had taken place at Hutton Hall, he told his coachman to stop outside the shop rather than at the door to his house. For Mrs Crombie, relishing a visit of the kind that had become so infrequent, this was a heaven-sent chance to hear the outcome of a fascinating case.

'Sir Samuel sounds a thoroughly unpleasant fellow,' Mrs Crombie said, when Foxe had completed telling her about his confrontation at Hutton Hall. 'No. That's putting it much too mildly. The man is a pompous, domineering, evil-minded bully; a man determined to have his own way, even at the expense of those who should be most dear to him. Did he really have his son murdered?'

'He did, Mrs Crombie. He as much as admitted it to me.'

'Then what I just said of him is still well short of the mark. To kill anyone is wicked and a mortal sin. To kill your own son is such a heinous crime it takes the breath away. God will punish him, Mr Foxe. If anyone is destined for hell, he is that person.'

'Valmar is all those things, Mrs Crombie,' Foxe said. 'You might also add cold and heartless. Even so . . .' He trailed off, staring idly at the old printing press his father had once used, the one which Charlie had now put back into working order. 'His mind has certainly become warped, there's no doubt of that. Yet, somehow . . .' He broke off again.

'It's his attitude to his family, isn't it?' Mrs Crombie suggested. 'It's like . . . Oh, I don't know! It's as if he had a malignancy growing inside him until it finally choked the life out of him.'

It wasn't like Mr Foxe to be lost for words, she thought. But then, he hadn't been himself for many days now; not since he'd made such a fool of himself with Lady Cockerham.

'Precisely,' Foxe said earnestly. 'It's not unusual for members of ancient families to be proud of their lineage. Nor is it uncommon for them to feel that somehow gives them greater standing among their peers. I have encountered many who felt in similar ways. Give them a chance to start talking about their ancestors, and they bore you to death. But Sir Samuel . . . All I can say is, he's . . . I don't know.'

'Obsessed?' Mrs Crombie suggested.

'That certainly. Completely consumed by ancestral pride. Yet there's even more than that.'

'It's the bit about him saying killing his son was like dealing with a horse that had turned vicious, isn't it?' she said.

'Exactly! Bless you, Mrs Crombie! You've hit on the exact point. It's as if his obsession has ... turned rancid; become a cancer eating away at him, just as you said. Changed from a harmless eccentric into a malevolent force: something capable of making him dismiss murder as no more than a necessity. All that balderdash about "bad blood!" Talking as if people were animals, to be improved by selecting the best bloodlines and keeping them untainted. Does that sound normal to you?'

'It certainly does not, Mr Foxe!' Mrs Crombie replied, now becoming heated herself. 'It sounds like the fantastic ideas of some deranged ranter in front of a group of radical dissenters. Either that, or one of the wretched delusions of the miserable creatures confined in Bedlam. Sir Samuel Valmar has become insane, hasn't he?'

'No, not quite mad. He couldn't run his estate or move in society if that were the case. Not mad, but not sane either. More like someone moving back and forth between delusion and sanity. Most of the time, his mind is probably quite sound; at least so far as you can say it of someone so domineering and dictatorial. Aye, and wicked with it. But let him come up against anything connected with his ancestry and the status of the Valmar family and the madness breaks out.'

For a few moments, the two of them sat in silence, each considering the dreadful fate which had befallen Sir Samuel and those about him. Then Foxe changed direction unexpectedly, his face becoming more animated and a good deal less grim.

'What do you know about Lady Valmar?' he asked. 'What is her background?'

'She's Sir Samuel's second wife,' Mrs Crombie replied, used by now to the way Foxe's mind could leap between topics. 'Did you know that? His first wife died within eighteen months of their marriage. Died in childbirth, I believe, and took the baby with her. To be honest, I know little about her, other than that it was said she was selected by the Valmar family based entirely on the size of her dowry. Before Sir Samuel married her, the Valmars had lost a great deal of their wealth. His grandfather had been something of a wastrel and a fool — a heavy drinker too. His father then compounded the losses through a number of rash speculations. By the time Sir Samuel himself inherited the estate, most of the family's money had been lost or frittered away and the lands mortgaged to the hilt. Even Hutton Hall itself was in a sad state. It didn't look anything like the building that's there today, I'm told. In the last ten years or so, the place has been almost completely rebuilt and remodelled.'

'I didn't know that,' Foxe said. 'Where did he get the money from?'

'Sir Samuel has proved a most able manager of the estate, greatly increasing the income from tenancies and buying extra land where he could. However, nearly all the money required to get him started came from the present Lady Valmar. She didn't start out amongst the gentry. Her father was a rich cloth merchant from Suffolk — or was it Essex? I can't recall exactly. Either way, he was determined to see that his only child, a daughter, should find a husband he judged would be worthy of her. She brought Sir Samuel a huge fortune, Mr Foxe. In return, she got a title and precious little else.'

'Her dowry paid off Sir Samuel's father's debts?'

'Yes, and far more than that. Whatever faults Sir Samuel has, Mr Foxe, no one could fail to admire his skill in dealing with money. He used what was left over from his wife's dowry to improve the estate, and then to buy more land. Whatever he had, he set out to ensure it paid him back handsomely. When Lady Valmar's father died some ten years ago, he left her all his wealth and business interests. Sir Samuel sold the businesses at a handsome profit and took the proceeds and the rest of her inheritance into his own hands. People say he's almost doubled the amount of her inheritance since then.'

'And that's the man who lectured me earlier on purity of bloodline!'

Foxe said. 'The man who showed such scorn for an honest tradesman like his son's father-in-law! It's unbelievable! What a hypocrite! Now I understand why he said he blamed his poor wife for the "bad blood" that had caused his son George to defy his wishes.'

'Families like the Valmars have always done that, Mr Foxe. Over the years, they deplete their own wealth. It's most often by gambling, drinking or whoring. Then they recoup their losses and more when one of their number manages to marry the heiress of some rich merchant. They forget that it's a constant influx of fresh blood and new money from the so-called lower classes which has kept them going throughout the centuries.'

'You're right, Mrs Crombie,' Foxe said, nodding his head energetically. 'That's also why Sir Samuel was so set on George Valmar marrying another heiress, as ill-favoured as she seems to have been. Two heiresses in successive generations! If George had repeated his father's success in adding to the family wealth in that way, the family might have become truly rich. Then the next generation would have had the means to do sufficient favours to people in the right places, to swap a mere baronet's title for an earldom at the least.'

'Yes,' Mrs Crombie agreed. 'He might have founded a truly aristocratic lineage, conveniently forgetting the means by which it was achieved.'

'Ah, but son George dashed those hopes, Mrs Crombie, didn't he?' Foxe said. 'Even worse, Sir Samuel has now learned that the next heir to his wealth and his title will be the grandson of a lowly cabinetmaker. No wonder that news hit him like a charging bull.'

'It's no more than he deserved,' Mrs Crombie replied. The severe tone of her voice and the stiffness of her posture spoke eloquently of her disapproval of such behaviour. 'He'd done much worse, hadn't he? Something unforgivable! He'd had his own son killed in defence of a senseless conception of family honour. It quite takes my breath away. God has brought him low, Mr Foxe, and Satan will do the rest. You may be sure of that. Whether in this life or the next, Sir Samuel Valmar will not escape what is due to someone whose wickedness must be so abhorrent to the eyes of the Almighty.'

'I fear it will have to be in the next life,' Foxe said sadly. 'He will not face a judge in this one. For all that he confessed his crime to me, no one else was present when he did so. If I tried to bring him to court, all he would need to escape would be to deny that he ever spoke in such a way. The same applies to the evidence offered by the actual assassin, Brunetti. This is an occasion when I wish I had your faith, Mrs Crombie. It might offer me some comfort. As it is, all I feel is frustration and impotent fury. It's enough to make me wish I had never become involved.'

'You are altogether too hard on yourself,' Mrs Crombie told him. 'Without you, Lady Valmar would have gone to her grave never knowing what had become of her eldest son. As it is, she can at least console herself that all her husband's plans have come to nothing. She also knows she has a grandson in whom she may place some hope for a better future.'

Foxe would not be comforted. 'I know you speak from kindness, Mrs Crombie,' he said, 'but it is Lady Valmar's plight which I find most unbearable of all. She's tied to a heartless brute of a man: the kind who demands total obedience and offers nothing in return, save more years of servitude to his crazed ideas. Still worse, if she obstructs him in any way he resorts to violence. I can do nothing save pity her from the depths of my heart.'

'You can pray for her, Mr Foxe,' Mrs Crombie said quietly. 'God can do what man finds impossible.'

'God and I have not been on speaking terms these many years, I fear,' Foxe replied. 'When I look at all the wickedness in this world, I doubt His very existence. I am a rationalist. My reason tells me men like Sir Samuel Valmar will continue to escape the justice they so readily impose on everybody else. Thus it has always been; and thus, it will continue.'

❦ 21 ❦

For the next day and the one after that, Foxe retreated more or
less completely within himself. He rose late, picked at his food
and even gave up his regular morning walks and visits to the
coffeehouse. Instead, he spent all day alone in his library, speaking to
no one. When Mrs Crombie enquired after him, and Captain Brock
came to visit, he told his servants to say he was sick and not able to
receive anybody. Most of Norwich enjoyed sunlight and warmth,
uncharacteristic of the time of year, while a dark cloud hung over
Foxe's home and shop. Even the customers felt it. Few lingered to
gossip or enquire after new titles, fewer than usual visited the circulating library and takings fell, adding still further to Mrs Crombie's
sense of impending doom.

Until now, she had never realised how much the success of the business still depended on Mr Foxe himself. He may have left nearly all the
running of the shop to her, but he was still its heart and soul. As a
result, she fretted and fumed. She dealt brusquely with the other staff
and became so severe with Charlie's tendency to daydream that he too
shut himself away in the stockroom whenever he could.

This pervasive sense of failure which now gripped Mr Foxe defied
all his efforts to shake it off. As he saw it, he had solved no less than

three puzzling killings, yet found no proper resolution to any of them. He could take no pleasure in such empty achievements. The young actor who had killed Lord Aylestone had reacted thoughtlessly to overwhelming provocation. As a result, he had killed a man by mistake. Now he must face judge and jury and admit publicly to what he has done. Foxe was sure he wouldn't face a murder charge. It would most likely be a case of involuntary manslaughter, even self-defence, followed by a stern lecture from the judge and a light sentence. Even so, his career as an actor would suffer a severe setback; possibly total collapse.

Dr Danson's death was also destined to go unavenged. In that case, the most likely culprit was already dead. Besides, Danson hadn't actually been murdered. He'd died from a heart attack, even if it was brought on by someone else. What bothered Foxe was less Danson's death than what must follow. Without an open listing of evidence in a trial and the subsequent delivery of a verdict, a cloud of suspicion would continue to hang over his young widow. There would always be those who claimed she had colluded with her brother — perhaps even urged him on; that he had helped her inherit a fortune and rid herself of an unwanted, elderly husband. Knowledge of this had already driven her to decide to leave Norwich as soon as she could. Yet even that might provide only a temporary respite. Before long, someone's inquisitive nature would fasten on the gossip and cause her past to follow her to her new home.

Worst of all, Sir Samuel Valmar, serial adulterer, wife-beater and killer of his eldest son, would escape justice altogether. He was destined to remain free to indulge in his insane fantasies about the purity of Valmar blood. To use his wealth and position to place every possible obstacle, legal or otherwise, in the way of his unwanted grandson inheriting what was due to him.

It mattered little to Foxe that he knew that the depth of Valmar's wickedness and madness had proceeded from some sickness of the soul, a sickness which had poisoned his life and the lives of all those around him. It was the same in Dr Danson's case where an obsession of hidden knowledge had led to his death. A disease of the soul had also caused Lord Aylestone to turn to religious bigotry and the

narrowest puritanism. It was that which caused his unjustified prejudice and violent outbursts against the theatre; and thus, produced his
death in due course. In all three cases, Foxe had managed to diagnose
the disease. He could even chart its destructive progress. Yet, in all
three cases, he was prevented from seeing the proper administration of
curative justice. That was what was required to heal wounds inflicted
on family and society. It was enough to make anyone — even someone
far less imaginative and dedicated to justice than Mr Foxe — fall into a
pit of deepest melancholy.

The third day dawned with no prospect of an improvement. Then
Charlie burst in to interrupt his master's fitful efforts to eat some
breakfast bringing the news that Bart, Mistress Tabby's servant and
gardener, had come with an urgent message.

'She wrote it on a slate, Master,' Charlie said, breathless from the
importance of the news that he was bringing. 'It says you must go to
see her right away. She has something of extreme importance to tell
you.'

'Has she indeed?' Foxe said in a dull voice. 'Tell him that I am
seeing no one and send him away.'

'I daren't do that,' the boy replied. 'She's also written that Bart is to
stay in this house until you leave with him, even if it should take all day
and more. He's sitting in the kitchen now. Surely even you dare not
ignore what the Cunning Woman wants? She'll probably put a curse on
you if you do!'

'Pah! What do I care for curses?' Foxe said.

'She also wrote something on the back of the slate,' Charlie went
on. 'It read, "No excuses! Come now! I mean it!!" That last bit was
underlined three times.'

Foxe knew the boy was right. No one in their right mind would
defy the Cunning Woman and hope to escape punishment. Foxe had
known her since his earliest childhood. First as his father's much-loved
mistress after his mother had died. Then, after his father's death, as his
own trusted guide into manhood. It was Mistress Tabby who had
taught him how to live well and manage his affairs. She was also the
one who had introduced him to the ways of women, shown him how to
give and receive pleasure — enriching her teaching with many practical

examples. Even though they had drifted apart until recently, for him to defy her was unthinkable. Without more ado, therefore, he got up, called for Alfred to bring him his outdoor clothing and set out. Bart followed closely behind him.

※※

THIRTY MINUTES LATER, FOXE STOOD IN FRONT OF MISTRESS TABBY, the Cunning Woman, hanging his head in anticipation of a sound scolding. He felt exactly as he had done as a lad of eleven or twelve, waiting to receive the just reward for his latest misdemeanour. Tabby let him stand there for a moment, then lent forward and cuffed him gently about the ears.

'I've been wanting to do that for several weeks now,' she said. 'What an idiot you are, Ash! Going about with your chin dragging on the ground, for all the world as if you had suffered some major disaster. In fact, all you have suffered is a blow to your pride and a little embarrassment; both of them due to your own stupidity. I remember your father telling me, many years ago, that he had to give you a good hiding from time to time to stop you getting above yourself. You're too big for me to do that now. Of course, I could always call Bart in to hold you down, then get my old carpet-beater and apply it to your backside — which is where you appear to keep what passes for your brains.'

She paused for breath. Foxe waited, knowing she had not yet finished. Truth be told, he was more than a little afraid that she would carry out her threat.

'Listen to me, Ashmole Foxe, and listen carefully! Your lifestyle of continual bed-hopping doesn't really suit you anymore, does it? I'm sure you get a great deal of short-term pleasure from all those pretty young women with their heads stuffed with dust and fluff. The trouble is, none of them are the kind of person you can talk with or hope might share your problems. When the Catt sisters were still in Norwich, you had the ideal arrangement. Young Kitty provided the glamour and excitement, she was easily kept sweet by vigorous bedding three or four times a week but her older sister, Gracie, listened to all your problems and gave you comfort — with a little bit of sex thrown in from time to time for good measure. When they left, you could find what Kitty had given you, but Gracie left a gap you haven't been able to fill — until recently that is. What did you do then? You behaved like an idiot to Lady Cockerham and, when she wouldn't listen to your nonsense, you stalked off in a huff. To make it even worse, since then you've been nursing your wounded pride and bringing misery on everyone about you.'

'I did what I thought was the honourable thing,' Foxe complained. 'She laughed at me!'

'I would have done the same thing in her place,' Mistress Tabby said. 'What on earth possessed you to think she would see you as an appropriate husband? Even if she wanted one, all she would have seen was a man prepared to go to bed with any pretty girl who crossed his path. Does that suggest suitable husband material to you? Grow up, Ash! If you want to persuade her to marry you, you'll have to prove you're worth it. That means behaving like a sensible and responsible person. One who isn't led astray by every young actress who comes to the theatre here.'

'That's hardly fair, is it? I mean ...'

'No more! Of course, it's fair! You know I'm right as well as I do! Why else have you been creeping around with a face like thunder, despite having solved all these baffling mysteries. You're lonely, Ash, that's your trouble. You've no one to talk to; no one to share your ideas with. Even your friend, Captain Brock, isn't as available now he's married and has responsibilities of his own elsewhere. Mrs Crombie will listen to you politely and make some helpful suggestions but even she's shown the good sense to keep relations between you on a purely business footing. Who else is there? Don't look at me! I've got many better things to do than wait around until you want me to soothe your fevered brow.'

'I suppose you may be correct, Tabby,' Foxe admitted. 'Maybe I did see in Lady Cockerham someone whom I could make an intimate friend. Then I spoiled it all by snatching at what I wanted without a moment's thought. Dammit! You're right, as usual. I know I'm capable of being a loving and reasonably faithful husband, even though my recent history is against me. At least, I think I know I could be faithful. To be honest, I've never tried it. There are so many beautiful women about to tempt me. It's probably hopeless. I don't expect I'm capable of changing.'

'By God, Ash, what on earth does it take to make you stop whining and moping? Perhaps I really do need to call Bart and beat some sense into you. You know what you have to do, so get on and do it! Swallow your pride. Go and see Lady Cockerham and beg her to forgive you — on your knees, if necessary. If you don't do it, I wash my hands of you and will never speak to you again! I mean it! You know I never threaten things unless I'm willing to carry them out.'

Foxe was horrified. What she said was perfectly true. The Cunning Woman was not the kind of person to make an idle threat, however much she might regret turning away from him for good. Foxe had already spent several years ignoring Mistress Tabby, in the mistaken belief that he didn't need her anymore, then lived to regret it. That time, she had been willing to forgive him. If he upset her again, there's no knowing what she would do. Whatever it was, he knew instantly that he didn't dare risk finding out.

'I promise I'll go and apologise to her,' he said at once. 'She'll probably turn me away, and I wouldn't blame her, but I'll still do it. On my knees, if I have to.'

'You know I'll hold you to that promise, Ash. I'll tell dear Bella Cockerham to expect you then. Soon, I mean! Now come here, give me a kiss and let us be friends again. It's time you told me all about how you finally solved the mystery surrounding George Valmar and what you intend to do next. Oh, by the way,' she added. 'Expect an important visitor in the next day or so.'

'How do you know that?'

'Never you mind. Just pay attention. Your mysteries aren't quite finished yet. There's more to come in at least two cases. Now, tell me what you've discovered since we saw each other last.'

THE NEXT MORNING, FOXE ROSE EARLY AND SET ABOUT PREPARING himself to make his promised visit to Lady Cockerham. He had slept badly. Now he picked at his breakfast, all the while dreading what lay before him. Setting his coffee aside, he went slowly to his dressing room, where he called Alfred to help him decide what he should wear.

If he dressed in his best clothes, he risked appearing proud and arrogant. If he wore more workaday garb, the lady might come to the conclusion he was not taking this visit with sufficient seriousness. He had dressed and undressed three times; Alfred's patience was nearly exhausted with fetching clothes and putting them away again when Molly knocked at the door to tell him he had a visitor.

She found him dressed for the fourth time in his second-best plum-coloured suit with the gold and silver embroidery down the front. Now he was standing considering himself in the long mirror and trying to decide whether he had at last found the right balance between penitence and elegance.

'A Mr Anthony Smith is downstairs, Master, asking to see you,' the maid said. 'He says it is a matter of great importance, so I've asked him to wait for you in the library. I hope that's right.'

'Please tell him I will be with him shortly,' Foxe replied. His curiosity was thoroughly aroused by this visit. Despite being on the brink of leaving for Pottergate, there was no way he was going to turn the man away. Besides, it offered an excellent excuse for him to delay his visit to Lady Cockerham a little further.

When he entered the library, Foxe found Mr Smith examining some of the books. Hearing him enter, the man turned around at once, full of embarrassment at having been discovered satisfying his curiosity in that way. They shook hands, each trying to decide how best to proceed. Smith took the lead at last, full of smiles and congratulations. He was, he said, eager to thank Foxe for finding the book that he had been looking for, despite its great rarity. Then, to Foxe's amazement, he put his hand into the pocket of his coat and drew out a small volume, handing it over for Foxe to examine.

'But . . . Isn't this . . . I mean . . . This is the book you asked me to find,' Foxe stammered. 'Where did you get it?'

'It's a long and sad story,' Smith said. 'Perhaps we might both be seated. Then I will tell you all that has taken place since my last visit.'

Foxe, recalled to his manners, invited his visitor to take a seat. He also rang the bell on his desk to call Molly to bring them some suitable refreshment. She had anticipated his request and entered the room almost at once, carrying a tray with a pot of fresh coffee, two cups and a plate of some of Mrs Whitbread's fresh-baked biscuits. All this time, though Foxe was still holding the book in his hand, he had failed to open it. When he did, he suffered such a shock he was unable to do more than stare at Mr Smith with his mouth open.

'You have seen the bookplate,' Smith said. 'Yes, that is indeed the book stolen from Dr Danson's library, exactly as you explained in your letter to me. I have come here today to explain and ask you to return it to the man's widow. The theft was not of our doing, Mr Foxe, I assure you. Nor are we willing to keep what has been obtained in such an illegal and underhanded manner.'

'So was Mr Cornelius Wake one of your number?' Foxe asked. 'Who is he? How did he know that Danson had a copy? Why did he come to Norwich after you had already asked me to look for it?'

'I said it was a long story, so let me start from the beginning,' Smith replied. 'Mr Cornelius Wake is a Dutchman. At least, his native tongue is Dutch. I believe he was actually born in Ghent. According to his own account, he was apprenticed to an apothecary there. When he had served his time, he moved on to Antwerp, where he established a similar business in his own right. All this time, his interest in alchemy and groups like the Rosicrucians was growing. He sought out information on them wherever he could find it. That was how he came to the notice of the local authorities.'

'Is he of the Roman persuasion in terms of religion?' Foxe asked. 'I believe that is prevalent in those areas of the Low Countries, is it not?'

'It has had a most troubled history, Mr Foxe, split between two Christian persuasions antagonistic to one another. Mr Wake claims to have been born a Christian and a protestant. He remained a protestant outwardly. Of his true beliefs, I cannot tell you much. His interest in so-called hidden knowledge affected all parts of his life. All I know for certain is that he became a Freemason. For the rest, he alone could explain what he believed in.

'That was his problem, I understand. His strange beliefs and his unwillingness to continue to hide them, finally resulted in a decision to leave that place. He says it was to seek a more tolerant society in England. Some of us believe the real reason was that he had lost interest in the trade of an apothecary. Instead, he had decided to take up the wandering life of a seller of magical cures and nostrums.'

'I thought he was still a young man,' Foxe said.

'He is. Still barely thirty years of age. It is a great deal to pack into such a short existence on this earth, is it not? You have put your finger on another one of the man's many difficulties. He is both restless and impatient. Nothing satisfies him for long.'

'How did you come into contact with him? I cannot imagine a man like yourself taking some seller of fake medicines seriously.'

'We knew nothing of that side of his life until much later, Mr Foxe. I hope you will believe me when I tell you Mr Wake is a most plausible fellow. He has the gift of discovering what kind of person you would like him to be, then adopting that guise in a moment. As to how we came to let him join our group, the answer lies here, with this little volume.

'The number of people, collectors I mean, with a serious interest in books of this type is small, as I'm sure you understand. From time to time, rumours circulate about titles thought to be especially desirable, like this one. We had already heard a suggestion that a copy might be found in Norwich, though we did not know precisely where. That was why I came to see you. It was in the hope that you might be able to discover where it was through your contacts and acquire it on our behalf.

'Mr Wake was still new to our group. Indeed, the rest of us had not yet decided whether or not to admit him as a full member. On the one hand, what he told us about himself suggested that he would have useful knowledge. According to his first account, he had been an apothecary at shops in Antwerp, then in the city of Utrecht. It was in Utrecht that he had developed a keen interest in alchemy and the writings of those who had practised that eccentric art in the past. Unfortunately, so he said, his interest had become known. The townsfolk became suspicious of him and accused him of dabbling in witchcraft and magic. When the ecclesiastical authorities threatened to charge him, he fled to England. Finally, he made his way to Cambridge. There, somehow, he heard about our group and approached one of our members in the hope of joining it. As you can see, it was a clever mixture of truths, half-truths and outright lies.'

Smith's story continued with Wake seeking to ingratiate himself by using his knowledge of alchemy to assist the group in their studies. He also suggested several books which he thought might be useful additions to their small library. That was how he heard about the group's decision to send Smith to Norwich to try to obtain a particularly rare volume.

'It was after I had left Cambridge that Wake claimed to have discovered exactly where the book was to be found. He already knew we were prepared to offer a significant price ...'

'How much were you going to offer?' Foxe said, interrupting. The gentle flow of Smith's narrative was becoming too slow for him.

'We were willing to pay up to ten pounds,' Smith replied.

Foxe whistled softly. 'An extraordinarily generous amount,' he said, 'and much more than I imagine the book is actually worth.'

'We did not think we should have to pay even half as much. The amount was chosen so that my hands would not be tied in negotiation. It would have taken too long to go back and forth to Cambridge to get permission to exceed a lower limit.'

Foxe nodded. Even so, to pay anywhere near ten pounds for a single volume struck him as foolish.

'Very few copies have survived,' Smith explained. 'As far as we know, the original printing produced only a hundred copies, only available by subscription. Unfortunately, barely a dozen people subscribed. The printer therefore decided to use the remaining, unbound copies to feed the stove in his workshop during an unusually cold winter. However, I must not be led aside, fascinating though the history of this book has proved to be. I was telling you about Wake.'

Wake, it appeared, had left for Norwich himself without telling anyone and without waiting for Smith to return. Nothing was seen of him again until several days after Smith had come back to Cambridge. Wake then presented himself at the next meeting of the group. He was holding the book and telling them that he had, with great difficulty, been able to persuade the owner, whose name he did not mention, to part with it. At first, they were overjoyed. Then they became suspicious. Especially when Wake told them he had been obliged to offer not ten pounds, but fifteen.

'That is a truly monstrous sum!' Foxe said, interrupting again. 'Was your group willing to give him the extra money to make up for what he said he had paid to obtain the book? I can scarcely believe it.'

'We were not, Mr Foxe. Not at once, anyway. As I said, our suspicions were aroused. Wake told us that the owner had allowed him to return with the book only on the promise that he would obtain the additional five pounds. Then he was to return at once to Norwich to complete the sale. Like you, we found this tale hard to believe. We told Mr Wake it would take us several days to collect the remaining money together. Then, after he had left, we quickly decided to refuse the book altogether. For a start, Wake carried out his transaction without our permission. Then we were unable to believe that a refugee, as he told us he was, would have ten pounds available to make the partial payment.'

It was in the period between Wake leaving and his return in the hope of claiming fifteen pounds, that Foxe's letter reached Mr Smith. As soon he had read it, he called the other members of the group together. Furious, they determined to confront Mr Wake with the charge of theft and murder, then hand him over to the university authorities. Within the area of the city occupied by the various colleges, Smith explained to Foxe, the university managed its own affairs. That included the preservation of law and order and the primary administration of justice.

'As you can imagine, Mr Foxe,' Smith continued, 'Cornelius Wake was horrified to discover we knew how he had obtained the book and were ready to hand him over to face justice. The theft alone would have sent him to the gallows. Committing murder would make his execution doubly certain. He fell on his knees before us, sobbing and pleading for mercy. Thus, it was that the true story came out. How he had discovered where the book was, he never told us. All he would say was that he had visited Dr Danson, exactly as you told me in your letter. There he hoped to purchase the book for a far lesser amount than we had said we were willing to pay. He planned to return, claiming to have paid the full ten pounds. The balance he would keep for his own use. On the way back to Cambridge, his greed got the better of him. He decided to ask for a still larger sum.'

'But how did he persuade Danson to sell?' Foxe asked. 'From all I have heard, Danson never sold any of his books, whatever people were willing to offer.'

'As I understand it,' Smith said, 'Wake persuaded Danson to let him examine the book. Then, when Danson refused to sell, he said he would take it anyway. Wake is a young man, sir, as I said. He thought the elderly Danson could easily be prevented from taking the book back again. According to his later story, it did not turn out like that. Danson sprang up from his chair and seized a dagger that was lying on his desk. Why he had such a thing in his library is beyond me.'

'He used it to slit the pages of new books, I believe,' Foxe said.

'I see. Well, Wake said Danson came towards him, holding the dagger in front of him and demanding that he hand over the volume. Wake claimed he was in fear of his life, though whether any of us believed him is far from certain. Either way, in order to escape, he punched Danson in the face. Danson staggered back and collapsed into his chair. At first, Wake said that he thought the man was merely stunned. A second look convinced him that the man had suffered either an apoplexy or a heart attack. Being an apothecary, he understood the signs to look for. That was when he slipped out of the house as quietly as he could, still carrying the book.'

'Was Dr Danson already dead?' Foxe asked.

'Your guess is as good as mine, Mr Foxe. I doubt Wake stayed long enough to be certain himself. He said it was clear the man's life could not be saved. Make of that what you will.'

Nobody knew Wake in Norwich, Smith continued, so he left as quickly as he could. His intention was to make his way back to Cambridge, extract the fifteen pounds, and use it to go somewhere he could evade justice. He would have probably returned to the life of a wandering quack-doctor.

'Did you believe what he had told you?' Foxe said.

'On balance, I think we did. It made little difference either way. He had confessed to theft and assault in front of us all. We sent one of our

number to summon the university proctors to take him into custody.
Meanwhile, he pleaded with us to allow him to cross the court to
where the privies stood. He said he needed to relieve himself to avoid
the added embarrassment of being taken into custody having wet his
trousers.'

'You agreed?'

'We did,' Smith said. 'Naturally we were suspicious, so one of our
members accompanied him to make sure he returned. Sadly, while they
were crossing the court, Wake tripped the man up, then ran hell for
leather for the main gates. Thus it was he managed to make good his
escape. No one has seen or heard of him since.'

'If it's any consolation, Dr Danson did die of a heart attack,' Foxe
said. 'The medical examiner said so at the inquest. If a man is found
with a dagger sticking out of his chest, most doctors would not look
elsewhere for the cause of death. What produced suspicion was the
lack of sufficient blood. Someone came into that library after Wake
had left, found Danson helpless in his chair, and used his own dagger
to stab him. He thought he was committing murder, even though he
was not.'

'Are you sure?' Smith asked.

'Sure enough, after all you have said. We will never be wholly sure
what took place. The person whom I now believe stabbed Dr Danson
is dead himself. Nonetheless, everything points to him as the killer.
Wake has escaped a charge of theft, and possibly one of common
assault. He is not a murderer.'

'A small consolation to my group,' Smith said, 'but I suppose it
must suffice. Will you take this book back to the widow on our behalf,
Mr Foxe? We cannot accept stolen property, especially if it was
obtained by murder.'

'Mrs Danson has asked me to sell the whole of her husband's
library on her behalf, Mr Smith. If you and your colleagues are still
keen to obtain this volume, I'm sure she will agree to sell it to you for a
far lesser sum than the one you mentioned. I think three pounds and
ten shillings would be a fair price in view of what you have told me of
the book, don't you?'

'Most fair,' Smith said, beaming. 'We will be more than happy to give you that sum. Of course, we will pay you a commission as well.'

'No need,' Foxe said. 'Mrs Danson has agreed to give me a suitable proportion of the money obtained for the books as recompense for my time and trouble.'

'You are an honest man, sir,' Smith said, now even more delighted, 'and it is a pleasure to do business with you. If you are selling the whole of the library, maybe there will be other books we would be interested in, either individually or as a group. Do you have a list of those volumes that are for sale?'

'Not yet. I will produce one shortly and be sure to send you a copy. Now, let me thank you for coming all this way to tell me what had happened and to return the volume. I am extremely grateful to you on both counts. Before you leave, may I be impertinent enough to ask you a personal question?' Smith nodded his agreement. 'Is Anthony Smith your real name?'

Smith's response was to burst out laughing. When he recovered himself, he gave his answer.

'Indeed, it is, Mr Foxe, though not all of it. I'm not surprised that you thought a stranger, introducing himself as Mr A. Smith, was operating under a pseudonym. Let me now introduce myself properly. I am Sir Anthony Foxley-Smith of Braidcote Manor. As I explained, when I came here the first time, the members of our small group at the University of Cambridge share an interest in tracing the early history of scientific endeavour. In the course of this, we have found it necessary to explore the writings of alchemists, Kabbalists, Freemasons, Rosicrucians and the like. Stripped of the obscure terminology and mystical baggage, many of these books point the way to genuine discoveries. Sadly, those of a superstitious turn of mind, let alone religious bigots, would not easily understand what we are doing. Several of the members of our group hold important positions within the university as Fellows of the various colleges. A few are independent scholars. Others are members of the clergy. That is why we prefer to conduct our activities out of the public view. It is not for any more sinister reason, I assure you. Now, I must be upon my way. My thanks to you again, Mr Foxe. I'm sure we will do business together on many future occasions.'

❧ 22 ❧

Because he had been delayed by his unexpected visitor, it was nearly two o'clock in the afternoon by the time Foxe was finally standing on the doorstep of Lady Cockerham's house. Even then, he hurried all the way so that he now felt flustered and somewhat disarranged. There was also a cold fear inside him that he might be denied entrance. His knock was therefore not the usual firm, double knock he gave to such a door. More of a tentative pair of light taps, as if this was the lair of some terrible dragon and he feared to awaken the wrath of the beast hidden within.

The door was answered by a young maidservant he had not met before. She stood aside to allow him in, took his visiting card and gravely asked him to wait in the hall. She would inquire whether her mistress was able to receive visitors.

Foxe, left standing alone, was now pray to even more irrational fears of rejection. It came as a considerable relief when the young maid returned and asked him to follow her to the mistress's parlour. Lady Cockerham was waiting to receive him.

On the way, Maria, Lady Cockerham's personal maid, appeared from nowhere. Then she stepped forward and kissed Foxe lightly on the cheek, wishing him "good luck!" as she did, before disappearing as silently as she had come.

On entering the room, Foxe found Lady Cockerham standing erect by the fireplace. The ray of early afternoon sun in which she was standing made her look like a Grecian statue of a goddess. She appeared at once heartbreakingly beautiful and as cold as the marble from which such statues were made. The stare she gave him as he entered was worthy of an affronted queen, not the youngest daughter of an insignificant Irish peer. Without hesitation, Foxe sank to his knees in front of her. There he began to stammer out the apologies he had been so carefully preparing.

Sadly, this dramatic tableau was quickly marred as the lady herself burst into a fit of helpless giggling.

'Do get up, Ash dear,' she said through her laughter. 'You look quite ridiculous down there. Mistress Tabby counselled me to be severe with you, but I am nowhere near a sufficiently good actress to maintain such an uncongenial role. There are no apologies needed, in any case. Your proposal of marriage did not offend me in any way. In fact, I thought it rather sweet of you. The reason I burst out into such unforgivable laughter was simply the way you looked as you delivered it. You were so serious and pompous! I was quite unable to restrain myself. Then you walked away in a bad temper without allowing me to explain or apologise, as I would have done given the opportunity. Now, do please sit down so that we may have a proper conversation like civilised people.'

Foxe slumped into the nearest chair, so overcome with relief that he could think of nothing to say in response. No words were needed from him. Lady Cockerham sat opposite, patted his knee, and continued to speak with barely a pause.

'Your absence, silly and regrettable though it was, may yet have proved to be of great benefit, at least to me. I used the time to think seriously about myself and my growing fondness for you. I also seized the opportunity for several long, intimate discussions with dear Mistress Tabby. She is indeed a wise woman, Ash, in reality as well as name. She also loves you deeply and is as much committed to your future welfare and happiness as any mother could be. Together, we reached the conclusion that it was high time I told you my most hidden secret. If I did not do that, things would never be on the correct footing between us. To be honest, I should have done this some time ago, but I was not certain of my own feelings until now.

'You know that I was married once before. That I did tell you. I also expect that you assumed that I was widowed young, thus accounting for the absence of a husband. That, I fear, is not the case. My husband is alive and well, though I am not quite sure where he is at the current time. Our marriage was very much the normal affair, arranged between the two families. Since I found him handsome and charming, I saw no reason to object in any way. It was not until shortly after the wedding itself that I discovered I had made a dreadful mistake. My husband then told me he preferred the company of young men in his bed to that of any woman. I should not, therefore, look for any physical satisfaction from him during the course of our marriage. A wife was just a means of concealing his real inclinations from the world at large. As I'm sure you understand, if they became known he would become an object of ridicule. He might even be subjected to a criminal trial and the threat of the death penalty. To have a wife, even one that was permanently absent, was thus much better than having none at all. That is why there has never been any possibility of a divorce or to have the marriage annulled. He managed — by what means I do not know — to consummate our marriage on our wedding night. However, he said he had no intention of ever repeating the experience. I was to be left as a wife in name only, honoured and well cared for, but deprived of the intimate companionship due between husband and wife. Meanwhile, he assured me that he was, by nature, a most prudent man. He would take care to pursue his various amours during the many journeys overseas which he was obliged to undertake in the course of his government duties. For the rest of the time, I might do as I wished, provided only that I did not betray my knowledge to anyone else, nor cause him any embarrassment. Thus far, I have followed his wishes in both respects.'

'What has changed?' Foxe asked.

'You have come into my life and I have fallen in love with you. There! I have said it. If my words have horrified you, you may walk away now. I will doubtless cry for a time, but I'm sure I will get over it.'

'My dearest, Bella,' Foxe said warmly, 'I will do nothing of the kind. I came here today having at last discovered my feelings for you and terrified that you would send me away. Now you tell me those feelings are reciprocated. I ought to be the happiest man in the world.'

'Ought to be? What stands in your way? I know you have bedded more women than I am probably able to count. I have set that aside already as a possible impediment. Don't, for goodness sake, tell me that you too have contracted a marriage at some time that I know nothing about.'

'Nothing like that, I assure you. It is far simpler. I do not know what to do. You cannot marry without exposing your husband to disgrace and danger. I have far too much regard for you to suggest any other arrangement.'

'You may have, Ash, but I do not,' Lady Cockerham said. 'Between us, Mistress Tabby and I have come up with a possible solution. I must warn you that it comes with certain firm conditions. I do not care a fig for what the world thinks of me. It will probably suit my husband very well to be able to tell his acquaintants he has sent me away because he found I had taken a younger lover. Very well, let us make that the truth. Not that he has sent me away, but the other part. If you agree, let us be husband-and-wife in all but name. We will keep our separate homes and establishments, since I am sure we both value our independence. For the rest, we will spend as much time together as we may, let the world think whatever it will. I imagine most men will envy you as much as most so-called respectable women will despise me. So be it! At least we can be happy in our own way.'

Foxe's mouth hung open in amazement. It had never occurred to him that any decent and outwardly conventional woman, let alone a titled lady, would be willing to enter into such an arrangement. He was still gathering his wits together to give an answer when she interrupted him.

'No! Wait before you speak! You have not yet heard my conditions.

If I am to offer you the love, companionship and devotion a man should expect of his wife, I expect to be treated as such. That means an end to your regrettable habit of jumping into bed with any young woman who smiles in your direction. We may not have exchanged vows of faithfulness in church, but I will hold you to such a vow none-theless. Can you keep it?'

'I do not know,' he said simply. Truth was the only thing that would serve at this point. 'I have never tried before. All I can promise is to do my best.'

Once again, Bella Cockerham began to giggle. 'Don't look so sad and solemn, Ash, dear. I know how difficult it will be for you, so I have decided to add a single exception. You were instrumental in intro-ducing me to Maria, who became my lady's maid. Since then, she has become most dear to me, as, I venture to say, I have to her. It is now impossible for me to treat her as a servant, so I have determined she will no longer be one. Since you came here last, she has become my lady companion. She is already well on her way to developing the grace and polished manners necessary to appear with me in public. I am well aware of what passed between you on various occasions before this. I also know that she harbours the deepest affection for you. I will there-fore continue to turn a blind eye whenever you need you feel a little variety and she decides to accommodate your needs. What do you say?'

'I don't know what to say, my lady —'

'It was Bella a moment ago. I much prefer that when we are together in private. I know my name is Arabella, but that is far too much of a mouthful, much as Ashmole is.'

Foxe grinned. 'Very well,' he said. 'Let it be Bella and Ash. What you have suggested will make me fortunate almost beyond the lot of mortal man. Of course, I agree. Who would not?'

It's almost exactly as it was with Gracie and Kitty, Foxe thought to himself. Maria, just like Kitty, will provide the youthful body, the fun and excitement. Bella will be my rock, just as Gracie was until she went away.

'In that case,' Lady Cockerham continued, 'let us retire together and seal our agreement in the most appropriate way possible. After that, I suggest you stay to dine with Maria and myself. I will send word via a servant to your household, telling them you will not return again until very late — if at all tonight.' Her smile was openly provocative. 'Provided, that is, you have sufficient stamina.'

'I have been accused of many things,' Foxe replied, 'but never of lacking that. The only thing I ask is that dinner should not be too heavy. I have found too much food detrimental to subsequent performance.'

'If I think it necessary,' the lady replied, 'I will deny you food altogether. Let us hope it does not come to that. You seem well-nourished enough to me, but I will take great care to keep up your strength. Now, no more words!'

She took his hand and led him towards the stairs.

❧

FOR THE NEXT TWO DAYS, FOXE WENT AROUND IN SOMETHING OF A mist of happiness and contentment. He spent large parts of each evening and night at Lady Cockerham's house. After breakfast, he returned to his own house. There he applied himself to his attempts to sell all of Mrs Danson's books as quickly as possible and for the best possible prices. He ate something light at midday, spent an hour or so with Mrs Crombie and Charlie, before returning either before or after dinner whence he had come. He gave up his walks around the market-place and even his visits to the coffeehouse. In the former case, he reasoned that walking to and from Lady Cockerham's house, coupled with those activities he undertook there requiring exercise and stamina, would more than suffice. He replaced his visits to the coffee-house with periods within which he might meet with his friend Brock or conduct other kinds of business.

He also took Charlie with him on a visit to Mr Lavender, the cathedral librarian. The lad had worked hard on the book Mr Lavender had entrusted to him to repair. Now he was finished and the volume could be returned to the library. Lavender was delighted with what Charlie had done and praised the lad in fulsome terms. Charlie blushed and beamed in response. Lavender even offered Charlie his own personal tour of the cathedral library and its treasures, followed by a lesson in the conservation of rare manuscripts.

'I shall have more work for you, my lad,' he promised the apprentice. 'That is, of course, if your master agrees. What you have done on this book has proved to me that you can be trusted to do your work carefully and well. To have your help will free me from a great many onerous tasks, and the cathedral chapter has ignored my requests for an assistant. With your help, albeit on an occasional basis, I think I may cope. In return, I will teach you what I can about the care of old and valuable volumes. Manuscripts too, though I doubt many of those will pass through your hands in the normal course of being a bookseller. Do you both agree with what I have suggested?'

Charlie nodded. He was too surprised and delighted to trust himself to speak.

'Of course, I agree, Lavender,' Foxe said. 'I know Charlie loves that type of work. It will make a nice change from the constant round of repairs occasioned by the careless way many of those who use our circulating library treat the books.'

It was on the third day after his visit to Lady Cockerham that Foxe received the news which put this idyllic style of life in danger of collapse. It was delivered by a breathless Mrs Crombie the moment he stepped into the shop.

'Have you heard, Mr Foxe?' she began. 'Sir Samuel Valmar is dead. The story is that he died yesterday evening after eating a dish containing bad oysters. I suppose that means that his young grandson will now succeed to the estate and the baronetcy.'

'Indeed, it will, Mrs Crombie,' Foxe replied, his mind full of the implications of this piece of news. 'I wonder how he came to be eating something of that kind?'

'It does happen sometimes,' Mrs Crombie said, 'especially towards the end of the season. It may also happen if they are left too long in the larder. Oysters can be chancy things at the best of times, if you ask me. I never liked them.'

'I can't say that I enjoy eating them either,' Foxe replied. 'Well, whatever the precise cause of the baronet's death, I expect it will be up to me to make sure his grandson receives what is due to him.'

With that, Foxe returned to his library to consider his next move. He expected no more surprises. When Alfred, his manservant, presented him with two letters that had just arrived, he simply threw them down on the desk to read later. It was only when, staring about himself somewhat idly, he noticed that the wax which sealed one of them bore an imprint of the Valmar crest; he took it up in haste and broke open the seal to read what was written inside.

My dear Mr Foxe,

I expect the news will by now have reached you that my husband died at around eleven o'clock last night. The physician was called and has decided his death was due to the dish of oysters that he had eaten at dinner. He has pronounced them bad, noting that my husband began to suffer severe stomach pains and vomiting within an hour of the meal. These pains steadily became worse until death was inevitable. He has told me that death was due to natural causes and no inquest is required before burial takes place. Then, in the manner of all of his kind, he offered me his deepest condolences, followed by telling me I would receive the bill for his services in due course.

My husband's death will be accepted as a sad accident by all who knew him. I certainly will not suggest anything else. He had not been eating properly since your visit — pangs of conscience, I presume — so I told cook to prepare him a dish of oysters, which were his favourite food. He ate those greedily enough.

I was standing on the other side of the door from the hall to the dining room throughout the time when you and my husband were talking. From there, I heard every word he said to you. I decided then I could not bear to live in the same house as a murderer, especially not the one who had brought about the death of my son, George. My exact role in my husband's last hours on this earth — if any such existed — will remain unknown to all but myself and my Maker. Your quick mind may well have jumped to a conclusion and formed what I will call an educated guess. It will remain a guess, since actual proof will never exist. Now I will write no more about it, save to point out that justice has been done. Let that be an end of it.

I have a favour to ask of you. I hope you will be willing to act as my emis-

sary and go-between to introduce me to my grandson, Henry, and the household in which he has been brought up. Let there be no doubt in anyone's mind that he is the rightful heir to the estate and the title. I have broken the news to my younger son, Frederick. As you can imagine, he is both disappointed and furious to discover that he has a nephew who will take precedence over him in the succession. I have assured him that my jointure will be generous enough for me to give him the means of moving elsewhere. For several hours, he stamped around in the most terrible temper. Then he announced his decision to emigrate to our colonies in America and begin a new life there. I have both approved of and encouraged that decision. It is possible that what has happened may turn out to be the making of that young man. Now that he must fend for himself, save for what help I can give him, he must exchange a life of idleness for one of purposeful and useful endeavour. On the other side of the Atlantic, there will be greater scope for him. He will also be able to put these unpleasant memories out of his mind.

As for myself, I will now dedicate my life to helping my grandson assume his proper place in society. Be assured that I will not ignore his other grandparents. They deserve my greatest esteem for all they have done for him after his mother's death and his father's disappearance. Provided they are willing, I will see that they have their proper place within our family. It is assuredly what they deserve.

My greatest thanks are reserved for you. Without your intelligence and perseverance, a dreadful wrong would have been committed. I would also never have learned of what happened to my darling Georgie. I hope he can now rest in peace, knowing that his son is being given the best of care. He too will be welcomed back into the family, if only posthumously. I shall commission a suitable memorial tablet to be placed in the chancel of our parish church, alongside the memorials to all his ancestors. The family tree of the Valmars, in which my late husband took such obsessive pleasure, may be largely the product of the imagination of past centuries, but my elder son still deserves his proper place in it.

Frederick, I hope, will forget all such nonsense. If he does not remain with his intention to go to live in one of our American colonies, I imagine he will settle down to being what my husband should have been: a respectable and useful inhabitant of this county. If he does not, whatever comes about will be his own fault.

God bless you for what you have done, Mr Foxe. You will always be a welcome visitor to this house, so long as I live and breathe.

I am, sir, your most grateful and appreciative servant,

Catherine, Dowager Lady Valmar.

P.S. I trust your face has fully recovered from the blow I gave it. Please forgive me. I was not myself that day and regret my intemperate action deeply.

FOXE GAVE A DEEP SIGH AT THE END, BEFORE READING THE TEXT through once again. Afterwards, he walked over to the fireplace, took down a candle from the sconce above there and lit the wick with his tinderbox. Finally, he held the flame to the paper and consigned Lady Valmar's letter to the fireplace below. It was better that way. Sometimes justice had to give way to mercy. Let the world think the Valmar family's problems were finally over. Sir Samuel had told him that a thoroughbred which turned vicious should be put down, lest it do any more harm to those around it. In time, Foxe hoped, his own conscience would surely grow quiet and come to accept he had done the best he could. No more members of the Valmar family would suffer from the death of that one of their number who had slipped into obsession and madness.

When he came to read the other letter, Foxe found something far less welcome. The missive came from Gracie Catt and had obviously been written in haste.

MY DEAREST ASH,

After a season of tumultuous successes in London and Dublin, dear Kitty is exhausted, and I am tired out trying to keep up with her. We have therefore decided to return to Norwich for some rest and relaxation before the autumn season starts the whole process off again. Expect us sometime within the next few days. We have borrowed suitable lodgings from a friend who is travelling abroad at the present time and expect to spend around two months in our old haunts. It will be delightful to see you again. I know Kitty joins with me in saying how much we are looking forward to renewing our previous close acquaintanceship, if only for a short period. We know we can rely upon you to keep us entertained and amused.

We both send you our love,
Gracie Catt

FOXE COULD HAVE WEPT!

ABOUT THE AUTHOR

William Savage is an author of British historical mysteries. All his books are set between 1760 and around 1800, a period of great turmoil in Britain, with constant wars, the revolutions in America and France and finally the titanic, 22-year struggle with Napoleon.

William graduated from Cambridge and spent his working life in various management and executive roles in Britain and the USA. He is now retired and lives in north Norfolk, England.

ALSO BY WILLIAM SAVAGE

THE ASHMOLE FOXE GEORGIAN MYSTERIES

THE FABRIC OF MURDER

Follow Mr Foxe through Norwich's teeming 18th-century streets as he seeks to prevent a disaster to the city's major industry and tracks down a killer with more than profit on his mind.

DARK THREADS OF VENGEANCE

Mr Ashmole Foxe, Georgian bookseller and confidential investigator, has a new case: to find the murderer of a prominent Norwich merchant and banker before his businesses collapse and the city is crippled by financial panic.

THIS PARODY OF DEATH

Eighteenth-century Norwich bookseller and dandy, Ashmole Foxe, is asked by the local bellringers to look into the death of their Tower Captain, found in the ringing chamber with his throat cut.

BAD BLOOD WILL OUT

Ashmole Foxe investigates two cases, both involving poisoned relationships from the past. A wealthy man dies amongst his own guests and a series of murders occupy centre stage at one of Norwich's main theatres.

THE DR ADAM BASCOM MYSTERIES

An Unlamented Death

The Code for Killing

A Shortcut to Murder

A Tincture of Secrets and Lies

Death of a Good Samaritan

Made in the USA
Coppell, TX
09 April 2021

53346633R00142